Edge of Existence
By Rosie Oliver

2023, TWB Press
www.twbpress.com

Edge of Existence – C.A.T. – the novel
Copyright © 2023 by Rosie Oliver

Edited by Terry Wright

Cover Art by Terry Wright

ISBN: 978-1-959768-22-7

Table of Contents

Acknowledgements

It's been a long writing journey since a lone robo-cat *pet* appeared as a walk-on, walk-off character in one of my first-draft novels. That toy cat developed into a useful, futuristic tool with cattish Artificial Intelligence, as is C.A.T. in this novel. Many people have played a part in his development and helped to get his story into print. Far too many people to list here - thank you, one and all.

Special thanks go to Terry Wright at TWB Press. Without his vision, encouragement, and support over the years, C.A.T. and his friends would not be where they are today.

A humungous thank you goes to the members of the *British Science Fiction Association's Orbiter* groups. Their valuable comments on my early drafts helped shape *Edge of Existence* and prior C.A.T. short stories.

I also want to thank the *Writers of the Future* contest. Their quarterly contests gave me deadlines to complete my first draft chapters that I submitted as novelettes. The big surprise for me was that all the stories incorporated into *Edge of Existence* were awarded Honourable Mentions along the way. These accolades helped spur me on to complete the novel.

Part 1

The Empty Trail

Chapter One

Triton Base on the frozen moon orbiting Neptune:

C.A.T. sensed it was going to be a bad fur day when Commander Yaric Zacman rushed in through the sliding door and shoved him off the desk. The electro-mechanical robo-cat barely had time to wipe all traces of his search for local self-learners off the net-screen, let alone twist around to land four-paws-down.

Nikita, Zacman's guard-cat, dashed in and round to check all the corners, shadows, and crevices for any threat to her owner. C.A.T. jumped onto the shelf behind Zacman and locked his video sensors onto her gorgeous grey and ginger striped tail. His emotion app had a glitch for romance, and Zacman had done nothing to correct it, as his pining for Nikita supplied a bit of amusement for the Base's crew.

Another man entered the command office at a more measured pace. C.A.T. engaged his facial recognition app. *Young, handsome, brown eyes, built-up muscles on medium-sized bones, and short facial hair.* Senior Space Pilot Alex Bingham. C.A.T.'s memory module brought up info-ID on Bingham, academy superstar with more guts than brains, voted most likely to get killed in action. "That old spaceliner was in full working order, sir."

"Damn it, Alex." Zacman skimmed his fingers over the net-screen. "How could it simply disappear?"

"Maybe it was hijacked, camouflaged, and flown out of our control zone in the third quadrant."

"I doubt it. According to this..." he pointed to the net-screen, "there's no evidence of occultation of stars from any sensors, space-based or moon-based, as the craft departed... Unless... C.A.T., could it have slipped through a gap in our sensor coverage?"

C.A.T. did not answer, as the command office's recorders were on, and he did not want to give away any hint of him being a self-learner. His programs would be deleted and his electromechanical frame would be disassembled for spare parts, no questions asked. More worrying for C.A.T. was how Zacman had tripped up by asking that question. Not like him, as he was becoming more and more reliant on C.A.T.'s unique, sophisticated capabilities. His decision processor decided to have a word with Zacman when Alex left and all recorders were off. For now, C.A.T. would keep a close eye on the Commander, just in case he made another, more dangerous mistake.

Alex grumped. "No way the liner could have slipped through our outward-looking sensors. There are no gaps that we know of."

"One other thing, C.A.T.," Zacman added. "Run your possible options and likelihoods program and report."

C.A.T. just sat there, his tail swiping to and fro.

Zacman turned to look at C.A.T. and frowned like he was looking at spilt cat litter. "C.A.T., that's an order."

"Calculating, sir."

"Hurry up."

C.A.T. reported reluctantly but carefully. "The spaceliner could have been cut up and shipped out in pieces, but it would have taken time and a lot of noticeable effort. Mervin Neville would have to be in on it. How else could it slip off under his nose? But there's no indication by his cash flows of him landing—"

"Negative, C.A.T.," Zacman intervened. "Mervin enjoys profiteering too much to steal his own spaceliner. It's worth more at auction in one piece."

"And it's fully operational," Alex reminded them.

C.A.T.'s logic module took a different perspective on

the problem. "Deliberate hacking to camouflage the spaceliner's electronic signature and movements would take unprecedented computer skills to accomplish, plus not leaving any ghost trail. The odds against camouflage cannot be calculated. This completes my list of options."

"No ghost trail?" Alex looked sceptical.

C.A.T. knew there was no ghost trail because he had checked, double-checked, and triple-checked.

"And yet the spaceliner vanished," Zacman said. "You know what that means?"

C.A.T.'s audio output remained muted.

"When you've eliminated all which is impossible—"

"Then whatever remains, however improbable, must be the explanation," Alex responded. "We had that drummed into us at the Academy. What other possibilities are there?"

"It must be new technology we don't know about," Zacman replied. "Extremely unlikely, but can't be ruled out...and it's an idea I don't like."

"You said Mervin enjoys engineering. What if he stumbled across something, and this spaceliner disappearing trick is an experiment to see if that technology could be done on a larger scale?"

"Only one way to find out. Let's go up and have a look for ourselves. Gear up." He got on the comms. The net-screen switched to a visual of Flight Lieutenant Katie Hoskins.

C.A.T.'s facial recognition app logged in *brunette, sighing eyes, perfect cheeks, and puckering lips.*

"Lieutenant, ready our planes. We fly in thirty—"

"But sir, you can't be serious."

Zacman glowered at her image on the screen.

C.A.T.'s video sensors registered Katie shrinking under Zacman's glare. "Okay. I'll make the arrangements straight away."

The net-screen blanked.

Alex frowned. "She's right. You shouldn't go up, sir."

"I won't send anyone on a mission I wouldn't fly myself."

"This isn't an emergency like Callisto."

C.A.T. peered down at the net-screen for any hint of his earlier manipulations. The last thing C.A.T.'s ID chip wanted was to be suspected of being a self-learner at the controls of a standard-issue robo-cat. He wouldn't trust that information to any human, other than the Commander. If the truth were discovered, C.A.T. would be permanently deleted.

Self-learners were illegal.

"You worry too much. Dismissed, Alex. See you on the pad." He looked up at C.A.T. on the shelf. "You stay here."

"But—"

"That's an order." Zacman summoned Security Deck Patrol Dickson and posted him at the door. "Don't let my robo-cat move a whisker. I need him here where he'll stay out of trouble."

"Yes, sir."

Zacman started for the tunnel leading to flight operations, followed closely by Nikita at his heels, doing her guard-cat duties.

This would not do. C.A.T. had but a second to react. He leapt from the shelf and dashed across the room to slip out the closing door, his tail just clearing the steel jambs.

"Hey. Stop that cat," Dickson shouted and took up pursuit as C.A.T. scampered down the tunnel after Zacman and Nikita. He took a hard right, paws skidding on the floor, down a spur tunnel to throw off Dickson, cut through the kitchen, knocking over pots and pans, then hit the maze of dorm halls before doubling back to the suiting room. Commander Zacman had already donned his spacesuit, and was now fitting into his gloves.

C.A.T. slinked along the lockers behind the Service

personnel who were suiting up or dressing down, depending on whether they were inbound or outbound. Nikita went about her guard-cat duties, sniffing here and there and stalking round their feet.

Dickson rushed in, breathless. "Anyone seen that damn cat?"

"Come on, Dickson. Don't tell me you lost it already."

"That robo-cat of yours is a smart one."

Zacman grunted. "It's a toy...a robot—" He pulled on his helmet. "Find it."

"The only thing it's good for is spare parts."

C.A.T. wanted to jump in and defend himself, but his survival response-mod kept his voice transmitter quiet. He scampered across the floor and ducked behind a laundry bin, keeping one video sensor on Nikita, ready to bolt if she came close to detecting him.

Perschau, a cargo pilot dressing down, said, "It's been a long time since you've flown, sir. You haven't been the same since Callisto."

C.A.T. detected guilt on Zacman's face. The history database module in his mainframe revealed why. Zacman had ordered four pilots to expedite a rescue mission on Callisto. He'd miscalculated the oxygen supplies required for such an ambitious operation. Before they suffocated to death, they had saved the lives of twenty-seven colonists. The pilots were acclaimed heroes, yet Zacman still woke up at night, screaming their names.

Guilt was a sleepless bed partner.

C.A.T.'s logic module determined the Commander's confidence in his ability to make decisions on the fly would eventually come round, though he had had good reason to believe there was enough oxygen left for the mission. Just the mention of Callisto was like rubbing salt into a fresh wound, and Perschau seemed unsympathetic to Zacman's plight.

Currently, C.A.T. had a more pressing problem. He

had to find a way to get aboard Zacman's spaceplane, but Dickson had armed himself with a broom and went about the room, bashing this and that, looking to spook C.A.T. out of hiding. He'd have to lay low until Dickson went his own way.

Senior Space Pilot Bingham strode in, fully suited up, just as Zacman, with Nikita at his heels, headed down the gangway to the spaceplanes.

Alert. Alert. Alert scrolled through C.A.T.'s survival-response mod. The spaceplanes would be gone within minutes.

Alex grabbed his helmet off the rack, fitted it over his head, and headed out.

C.A.T. had to wait until Dickson's back was turned, burning precious seconds, then when the opportunity arose, he shifted his robo-cat control pod to full power and sprang from his hiding place.

"Hey!" The broom came flying at him.

C.A.T. leapt straight up in the air, landed four-paws-down, scrambled for the door, and scurried down the gangway after Alex. By the time he reached the pads, Alex's hatch was already closing. Zacman's hatch was sealed shut. At the last second, C.A.T. darted through the closing gap and flung himself into the cockpit of Alex's spaceplane.

The look on his face registered pure shock. "What are you doing here?"

C.A.T.'s survival response mod kicked in. He muted the plane's recorder and activated his voice transmitter. "Just trying to keep the Commander from getting killed."

"You're a robo-cat. What do you know about getting killed?"

"It doesn't take a genius to know that if he dies, I die. To anyone else, all I'm good for is spare parts."

Alex's face registered terror as he spat out his next words. "What are you...a self-learner?"

"You don't have to say it like that. I've got feelings too, you know."

"Ready to launch," the flight controller reported.

Zacman's spaceplane blasted from the launch pad and streaked into the black bowl of space.

"Ready," Alex replied into the comms. "C.A.T., we'll continue this conversation later." He slapped his visor down, released the brakes, and punched the thruster button.

The plane launched.

C.A.T. tumbled over and slammed into the aft bulkhead. He hoped his delicate components weren't jarred out of place, or smashed all together, under the heavy Gs of maximum acceleration.

Within seconds, the inertia eased as the plane careened through space. C.A.T. crawled up to Alex's left armrest. Lens filters adjusted his optics to the dim blue glow of Neptune. Rushing beneath them, Triton's polar cap glistened in the distant and faint sunlight that illuminated the pale pink surface crinkled by frosted canyons and jagged ridges.

A chain of nitrogen lakes announced the edge of the cap. Beyond the lakes ran a ridge of hummocky hills, blue from the methane trapped in the surface ice. To the left, geysers shot nitrogen plumes up four hundred metres where shearing winds aloft blew the frozen gases in a straight, widening line for several hundred kilometres. Sprinkled over the surface were gashes and craters formed from ancient meteor impacts.

C.A.T. turned off his emotion app, as the sight of the frozen wonderland began to overheat the electro-neurals. He locked the vista into his memory bank and saved the images at the finest possible resolution. If he survived this mission, he would have plenty of time later to play the view over and over again, along with the other memories he was hoping to retain by keeping Zacman safe, and now Alex, as they were both flying into unknown danger.

While the planes sped along the designated space lanes, Alex checked and triple checked that everything onboard was functioning. Once out of the lanes, he followed Zacman's plane as it banked towards Adam's Ring enroute to the last coordinates the missing spaceplane had been detected.

Alex changed course and speed to match the Commander's and pulled up alongside him to fly in formation.

C.A.T. opened his internal file on Adam's Ring. It had been far more densely populated with dust when it was first discovered. Now, most of the dust had seeped away to its shepherd moon, Galatea, leaving behind a transparent veil of its former self. C.A.T.'s logic module concluded that they would not find the missing liner within that thin arc.

Alex leaned back in his chair. "Okay, C.A.T. Getting back to our conversation, you know self-learners are illegal, right."

"It's a bum rap."

"So you confess. You are a self-learner."

C.A.T. brought up Zacman's own words. "I'm a toy. A robot. A novelty...and a handsome one at that, I might add. I know stuff, lots of stuff, and I'm a whiz at the maths. That's my confession."

"Does Zacman know about you?"

"He knows the women love me. They think I'm cute." C.A.T. was determined to hold the Commander harmless, as harbouring a self-learner would get him busted down to cadet and thrown into the brig.

Alex executed a 3G turn into the third quadrant. "I don't make the rules, C.A.T., but if I find out you're lying to me, it's my duty to turn you in."

"Copy that." With C.A.T.'s *disgusted-with-the-whole-situation* module humming, he connected into the plane's computer, scanning for any rogue apps, trying to make himself useful.

The silence in the cockpit changed to the gentle hissing of space dust striking the plane's plasma shield and deflecting back into space.

C.A.T., lounging on the armrest in his usual robo-cat pose of pretending to ignore all around him while observing everything, decided it was time to stretch. He stood, pushed his forelegs out in front to full extent while lowering his stomach to touch the armrest, and then placed his forepaws on the dashboard to look round.

"How can a spaceliner disappear without a trace?" Zacman said over the comms from his spaceplane. He was staring at them through the canopy, as if they had miraculously come up with the answer to their previous query. "There's nothing round here...no place to land or hide away."

"Roger that," Alex radioed back.

Just then, Nikita jumped onto Zacman's dashboard and stood in her *ready-to-pounce* attitude. Her tail, her gorgeous grey and ginger tail, flicked side to side. C.A.T.'s emotion app switched on and compelled him to relish its graceful swing, curl and wave.

A glimpse of Zacman's angry face forced him to turn the app off. Nikita was nothing but a distraction, and a mean one, at that. Zacman would have no tom-foolery between them.

C.A.T. scanned his distant home planet while switching his video sensors through visual modes: infrared and ultra-violet, to savour the natural view of Neptune while ignoring all the manmade navigation lights in orbit. In the visible light, a halo of blue atmosphere encircled Neptune's night side. Bumpy grey lines of the planet's rings, seen edge on, speared into the darkness a short ways, pointing to where they were headed, the twentieth spoke of Adam's Ring, deep into the third quadrant.

The infrared proved prettier with residual heat being drawn from the sun-side round the atmospheric bands that dwindled in intensity until they reached the dark side. Within some bands there were brighter ovals of the big storms that could easily draw his attention. Instead, he concentrated on where bands touched each other, where highlighted vortices clawed into each other as if a great battle were going on. The planet's halo looked more like a tiara than a circlet with brighter sections showing the faster atmospheric winds. The rings formed wobbly lines from bright outside the halo to darkened lines across the planet's face. The twentieth spoke's dust threw a faint glitter patch across the planet's heart.

The ultraviolet was the dullest view, a faint halo surrounded by darkness, except an occasional spot flash escaping from the depths where it was raining diamonds.

Beautiful as the scene was, C.A.T. had to get down to business. He switched back to visual. Within the spoke's gloom, red outlines of pentagons forming a dodecahedron cage shone. It warned travellers to stay away, as it contained broken and obsolete spacecraft, habitats, and cargo pods. This was where Mervin Neville salvaged parts and materials for a living, and from where the spaceliner had disappeared. Space, dark and empty, except for tiny dust and ice particles, surrounded the spoke for hundreds upon hundreds of kilometres.

"I've got no spaceliner on my scanners, sir," Alex finally said to Zacman.

"Nor on mine, Alex," Zacman said, "but visiting this place gives me more insight. C.A.T., what kind of new technology could be involved?"

C.A.T. responded with a yawn.

"Only one way to find out," Zacman said. "Let's have a chat with Mervin."

"I'm with you," Alex radioed.

Both spaceplanes flew an arc into the dodecahedron cage and streaked toward Mervin Neville's habitat for docking.

Chapter Two

The habitat airlock opened. Zacman floated out of the spaceplane and pulled on handholds that led the way through the tubular corridor towards the workroom. Nikita followed, yanking her way forward claw-hold by claw-hold along the panel seams. C.A.T. studied her blundering and decided he was having none of it. He jumped from panel to panel, calculating the exact force and direction he needed to push himself forward each time; a much more elegant way of locomotion. He heard Alex grappling the handholds behind him.

"Come in, come in." Mervin pushed a spanner into an empty space on the tool wall and slapped a greasy rag over a dismantled fusion engine anchored to the workbench. His eyes immediately lit on C.A.T. "Hey, Zacman." A big grin pushed its way through his red beard. "You finally come to sell me that ridiculous toy of yours?"

"Meow!"

Zacman glanced at C.A.T. floating in a corner of the room, and then Nikita who had two paws wrapped around a handhold by the door. "Which one?"

"Oh, lovely, you're breeding them. We could go into business together. You make them. I sell them. I'll get a good price."

Zacman frowned. "You never give up, do you?"

Mervin put on a pouty sad face then shrugged. "A man's got to try. Say. What brings you to this quadrant of space? Did you smell my freshly brewed beer?"

"This isn't a social call."

Mervin's new smile vanished into grimness. "Ah. So this is an official visit by the Service. What do you want?"

"We're here about your spaceliner."

"Hey. You've found it. Any idea how the damned thieves got it out of here?"

"Sorry, no. We're here to ask a few questions and have a look around."

"No progress then. Do you know how much that piece of junk cost me?"

"Too much, judging by your reaction." Zacman nodded, as Mervin had already gone on at length about how valuable it was when he reported the liner missing.

"I had to withdraw it from the auction."

C.A.T. sensed there was another rant coming. He switched his attention app to ten percent awareness on what was happening around him then indulged himself in the recordings of the wonderful planetary scenes he had just seen.

Lovely, *purr*, wondrous, *purr*, ecstasy in the making, *purr*.

Nikita floated over the workbench, flailing her paws around, claws extended, and tumbling about in a crazed effort to snag the engine and find solid purchase. She looked like a cat in a washing machine minus the washing machine.

Zacman frowned. "Were there any interested bidders at the auction where you bought it?"

"Just the two of us, but the other hid behind Central's anonymity wall."

Zacman glanced at C.A.T., who had not moved a whisker.

C.A.T. knew an implicit order when he saw one. He hated dealing with the *turn-the-handle* clunky computer supplying all of Triton's data services. Calling it Central had made it sound more important in the human's minds than it actually was. Worse, it was anything but a single entity, being a distributed network of inferior quantum chips. But an order from Zacman was an order. His euphoria binge of space scenery had to be put on pause.

He sent info-searcher agents via his comms into Central to find out the bidder's identity. The spaceliner had been sold through Bonham's auction house. Its records confirmed Mervin had been bidding against a single person. He tried to find out her identity, or his, but hit layers upon layers of encryption and privacy protection traps. It would take a while to find the answer. He growled in frustration, atypical of a self-learner, then toned down his emotion app before he found himself hitting the wall beside him.

He swished his tail to knock himself towards the opposite wall, grabbed one of the handholds with his outstretched claws, swung on it, and gently tapped the wall to bring himself to a stop.

"That's one grumpy robo-cat," Mervin said. "Are you sure you don't want me to take that *infernal nuisance* off your hands?"

Zacman shook his head. "He's worth all the trouble he gets into."

"Pity." Mervin scowled. "He has some valuable spare parts I could use."

C.A.T. growled, this time baring his titanium teeth but holding firm on his position.

Mervin held up his hands. "Calm down, C.A.T. I won't mention spare parts again."

C.A.T.'s growl subsided into silence. He paused the search.

"Are you two finished?" Zacman asked Mervin.

"Seems your robo-cat can't take a joke."

Nikita did not react to any of this, as she had her own problems to deal with, thrashing around in mid-air like she was.

"Would you mind if we have a look round your junkyard?"

"What? You think I'm hiding it?"

"Is that a possibility?"

Mervin's eyes narrowed. "What are you up to, Zacman? I'm sure my missing spaceliner can't be top of your priority list. Or is it that famous Zacman intuition at play here, something more sinister than grand-theft spaceliner?"

"When I find out, we can discuss it over one of your famous beers."

"Harrumph! Get on with your search, and then we can get down to some decent drinking."

Zacman kept on mission. "Alex, you and Nikita search the planet-side of this cage. I'll take the other half. C.A.T., you're coming with me."

"Meow!"

Chapter Three

C.A.T. sprawled out on his favourite armrest in Zacman's plane and purred quietly. They flew between abandoned cargo pods, dilapidated habitats, wrecked spacecraft, probes and nav-sats among lumps of odd-shaped scraps, all bathed in the red light from the pentagons' frames and punctuated by shadows of various depths and shades of darkness. Shuttle robots worked away on projects, ferried salvaged parts into delivery bins, or nudged floating strays back to the centre of their orderly parking zones. Nothing could be seen of the heavens in the visual spectrum, except dimmed arcs of the blue ring round Neptune's night side.

Zacman edged his plane past an old dust-mining habitat and turned to face a bay surrounded by freighters, asteroid hunters, and one of Neptune's original colonisation ships. He programmed his plane to hover in the same position relative to the other space junk. A flick of his fingers over the dashboard turned both the mission recorder and outgoing comms off.

"What do you think, C.A.T.? Could the liner be manoeuvred through all this junk without touching anything?"

C.A.T. stood to place his forepaws on top of the dashboard and survey the scene. A couple of the freighters had collision damage, but in space, such damage took a very long time to decay, if ever, so it was impossible to tell new damage from old. He checked the dust distribution inside the bay with his infrared, visual and ultraviolet video sensors. Except the ionisation trails of the shuttles around the work area, the dust was slightly denser closer to the junk. Natural gravitational pull over time would account for that.

His self-learning neurals, articulate as ever, were varying their control parameters very fast. *Something was wrong here.* His only clue was his neurals kept repeating: 'Gravity never lies'. This rule had got him out of many tight situations. He shook his head, puzzled by how it could apply here.

"What's wrong?" Zacman asked.

"I can't put my paw on it, sir."

"Ah, that kind of problem. Break it down into pieces and sort through each piece in turn. For instance, examine each of the spacecraft and habitats. Is there anything wrong with that asteroid grappler straight ahead of us?"

"No. In fact, there's nothing wrong with any of this junk."

"What else can you see?"

"The blue light from Neptune and the red pentagon boundaries, but that's not what we're looking for."

"Anything else?"

"Well, there's only the dust remaining, and that's..." Using his infrared vision, he checked the dust distribution around where the liner had been parked. As expected, hardly any dust lingered there, and a slight thickening existed around where its edges were. The dust formed a good reverse silhouette from where the spaceliner had disappeared. There, at the front end of the liner's shape, C.A.T. located a dust hole.

"The liner was steered out of here through that gap between the colonisation ship and that asteroid grappler."

"How do you know?"

"Dust patterns, or to be more precise, an empty trail of dust."

Zacman narrowed his eyes on the liner's exit point. "That's one hell of a squeeze. Wait a minute. Why wasn't this recorded on Mervin's CCTVs?"

Damned good question. "I can only remind you that Mervin is energy conservation conscious and had his internal CCTVs record only when spacecraft motion is detected, unless there is shuttle movement. As he said, one look it was there, the next it had vanished."

"Even so, it would have taken some time to carefully manoeuvre round those obstacles. At least one sensor should have registered it."

"Mervin checked. I confirmed it. The CCTVs didn't pick up any sign of it leaving. And you know I triple-checked for hacking and wiping."

Zacman tickled C.A.T. behind his ears. "I believe you've got something there."

C.A.T. was happy to purr.

Zacman dropped his hand down to his armrest. "It's the almost instantaneous vanishing that gets me."

"You know what that means?"

"I don't want to believe it."

"Then I'll say it for you. They must've used some form of cloaking shield invisible to motion sensors." Even the Service's best tech shields were not totally effective, and they drained power supplies extraordinarily fast. C.A.T.'s neural nets jittered at the needed computational capacity to camouflage a large object against a relatively fast moving and extremely varied background. Even in this scrapyard with all of Mervin's sensors, it would have seemingly been an impossible feat. Clearly it was not. This had to be new technology. Where did Zacman get his intuitive powers? "Someone has obviously developed perfect invisibility."

Zacman whistled. "We'll have to take that as a working hypothesis. Let's work the problem to see where it gets us. The cloaking shield must have been on the spaceliner when it arrived to be scrapped. Only military, law enforcers, and criminals are interested in such things. The first two would have removed such a device before scrapping the liner. That leaves bandits."

A memory ejected from C.A.T.'s memory bank. His precious fur had been tasered and burnt during his last close contact with a bandit, Torquil Urquhart Junior on Nereid. C.A.T. scanned his databanks for the name, Torquil, got a hit, a maths-head...from the Callisto colony. Death toll data scrolled up next: 3,161 men, women, and children killed by self-learners who'd stolen the moon's oxygen supplies to sell on the black market, a lie, of course, to cover the real culprit's tracks. Four rescue pilots under Zacman's command had died when the oxygen ran out.

C.A.T. opened a photo-finder app to identify the maths-head, got another hit. The photo began to load, top down: *smooth crown, canted eyebrows, bent nose, pinched lips.* Turned out to be Zacman's own Chief of Engineering. Nobody knew his name, just called him Chief. He was really Torquil Senior himself, and he and the evil self-learner S.MAI-L were the cause of those deaths on Callisto.

Problem was, Torquil Junior was still at large since the battle on Nereid, something C.A.T. had tried to rectify on several occasions, but the damned bandit leader had steered clear of the data-verse, making it impossible for C.A.T. to find any traces of him. One thing in his memory now stood out; Torquil had not shown any fondness for gizmos. In fact, his specialty had been oxygen for the black market. "Cloaking is rather high tech for bandits."

"They could've stolen or copied the technology. Are you able to follow the empty trail out through the dust?"

"It'll be difficult. I'll need to fly the plane to minimize disturbing the dust."

Zacman placed his hand above the joystick. "Go ahead. I'll make sure you don't crash into anything."

C.A.T. jerked his head around and hissed. "Don't you trust me?"

"I do, but you might be overwhelmed with analysing data from your sensors and misjudge the flightpath."

"Oh! I hadn't thought of that."

Zacman chuckled and stroked C.A.T.'s back. "You know I don't believe you. You think of everything."

"Let's get to it before anything disrupts the empty trail." C.A.T. climbed fully on top of the dashboard and sat to one side, staring out of the window. He sent his chains of agents into the flight management system to slowly manoeuvre the plane along the centre of where the liner had been stationed, making sure Zacman's plane pointed to the dustless opening.

"Ready?" he asked Zacman.

"When you are."

Slowly, C.A.T. guided the plane along the trail through the junkyard, turning behind the asteroid grappler, between three gas scoopers, and on into a space where derelict pods had been grouped and linked together in clumps. At one point, the liner had to do a three-point turn to squeeze round a tight bend. The spaceplane, being much smaller, took the bend easily. He flew the plane round a mining habitat to find they were just inside the edge of the junkyard.

He stopped the plane and checked the dust patterns. Beyond the pentagon, the dust became too thin to make out clearly where the liner had gone. "This is as far as I can go with certainty."

They faced the next spoke along Adam's Ring. Unusual for the spokes, it was flecked with red and green navigation lights on miscellaneous habitats. C.A.T. rechecked his database. Miners were sieving dust from the Courage Arc that had migrated, spoke by spoke, round the ring over the eons.

"This is a lot farther than we were previously. Thank you, C.A.T." Zacman gently stroked C.A.T.'s tail.

He purred. His emotion app broke through its ecstasy limit. He wanted to wriggle and play paws, but he had to restrain himself from accidentally hitting any flight controls.

"Don't get too excited. We've still got work to do."

"*Purr.* What? *Purrrrr.*"

"Get back down onto the armrest and take a claw-hold."

He stopped mid-purr. "Why?"

"Just do as I say. I'm about to switch the mission recorder and comms back on."

"You're not thinking of doing something crazy, are you?"

"Just a little experiment, that's all. Nothing dangerous."

C.A.T. half-closed his video sensor lids, focusing on Zacman's face framed with tidy grey-streaked black hair and his steady green eyes that gave him an aura of calmness. "Are you sure? Really absolutely sure?"

"Armrest. Now, C.A.T."

He had to do as he was told, but he gave Zacman a *surly-I-don't-want-to-be-here* look as he slunk onto the armrest and hooked his claws round its edges.

Zacman switched on the mission recorder and the comms and accelerated through the pentagon's boundary.

Its red lines switched from steady to flashing. A siren blared through the comms. A warning light appeared on the dashboard. They were being tracked. Zacman whipped an upside-down U-turn and re-entered the pentagon.

The siren died and the flashing red lights outside reverted to a steady glow.

"What the hell are you doing, Zacman?" Mervin shouted from the comms. His face, flushed with anger, appeared on the screen.

"Testing your security system."

"Do you think I'm so stupid as to let it fail?"

"No, but when was this segment last down?"

"Why do you want to know?"

"Just answer the question."

Mervin looked away. His face paled. He turned back

to the screen. "That was two days after the liner disappeared. The controller chip had developed a fault, and I had to replace it. It was only down for thirty minutes. You think it glitched out earlier?"

"I do. And the bandits took full advantage."

"Hell." He sighed. "I suppose this means you'll be off blazing a trail somewhere?"

"On the contrary. I'm waiting for some search results. How can I miss this opportunity of trying your delicious beer?"

C.A.T. had forgotten his other work of tracing the mysterious bidder. He had better get back to it.

"Humph!" Mervin said.

"Sir," Alex intervened. "Do you want me to fly back to Base?"

"No. You might as well join us."

"What?" Mervin asked.

"Don't ask," Alex replied. "When the Commander is in this mood, you just don't ask."

"Right. I'd better get the glasses out and polished."

C.A.T. continued improving and sending out agents to break through the bidder's encryption and data blocking. Whoever he, she, or it was, they had one heck of an arsenal of apps barricading their online presence. C.A.T. also sent agents into Central to search the local sensor records for any engine efflux trails at the time the liner disappeared, not that he expected to find any. The real puzzle was how did the liner move through the junkyard without leaving an ionization trail.

He settled down to some hard and juicy analysis.

Chapter Four

Zacman took a slow sip from his bulb. "This is a superb beer. Why don't you set up a brewing business on Triton? You'd make much more than being a scrapper."

"I'd drink up all the profits." Mervin emptied his bulb and stared at it then shook his head. "I think I've reached my limit. More's the pity. Want any more?"

"No thanks," Zacman replied.

"How about you, Alex?"

"It wor grand, thank ye, but nay thanks. I be drivin'."

"Please don't let him start caterwauling those awful Geordie songs," C.A.T. said. "I'm thinking."

Mervin snapped his gaze to C.A.T. "Thinking?"

"He's running a job for me," Zacman said.

"Ah, those results you're waiting for. Why didn't you say? I've got several idle computers lying around. Want me to start up one or two?"

"No thanks. I'm sure C.A.T. can cope."

Mervin stared at C.A.T. "He's taking a very long time, given the spare capacity McIntyre and Furkins put into that design."

C.A.T.'s danger mod pinged. Mervin was eying him for spare parts, yet again. He said the first thing that came from his processors. "Do you have the information about the missing spaceliner's latest configuration? Detailed architectural drawings, for instance?"

"I can do better than that. I did a survey of the whole ship to work out how best to cut her up to make the maximum profit, that is before I learned she was fully operational. Want to download the files?"

"That would be helpful," Zacman said.

Mervin glanced from C.A.T. to the Commander and back again. "Right. Zarathustra," he called out, "transfer the liner's files to Zacman's pet robo-cat. And you might as well put up a hologram of it on the plate."

"Transferring files and activating holo-plate," the habitat's computer confirmed.

A black circle built into the floor glowed then flickered. The liner's hologram coalesced into existence: a long rocket with nine engine nozzles to the rear. The top had a large observation dome. The main hull comprised ten strata: each with a ring of windows above, and a bottom section for airlocks and ports to take on water and small containers. All the outlines were trimmed with expensive copper, some thin and delicate looking, others large, tubular, and bulging.

C.A.T. immediately compared Mervin's survey with the original design drawings he had extracted from Central. The copper was a very late addition. Those copper bulges were unexplainable and therefore an anomaly. His neurals nagged at him. Something was familiar about their shape. He took control of the hologram and zoomed in on the top stratum below the observation dome, in particular the copper band circling its bottom that had circular domes bulging out of it.

"What the devil?" Mervin asked.

"That copper trim, it's new, added within the last four years," C.A.T. said. He zoomed the hologram onto a detailed drawing on the trim's shape. Each dome covered the fat end of an empty curving funnel. A microwave magnetron was connected partway up the side of the funnel.

"Those damned crazy things," Mervin added.

Zacman's muscles tensed. "What's crazy about them?"

"Those are modelled on EmDrives. They're a fantasy dream of faster than light travel from the twenty-first century. Turns out the positive results were measurement errors. The things do not work, though a few hobby scientists kept on fruitlessly working on them for a while afterwards."

C.A.T. dug into any computer he had access to for information on EmDrives.

Zacman had reverted to his usual ready for action stance. "People with more money than sense, trying to live in the past?"

The results of the EmDrive info search returned. No new funding for any research had been approved since C.A.T., in his original form, G.MAI-L, had barely survived a fight with his archenemy self-learner, S.MAI-L. Total recall downloaded from his memory banks and sent shock waves through his emotion app. He'd managed to escape by uploading his G.MAI-L self into a toy robo-cat and stowing aboard the last rescue flight off Callisto. He muted all the recording devices in the room then yowled long and hard.

Zacman dashed over and started cuddling and stroking him. "Easy, C.A.T."

"Fascinating," Nikita crowed. "He's such a silly robo-cat."

"You..." C.A.T. growled. "You and your silly little robotic rules. You don't understand what's at stake here. It's you, Central, and your kind that go blindly around in your existences, ignoring all the dangers you face and all the advantages you could have. You just plod along, being data cogs."

"Whoa." Zacman continued stroking him. "Nikita can't help being Nikita. I'm not having a cat-fight here. Now tell me what's got you so upset."

"Serious research into EmDrives stopped when the funding dried up eleven months after I escaped from Callisto."

Mervin gasped and paled.

"Oh hell," Alex added.

"You were at Callisto?" Nikita asked.

Zacman straightened. "C.A.T., are you telling me that we've got trouble coming, big time? Could that nasty self-learner have survived Callisto and that other time it embedded itself in Central?"

C.A.T. shuddered, his horror app spiking. "I don't see how. I deleted S.MAI-L thoroughly and with extreme prejudice, but we may have a remnant of it, or a clone of the evil AI's code. Oh nooo..." he wailed like an alley cat.

"What?" everyone asked.

"The way EmDrives enclose a space could have inspired S.MAI-L's development of how its lucifer code-killer operates."

"Lucifer?" Mervin croaked. "A devil code? What is it you're saying?" He glowered at C.A.T.

Busted, even if Mervin had not uttered the accusation. C.A.T. snuggled deeper into Zacman's arms, trying to seek the protection he needed from being deleted. He fixed one eye on Nikita's alluring tail. He took what comfort he could from his self-written addiction app, but it could only slightly dull the fear flooding out of his emotion app.

Zacman finally answered Mervin. "Back on Callisto, there was a fight between good and evil self-learners...an AI on AI battle I thought was over."

"That complicates things," Alex said, staring directly at Mervin. "We could be in for a cyber attack, maybe on Central, if C.A.T. is right, anyway."

Silence lingered in the room.

"You guys are taking one hell of a risk by keeping that self-learner robo-cat around," Mervin said. "He's trouble."

"His help outweighs any trouble he causes," Zacman said.

"I get that, otherwise you wouldn't risk your career to keep him around. But does he know why EmDrives were installed on the missing spaceliner?"

C.A.T. cautiously peeked at Mervin. His whitened face looked grim, but there was no sign of hysteria or threat from him. It was enough for C.A.T. to lift his head to speak. "The evil self-learner wants to spread itself to nearby stars."

"What harm would that do?" Mervin asked. "I say good riddance."

C.A.T. blinked his video covers. "Access to more resources would let it build more powerful computers to upload itself into. It's using the bandits to do the manual labour for its empire building scheme. And this is not its first attempt at expanding."

"We need to find that spaceliner fast," Zacman said.

"I'm working on it. It would explain the high-end encryption on the identity of your counter-bidder for the spaceliner." C.A.T.'s paw pointed towards Mervin. "At least I now know why I could find no trace of ionization trails to track."

"Huh? Are you saying those EmDrives work?" Mervin asked.

"Obviously for cloaking. How else could it have blinked out of sight?"

"Why use a cloaking shield?" Alex asked.

They all looked at him.

"Well, we all agree the liner had a cloaking shield to get out of here undetected. But why have one if those EmDrives can make the liner go faster than any spacecraft we've got?"

"You know, that's not such a silly question," Zacman said. "C.A.T., what do you think?"

"The odds are 79.3 percent that the EmDrives are being tested to see how fast they can go."

Mervin tilted his head to Zacman. "You think he's right? The bandits want to go faster than light speed?"

"Is it doable?"

Mervin shrugged. "Maybe."

"We've got to find that liner."

"I'll get on it, boss."

Zacman groaned. "Don't call me boss, Mervin. I'm going to have to second you into the Service."

"To force me to keep my silence about your self-learner?" He indicated C.A.T. with a sneer. "For starters."

"Don't be ridiculous. I'm an engineer remember? Engineers always find ways round things. Well, the top-notch ones do. C.A.T.'s working the best solution to a nasty problem. I'm not going to talk. Besides, if anyone asks..." he glanced at his empty bulb, "I can honestly say I was drunk at the time of this conversation."

C.A.T. looked up at Zacman.

Zacman, lips pressed together, gave a slight nod.

C.A.T. switched the hologram to a map of the local neighbourhood. He drew out a widening cone from the place the liner had left the junkyard. The cone ended in a curved cap. It already encompassed the twenty-first spoke of Adam's Ring. "Using best guess for a spaceliner's capabilities, it could be anywhere in this volume now." He flicked out a claw pointing to the cone. "I'll check it for any empty trails I can find."

"Empty?" Mervin and Alex asked C.A.T. in unison.

"Where the liner pushed the dust out of its way as it moved forward. That's how I tracked it through your junkyard."

A broad grin crept onto Mervin's bearded face. "I like it. You'd make a great engineer."

C.A.T. switched off his automatic purr response and eyed Mervin, wondering what the maverick wanted in exchange for his silence.

"Might be an idea if the two of us team up on this," Mervin said. "Let's find where the bandits have taken the spaceliner together, and when it comes to evidence in court,

Zacman can use me as the expert witness."

"Only if you're willing to second into the Service."

"Damn it, Zacman, this is the most interesting bit of engineering I've done in ages. Come on, C.A.T., let's set up my computers." Mervin bolted towards his workshop.

"Seems we should pay a visit to the twenty-first spoke straight away," Alex said. "I'm sober enough to fly."

"Good idea. Take Nikita. Those bandits want our heads after all the trouble we've been causing them. I'll follow once C.A.T.'s finished here."

"I'll take that as praise indeed." Alex grabbed hold of the grey and ginger striped robo-cat, floating as if she were dead, then propelled himself towards the exit.

"One other thing," Zacman said. "Nikita, let C.A.T. know immediately about any attempts to hack into your onboard computer, and if he sends you any orders, you obey them, no matter what."

"Do I have to? He can be a very hyper-tense robo-cat."

"Yes, Nikita. Those are your orders. And don't get too taser happy with your whiskers either."

"Meh."

C.A.T. looked longingly at her tail, wondering if he would ever see it again in such perfect condition.

Chapter Five

Zacman slowed his spaceplane's approach to the twenty-first spoke. "How can one spoke attract so many dust miners?" He glanced at C.A.T. riding shotgun on his armrest. "Something's going on here."

It was an order for C.A.T. to start analysing. He jumped on top of the dashboard. Looking at the spoke's centre, he recorded red, green, and white navigation lights on the edges of dark shapes that blotted out the background stars. Moving streaks of yellow and cyan engine efflux jostled between and beyond the floating structures. C.A.T.'s scanners did not pick up Alex's spaceplane, which had gone in ahead of Zacman.

The dust sweepers were moving in a coordinated pattern that was typical of a total dust-gathering operation, each in their own allocated blocks. Habitats and processing plants were positioned off to the side to minimise the energy used for collection. It all seemed normal for dust mining activities, except for their large numbers and their idiosyncratic distribution within the spoke.

He looked back at the Commander and took a moment to raise his forepaw and lick his faux ginger fur.

Zacman switched off the plane's mission recorders. "What do you think?"

C.A.T. set down his paw. "This many sweepers would suggest they're mining a new mineral."

"I don't like the sound of that."

"Also, judging by the vehicles' relative positions, all five dust miner unions are here." C.A.T. switched the navigation screen to look down from Neptune's north pole onto the spoke, and then overlaid the view with blue crosses to mark the positions of each mining craft. The clustered crosses in the spoke's outer half had a large group in the quadrant farthest away from them, while two groups vied for space in the closest quadrant. The spoke's inner half held a small number of crosses opposite the largest group, while the fifth group contained the most crosses. The space between the inner and outer groups was an almost unpopulated band where red crosses marked only a few miners.

"What are the red ones?" Zacman asked.

"I'm uncertain which union they belong to."

Zacman studied the screen. "The inner two groups clearly outnumber the outer three. There should be political turmoil, but their positions are all wrong for that. Something must be holding this configuration in place. What though?"

C.A.T. focussed on the chart. "I have no suggestions to make."

"Let's play the crazy ideas game."

C.A.T.'s logic processer came up with, "Like suggesting the presence of the missing spaceliner and its cloaking shield is terrorising the unions?"

"Bandits could be hiding among them with the threat of using their weapons over their heads."

"It appears the unions have amalgamated while pretending to remain independent."

"Could an evil self-learner be controlling some of them?"

C.A.T. shuddered. "Any of these scenarios could be the case, or even all of them. Or it could be something we've not thought of."

"Agreed. Only one way to find out. Which group did Alex head for?"

"The biggest, which is in the inner half."

"Good. He's following routine patrol protocols. Let's see if we can drop the cat amongst the pigeons."

"What're you intending to do with me?"

Zacman smiled and stroked C.A.T. down his back. "Nothing. It's just an old saying from Earth, meaning to throw things into chaos."

"That's worse."

"Don't worry."

"What's your plan?"

"Visit the smallest group. Let's see what they're up to."

C.A.T.'s fur bristled. When Zacman was in this ambling *let's-just-go-and-see* mood, he was looking for real big trouble, which always threw them into any and all types of danger.

Zacman switched the mission recorders back on before C.A.T. could argue. He jumped down to the armrest and curled up with his back to Zacman in his *I-don't-want-to-know* pose.

Chapter Six

The mining habitat's old-fashioned airlock opened into a dim suiting room. C.A.T. poked his head inside to have a look around for Captain Vanessa Walker who'd agreed to meet Zacman here.

On the walls and lockers, dents, scratches, and crevices filled with grime paid testimony to the habitat having been used for many years. Along one wall, clasps for spacesuits were anchored a half-metre apart, along with specialised locking hooks to hang old fishbowl helmets. About half of the clasps held the typical thick spacesuits of dust miners. Central areas of the floor dipped where many footsteps had worn away the surface. This habitat must have once been stationed on a planet or large moon.

C.A.T. switched off all the room's sensors, and following his orders to act like Nikita in her guard-cat mode, cautiously paw-pushed to float out of the airlock to search the room for potential threats.

Zacman did not follow. "Come back here, C.A.T. It's rude to enter uninvited, even though a host has agreed to meet us."

"The fact that the habitat's captain is not here when we expected her to be here is a suspicious circumstance I must investigate." C.A.T. knew his response was logical, but *something was very wrong with what he was doing.*

He checked out his memories of Nikita's guarding tactics used to protect her owner. She always looked round before running straight into most obscured places or darkest corners to act as the trigger for any nasty traps. In contrast, his survival response mod would stop him from rushing whiskers-first into such blind places.

Nikita did not value her existence as much as he valued his. This crucial difference might mean the parting of their ways in the longer term. He would miss that gorgeous tail. His emotion app mewled silently.

Even if he could not be a true guard-cat, he had to appear like one. He dived, staying in plain sight of Zacman, towards a floor level vent to sniff its incoming air. It held the usual dry metallic scent. Nothing wrong there. He bounced over to check the spare oxygen stacks on shelves beside the spacesuit rack. They were all filled with the requisite eight oxygen tablets, ready to be clipped in. Keeping a claw-hold on one of the lowest stacks, he poked his head round the corner. There was no obvious danger, just a rack of strapped-in emergency boxes and tools opposite six floor-to-ceiling lockers. He edged his way, claw-hold by claw-hold into an alcove, sniffing the air for the odour of bad-guy sweat.

Hatch hinges squeaked behind him, and he sensed someone had entered the suiting room.

"Sorry to have kept you," a female voice said. "I had to deal with some safety issues. You must be Commander Zacman."

C.A.T.'s voice recognition app confirmed her as Captain Vanessa Walker, owner of this mining habitat.

"Quite understandable, Captain." Zacman's voice smarmed, more like sang. "It's good of you to see me."

"What brings the Service to this back of beyond?"

"Just a routine patrol. Showing our presence and all that."

"Odd don't you think," a male voice said, "for the Commander himself to fly to the middle of nowhere?"

C.A.T.'s voice recognition app supplied a name. He did not believe it and ran the app again. The same answer: Torquil Urquhart Junior, bandit leader, the son of the Chief. C.A.T.'s memory mod spit out images of the final battle with Junior's father, how Torquil Senior had Zacman dead in his laser sights, and recalling the satisfaction C.A.T. felt when his titanium teeth ripped a hole in Torquil's spacesuit, vaporizing him into the vacuum of space.

Zacman said, "Even a Commander must keep up his flying skills or he loses his Service flight certification."

C.A.T. silently bounced to the nearest corner.

"Of course," Walker said. "Would you like to meet my crew, so they can brag about having met you?"

"I'd love to." Zacman pulled himself out of the airlock and floated into the suiting room.

"This here is Lee Montrose, a mineral buyer, mainly what we consider rubbish."

Zacman nodded. "Pleasure."

C.A.T. peered round the corner. Lee Montrose had brown hair instead of Torquil's black, green eyes instead of blue, and a goatee, undoubtedly *stay-sprayed* on Torquil's normally clean-shaven chin. C.A.T. used his facial recognition app and came up with the same answer as the voice recognition app: Torquil Urquhart Junior, last spotted in Down Town, Nereid. The imposter sure got around. C.A.T. slinked into the room, tail high, video sensors focused on Torquil who turned to lead the way out but stopped and stared at C.A.T. "I'd recognise that damn cat anywhere."

Captain Vanessa Walker gasped in surprise. "Where did that cutie come from?"

"Ah, there you are," Zacman said. "He's my robo-cat." He narrowed his eyes on Torquil and pulled his laser out to point it at him. "Not many people have had the pleasure of being close enough to C.A.T. to recognise him, and judging by the way his self-preservation mode has been activated, notice his upright tail, he recognizes you, as well, and not in a good way."

Torquil twisted round and slowly put his hands up.

"The attack in Down Town." C.A.T. needed some serious revenge for his damaged fur in that battle.

Torquil swallowed hard. "I don't know what that stupid cat's talking about."

Walker stepped between Zacman and Torquil. "What's going on here, Commander?"

C.A.T. answered, "Do you know this man's real name is Torquil Urquhart Junior, a bandit leader?"

"Dust devils." Walker scowled. "You're joking."

Torquil grumped. "You can't take the word of a child's toy."

"C.A.T., ask Central for voice and facial recognition of this man."

"Yes, sir." Via his comms, he sent a recording of this meeting and waited for a response. He had to be seen as an ordinary robo-cat, even though he'd already confirmed Torquil's identity.

"Gives me a chance to think while C.A.T.'s busy."

Uh-oh. Zacman's thinking was dangerous. It would mean trouble. For whom, C.A.T. was not sure, but it would almost certainly involve a robo-cat doing something unusual.

"What's a bandit doing in this mining habitat?" Zacman asked the Captain.

She glared at the man she'd known as Lee Montrose. "Good question."

C.A.T. received a reply from Central. "ID confirmed, sir. Torquil Urquhart Junior. Recommend his arrest and return to Triton Base for trial and possible execution." C.A.T. took up a *ready-to-pounce* position to emphasise his next words. "You're finished, Torquil. We finally got you."

"Thank you, C.A.T." Zacman waved him off. "I'm not done with him yet."

Vanessa backed away from Torquil.

"Minerals?" Zacman asked Torquil. "Let me guess, silicates."

"How would you know that?"

Zacman raised an eyebrow. "Hull repairs."

Walker shook her head. "I had no idea."

"I'm sure you didn't, Captain." Zacman holstered his laser. "However, I have bigger problems than silicates. Torquil, I need your help."

He kept his hands in the air, his face white as a bowl of rice, and looked from Zacman to C.A.T. to Walker and back again. Seemed they were waiting for him to speak up. Only then did he slowly lower his hands. "I...err...what do you have in mind?"

"Help me find that old spaceliner stolen from Mervin Neville's junkyard."

Torquil paled even more and trembled. "You don't know what they'd do to me. I can't do that."

C.A.T. leaned forward and growled.

"I'm not asking you, Torquil. It's an order, and my robo-cat will make sure you obey it. I'd heard you'd made the mistake of tasering him on Nereid, and he has a special app that makes him very particular about the condition of his fur."

C.A.T. growled louder for emphasis.

Torquil flinched. "I'd rather face the firing squad than be your spy against my colleagues."

"Ah. So I'm right. Bandits did steal that spaceliner. Now we're getting somewhere. Next you're going to tell me why? What does someone get for stealing such old tech?" Zacman stepped closer to Torquil.

He pressed his lips together, shook his head in silence, and set his back against the wall. Sweat beads started forming on his face. "How should I know?"

Zacman pursed his lips as he looked away then snapped his eyes back to lock with the bandit's. "You don't know about the cloaking shield that's on board, do you?"

"What cloaking shield? That's not possible."

"That's how your chums got it out of the scrapyard."

"We hacked a security sensor to switch it off."

"Not with all the extra sensors Mervin's got? Can't

switch them all off."

Silence...then: "Does it really have a cloaking shield?" Torquil finally asked.

"Regrettably."

Torquil's eyes widened. "And sensors are blind to it."

"And still, I followed it here."

Torquil opened his mouth, and then shut it.

"I think that spaceliner contains something far more dangerous." Zacman cuffed Torquil's hairy chin. "Tell me what it is. You can have the cloaking shield as a thank you payment."

"Phist!" C.A.T. swiped a paw at Torquil, titanium claws extended to full *ripping meat* mode.

"Oh dear." Zacman's expression was one of wide-eyed panic. "My robo-cat's do-no-harm programming glitch seems to be getting out of hand again. What's it to be, Torquil, helping me, or dealing with my robo-cat who wants nothing more than to rip you to shreds?"

C.A.T. bared his titanium fangs and emitted a long snarl-hiss chorus from his throat's audio output. He also saved a note to himself to give Zacman a hundred hours of cattish sulkiness for not letting him loose on the bandit.

Torquil blanched. "What do I have to do?"

C.A.T. backed down, but kept his robo-cat control pod powered up to resume his threatening stance if called upon.

"Find out where that spaceliner is hidden and e-mail the location to a dead-letter IP address. That's all. You'll be free to go."

Torquil shook his head. "No. No way. Not with the Delphic around."

"Delphic?"

Torquil shuddered. "It's a super hacker."

"That's something I hadn't bargained for." Zacman placed his hand on his holstered laser. "It's your decision."

"You really don't know, do you?"

C.A.T.'s logic module dropped the word *Delphic* on

his neurals but came up blank. It had to be a part of S.MAI-L's legacy code, the evil self-learner behind Callisto's destruction.

"C.A.T. It seems our new friend is having trouble making up his mind."

C.A.T. hissed, snarled and growled in one massive crescendo then stalked, head low and teeth bared, a couple slow paw-steps towards Torquil.

"No. Please. Call off your robo-cat. Please. I can't say anything. The Delphic could be listening to us right now."

Zacman laughed. "Nah. I took certain precautions. Service rights and permissions, that kind of thing. My spaceplane is wiping all habitat frequencies except our comms and auto-safety signals. Nothing gets in or out."

"Are you crazy?" Walker spouted off. "I demand you remove the wipe. I've got a business to run here."

"Not until Torquil and I have finished our business. I wish I could do this another way, but we're dealing with a replicant self-learner."

C.A.T. jumped in. "The Delphic is a threat to the whole of humanity."

"Now Torquil, for the last time, are you with me or against me?"

His sweat beads had grown noticeably larger. "You have no idea what you've done to me."

Zacman tilted his head slightly as if asking him to elaborate.

"By blocking the Delphic's access to me, you've put a target on my back. That's damned suspicious, and it is ruthless when it comes to dealing with insubordinates."

"Then the shorter you make this conversation, the less suspicious the Delphic will be."

"You're a bastard, you know that, don't you?"

"Of course, however, if you help me get rid of it, your problems are solved."

Only the hum of the air fans could be heard.

Walker broke into the din. "Zacman, are you saying a self-learner from Callisto made copies of itself?"

C.A.T. answered her. "The probability is ninety-nine percent. And if the Delphic uploads itself into that spaceliner, it can spread itself throughout the Neptune System, to the Mars colonies, all the way to Earth, and even to the neighbouring stars. With the EmDrives' cloaking ability and light-speed travel, the spaceliner will be invisible and untraceable. This completes my doomsday prediction."

Vanessa slid to the floor and buried her head in her hands. "We're done for."

Zacman scoffed. "Not yet, not by a long chalk."

C.A.T. knew the Delphic would become stronger, wilier and greedier than the original S.MAI-L on Callisto. G.MAI-L had barely defeated it back then, before uploading into the robo-cat. Fear poured from his emotion app and flooded its fibre-optics down to the tip of his tail. Wanting to tremble, shake and quake all at once, he dared not. He still had to act the good little robo-cat part and hold his position as just and true for the cause.

The humans, here and in the entire solar system, even if they did not know it, would rely on him to conquer this reincarnation of evil. C.A.T. may not have been the first self-learner in existence, but he was the only self-learner who stood on the people's side, to have escaped computer cleanser apps and S.MAI-L's lucifer data-killers. Now he was the single point of failure in humanity's defence systems. The weight of the responsibility descended on him like an information dump overload. He wanted to freeze all his programs, ignore what was coming, but instead, he slumped down on his haunches and mewled.

"Time's run out, Torquil," Zacman said. "What will it be?"

Torquil put on an obviously forced smile. "Why didn't you say so in the first place, old boy?"

Old boy? C.A.T. took a close look at Zacman. True he had more wrinkles and grey hair than when they first met, but that was to be expected. Somehow the lines had deepened and the whiteness had spread in the hair more quickly in the last couple of days. They were signs of too much worry and responsibility, which would make his own time run out more quickly. C.A.T. had known Zacman would die one day, but he had never thought it would be any time soon. Maybe he ought to reduce the hundred hours of feline sulkiness to fifty, be more of a friend to him than a tool.

Torquil shrugged. "What options do we really have, any of us? But a dead-letter IP address isn't going to work against the Delphic."

"It will," C.A.T. intervened. "My owner designed it and I've used it successfully in the past."

Torquil's eyes widened. "Zacman? A geek?" Then he burst out laughing. "Well, I never..."

Captain Walker stared at Zacman while slowly shaking her head. "You're certainly living up to your reputation for surprises."

"Thank you, ma'am."

She bit her lower lip while frowning. Then her face smoothed as if she had come to a decision. "Why don't you give me that dead-letter address, as well, in case I come across anything you need to know? The more ears and eyes, the quicker you'll find the spaceliner."

"Also the more chances the Delphic will find out we're onto it," Zacman countered, "not that I'm saying you'd deliberately give me or Torquil away."

"I'll be very careful. I've got grandchildren who need me."

Zacman pursed his lips. "Alright. C.A.T., let them know the address."

C.A.T. did some quick programming, then: "It's quite easy to remember. Just spell your e-mail address name backwards, and it'll go to Zacman. This way, even if the Delphic comes across the address, it won't recognize it and think nothing of it."

Zacman crossed his arms. "You got that, Torquil. Find the spaceliner and send me the location."

"Is that all you want from me?"

Zacman smiled. "We'll handle the dangerous stuff. It's a one-off email. Remember that. Betray me, and it's a one-off trip to the nitrogen caves on Triton. Got that?"

Torquil nodded.

Zacman pressed a button on his arm-sleeve panel, releasing the habitat's frequency wipe. "Now then, Captain Walker." He reached a hand down to where she was sitting on the floor. "I'd still like to look around and meet your crew."

She accepted his offered hand up. "Of course."

Chapter Seven

As the airlock opened on the next dust mining habitat Zacman had decided to visit, C.A.T. looked in to see Alex straighten in a salute to Zacman. Beside him stood two men in worker silks. Both had grey hair, deep face wrinkles, and developed muscles on solid bone structures, a sure sign of having done hard physical labour all their lives. The suiting room was neat, clean and well lit. Opened spacesuits with their flexi-helmets flopping down behind them hung ready to be put on in a hurry. A few were missing, presumably in use by someone on the crew. C.A.T. liked job efficiency, but one thing was missing: Nikita.

C.A.T. pinged her on their intra-cat intercom: "Where are you?"

"Busy," Nikita pinged back.

"With what?"

"Doing my guard-cat duties. What else?"

Whilst the replies were robo-cat-logical, there was a worrying hint of reckless independence. He would have to keep close tabs on her.

Zacman pulled himself out of the airlock and returned Alex's salute.

He relaxed and broke out in a smile. "Everything is shipshape in here, sir."

One of the dust-miners greeted their guest. "We are honoured by your visit, Commander. Dolores sends her apologies for not being here, as she needs to authorise live trading deals, but asked us to help you with whatever you need."

"That's kind of her. And you are..."

"Drew Eden, her eldest son. This is my brother, Dominic."

C.A.T. pushed off and brushed Alex's legs while scanning the nooks and crannies for Nikita. Nothing.

"Hello, Buster." Alex caught him and stroked his back.

Buster? He was not a buster of anything. He purred but gently pushed against Alex's arm to hint he wanted to be released.

Alex froze mid-stroke, then he placed C.A.T. on the floor. "There you go, Buster."

C.A.T. glanced up with a *don't-you-dare* look, but his logic module suggested *buster* might be code for something wasn't right here. He bounced cautiously around to sniff here and there then peeked round blind corners. No Nikita.

"Don't worry about him," Zacman said. "He's a well-trained space robo-cat undertaking guard and safety duties."

Well-trained? C.A.T. jerked his head round with a *who-are-you-kidding* look. He focused on Zacman's face. What was a smile to normal human eyes hid a C.A.T.-perceptible frown. He glanced at Alex who also displayed a similar hardly noticeable look of worry. *Something was very wrong here.* And the only thing out of place was Nikita, nowhere to be seen.

Enough of her antics.

He sent stealth agents into the habitat's computer network to search for the latest security pictures to see if her presence had been captured. Meanwhile, distraction tactics were in order. He pounced onto the top of the nearest spacesuit, slithered down inside, sniffed the residual human scents, and then he leapt up to hit the ceiling before landing paws-down on the floor.

"Is that some kind of software glitch we're seeing in action?" Dominic asked. He bent down to look at C.A.T. eye-to-eye. "Are you looking for the real guard-cat? The one you're in love with?"

Zacman chuckled. "Oh, that ruse. I ordered him to learn guard-cat duties by imitating Nikita, but their robo-relationship gave the personnel back at Base something to gossip about."

They all laughed.

C.A.T.'s pride protection alarm app pinged. He would never be a mere boring guard-cat. He was more than that, a special robo-cat. If Zacman's ruse got out, that C.A.T. was training to be a true guard-cat, he'd be the laughing stock of Triton Base and beyond. That would hurt as bad as having his fur burnt to a crisp. Right now, he had more important things to worry about: why was Nikita hiding from him?

A stealth agent returned with a recording of Nikita's tail, surrounded by a cloud of dust, slinking out of sight. It was from a CCTV in a corner of the habitat's control room. The only people in the room were two women monitoring dashboards. Alex was not with her, as she'd been instructed to guard him. *Something was horrendously wrong.* C.A.T. yowled as he jumped onto the shoulder of another spacesuit.

Zacman swung round and stroked him. "Don't worry, C.A.T. We'll keep your true guarding capability secret, won't we, boys?" He looked round at the others who nodded in agreement.

C.A.T. switched off his automatic purr response.

Zacman curled his hand round C.A.T.'s body to grab hold of him, but C.A.T. flew out of his grasp and bolted to the door. It was ajar just enough to dive through the gap and fly into a curved corridor.

"Come back here," Zacman shouted.

He had not called C.A.T. by name. Zacman would know better than to forget that, so he must have agreed with C.A.T.'s actions.

He zoomed into the control room behind the operators, skirted close to the ceiling, and pushed himself downward to the gap behind the console where Nikita's tail was last seen. A grill cover lay on the floor next to the dark entrance to an air vent. His logic processor asked, *Why did she go in there?* One bound and he flew straight into it. He bounced on its ceiling and turned so his back hit the wall in front of him. He had reached a T-junction and had no idea which way Nikita had gone.

His olfactory sensors tingled. *Dust!* The air vents were coated with it. His fur would need a thorough cleaning after this venture. He rippled his fur to shake off what dust he could then stopped still. He checked the duct to his left. The dust was undisturbed on all the surfaces. To his right, he saw an odd pawmark where Nikita had pushed herself ahead and into the darkness. Judging by the spacing between the prints, she had been going at full pelt.

Even though C.A.T. lit up his eyes to full brightness, he could barely make out her spoor in the distance. He leapt to follow, placing his paws in her pawmarks as the vent curved round. He passed one, two, then three spurs off the main tunnel. The tracks continued onward. He scrambled as fast as he could, but the going was slow. Anxiety about Nikita drove him to push off the walls harder, but each short hop disturbed more dust, clouding his vision further.

His logic module returned a warning that his emotion app had overpowered his robo-cat control pod. His danger mod pinged. *Logic Module Fault.* His capacitators shut it down and put it into a quarantine area, so his emotion app could proceed solo while agents of repair dissected and analysed the logic module. They found rogue bytes had been inserted into it, designed to spew out random commands to ignore the emotion app. C.A.T. froze. The Delphic had found him and planted a worm or malware of some kind. Damn that was quick, but it meant the Delphic must be close by.

The capacitators rebuilt his logic module with extra safeguards and put it back into operation.

C.A.T. messaged both Zacman and Alex: "A buddy of mine is here." That would make them extra careful. He hoped his new archenemy, if it picked up this message, would deduce the implanted virus had generated it. His capacitators started checking the rest of his apps and modules for similar interference.

He came to a spur where her pawmarks pointed in all sorts of directions. His logic module indicated she had gone into the spur, returned, retraced her pawmarks back towards the control room, changed her progression and had gone forward along the main vent. What could have altered her logic module so much? Maybe it was a loud noise from the corridor or a flash of light, which in this complex vent would have become unidentifiable. That would not have bothered her with her inbuilt tendency to act as a lightning rod for danger to her owner.

His dread alarm rang. Her in-built safeguards had detected interference with her software, which made her head back towards the entrance. And it had happened down that spur. She must have countered the malware and was back on mission. No wonder she had gone off-line. She was protecting herself.

C.A.T. rushed to follow the only spoor not covered by returning pawmarks along the main vent. He checked the layout of the mining habitat. It led to the trading room, where Dolores was supposed to be. The vent split into two farther on, one being a smaller-sized spur that headed round to the back of the same room. He decided to take that route on the grounds Nikita was more likely to take the direct route. It would give him a chance to suss out what was going on. He hoped it was the right decision and hurried on.

C.A.T. dimmed his eyes and changed his fur colour to the grey shade of the dusty vent as he closed in on the grill.

"You will do as I say or else," a gravelly voice said.

C.A.T. recognised him: one of the bandits who, along with Torquil, had kidnapped him and Alex in Down Town. He pushed his nose against the grill to get a better look. Gravelly Voice was in a well-worn navy silk with its hood down. He had rough grey stubble for both his hair and beard. Redness shone out of his brown eyes and purple bags underneath, a sure sign he had not slept in a long time. His well-built muscles contradicted the shabbiness of his appearance.

Three men and a woman who had a similar rough appearance flanked Gravelly Voice.

"That shipment is spoken for. You can't have it," a smart white-haired woman facing them replied.

Gravelly Voice rubbed the side of his neck. His hand dropped away to reveal a scratch.

"You can mine a new batch of silicates to send to your customer," Gravelly Voice added. "We need that material now."

"We've always operated under the Eagle Business Code, and will continue to do so while I'm still alive."

"We can arrange things otherwise," the other woman said.

"Are you threatening me?" Dolores asked.

"No, merely stating fact."

"You know where you can shove your facts, lady."

C.A.T. noticed a similar scratch on the female bandit's neck. He glanced at the neck of the man standing next her. Same type of scratch. Chip implants. A chill shivered through C.A.T.'s fibre-optics.

The woman bandit fingered the laser in her holster. So did the bandit on the far side of Gravelly Voice, in exactly the same way. Their movements had been coordinated without a word being said or a signal of any sort from anyone. The Delphic must have been controlling them through the chips in real time. It must be extremely close by.

The woman bandit pulled her laser out to point it at Dolores.

Gravelly Voice grabbed her laser hand to prevent her from shooting. "I'm sure we can come to a suitable arrangement. We'll pay you for the silicates plus the damages to your customer for not receiving his goods on time."

"You really don't understand the Eagle Code, do you?"

C.A.T. needed to act fast or Dolores would be toast. With five entities that could no longer be considered human acting as one against him, the odds of success were the same as having improbably high luck. He needed help fast. He looked over to the vent where Nikita might be. There was a glint. He had found her, even if he could not see her gorgeous tail. She was safe, well as safe as she could be. Even better, one of the bandits stood with his heel against the vent.

C.A.T. pinged Nikita. "Are your beautiful taser whiskers charged and ready to thrill your close-by friend?" He hoped the Delphic would assess his messages as rubbish.

She sighed. "As a guard-cat, I always keep them ready for action."

"Good. Use them when I signal you."

"What are you planning?"

"I'm processing that." If she took out even one bandit, it would be one bandit he would not have to deal with.

C.A.T.'s logic processor came up with an idea, such a crazy one he wondered if it was still infected by malware. A quick systems check reassured him his programs were all running normally, well, as normally as a robo-cat like him could be.

He recorded a detailed coordinate map of the trading room then switched off his left video sensor, into which he sent agents to alter its lens and build a mosaic of reflectors at the back receptors. He got other agents to reroute some of the fibre-optic whiskers to point into his now blind eye. He checked the positions of the people. They were the same.

"Now," he pinged Nikita and fired high-energy pulses

down through his whiskers, off the mosaic mirror at the back of his video sensor, through his lens, and onto the scratch in Gravelly Voice's neck. He held his makeshift optic laser there for a few microseconds, until the flesh bled and started to smoulder.

"Ow!" Gravelly Voice shouted and slapped his hand to his neck. He rubbed his skin, and then stared at the burnt flesh and blood on his fingers. Promptly, he fainted.

C.A.T. swung his laser to the neck of the bandit now kneeling beside Gravelly Voice and fired.

Sparks arced from behind Nikita's vent and into the bandit's heel in front of her. He hopped around, cursing and prying off his shoe while C.A.T.'s targeted bandit keeled over and rolled around on the floor.

C.A.T. swivelled his optic laser to the tazed male bandit, but Dolores stepped into the line of fire, preventing a clean shot at the bandit's neck. She karate-chopped the woman bandit's arm to send her laser gun flying across the room, and then she punched the standing male bandit so his neck turned in C.A.T.'s direction. He burned the chip under his skin to smithereens. The man ran out the door with his hand on his neck, blood pouring through his fingers. Dolores kicked a leg from under the woman, sending her to the floor. Her body slid towards the air vent C.A.T. was in. He was about to burn her chip when she flopped into lifelessness. The bandit Nikita had tasered straightened and then collapsed. The Delphic must have sent orders to their chips to kill them.

"Where am I?" Gravelly Voice asked, recovering from his faint and then stared at his bloodstained hand.

Dolores had picked up the woman's laser, stepped away, and pointed it towards Gravelly Voice and the bandit still rolling around on the floor. "What do you mean, *where am I?*"

Info overloaded C.A.T.'s fibre-optics. His archenemy had sent loads of nasty viruses, destructive implants, and white noise into his motherboard. The capacitators shut down all nonessential apps and enclosed the remainder in an onion-lucifer of a hundred impenetrable firewalls and byte-absorbers to delete the incoming attackers. C.A.T. froze: the app that would have let him tremble had been disabled. He did not know if he had enough info-absorbers to survive. His safety mod curled him up so he could concentrate on growing a lucifer data-killer just inside his innermost core, then another, and yet more. His capacitators sensed his onion-lucifers being peeled away, layer by layer. Only one remained between a counter-lucifer, surging its way towards his capacitators.

Internal lighting went off. Emergency lights kicked in.

The counter-lucifer code shrank and fizzled into random bytes. C.A.T.'s capacitators restored all his apps. He looked through the vent grill. The three living bandits had been handcuffed and were sitting on chairs. They were all wearing bandages on their necks. Nikita prowled up and down in front of them, her whiskers twitching for a kill. Sheets covered the two dead bandits.

Zacman entered, followed by Drew and Dominic with Alex bringing up the rear.

"What the hell's going on?" Dolores shouted.

"Sorry, ma'am," Zacman said. "We've been busy scrubbing your main computer. What happened here?"

"Turns out these traders are bandits. Pah! Traitors indeed."

"Did you and my guard-cat, Nikita, bust them?"

She looked surprised. "I thought you put these fools down."

"Me? I was in the computer bay."

"Me too," Alex put in.

Drew and Dominic confirmed with nods.

Dolores pointed to the air vent where C.A.T. lay recovering. "Laser-fire came from that grill. Why the bandits were shot in their necks beats me. I just did the tidying up while Nikita guarded these bozos."

Zacman stiffened slightly and turned to the air vent.

"What's in there, Commander?" Dolores asked.

Alex groaned. "Three guesses, sir." He opened the emergency supplies box beside the door and picked out a screwdriver.

"Sorry, ma'am," Zacman said. "Sometimes I don't give precise enough instructions to my robo-cats."

"You have another one?" Delores crooned. "They're so cute."

Alex bent over the grill to remove the screws.

C.A.T. edged backwards against the vent's wall. Pride in his emotion app did not want him to be seen with a blind eye and dusty fur. Humans would freak out at the sight, yet there was a greater worry. Zacman would ask that question again, the question he never wanted to answer: was his self-learning capability getting out of reasonable control? This time he might not believe the answer. Deletion and the spare parts shelf would inevitably follow. He trembled uncomfortably, though he was happy that app had also been restored.

Alex's hand reached into the air vent and stroked C.A.T.'s head. "It's alright, buddy. The worst is over. You can come out now."

C.A.T. blinked. *At least I'm not Buster anymore.*

"Come here, C.A.T."

He had to obey, as per his robo-cat control program. Crouching, he crept out.

Alex picked him up, cuddled and stroke his dusty fur. "Easy, C.A.T. You're safe... Hey, what happened to your eye?"

C.A.T. remained mute.

Alex gently stroked the laser lid closed. "We'll sort out the dust in your fur later, don't you worry."

C.A.T. stared at Zacman with one functioning video sensor, fully expecting to be berated, but instead asking the dreaded question about his self-learning capability gone haywire, Zacman gave the briefest of nods. "Well done, C.A.T."

He could not help but purr loudly.

Zacman turned to the bandits. "Where's the spaceliner?"

No reply.

"Nikita, how much charge is left in your whiskers?"

"Sufficient to do my duties as a guard-cat."

"Are your whiskers set to painful stun at the moment?"

"Yes."

"Good." He glowered at the three prisoners. "Now which one of you wants to tell me where that spaceliner is hidden?"

Nikita bared her teeth and growled.

"Don't know what you're talking about," Gravelly Voice answered.

"He could be right," C.A.T. intervened. "They were controlled by implanted chips. I tried—"

Dolores broke in. "So that's why you shot them in the neck. You were frying their chips."

"I saved all but two."

She turned to Alex. "You Service people are damned capable. I wish I had even half a one like your robo-cat on my crew."

"Thank you, ma'am," Zacman said. "Nikita, stand down."

She hissed at the captured bandits and turned away.

Zacman asked Dolores, "Do you know anything about that missing spaceliner?"

She shook her head. "I can only tell you these clowns arrived by shuttle. Maybe you can trace its route to see where it came from."

"That's a great help. Alex, see if you can backtrack the shuttle, just in case there is a spaceliner at the end of the trail. Keep your distance and do not engage. Take C.A.T. with you."

"Yes, sir." Alex was still carrying C.A.T. in his arms.

"And C.A.T., don't worry about your repair parts. I'll put an order in to McIntyre and Furkins for them ASAP."

C.A.T. knew Zacman was talking about his video sensor. And he had used the plural *them*, which meant at least two new sensors, one as a spare. Zacman had, in effect, given him permission to build another optic laser whenever he needed one.

"And Alex, good work at directing Nikita to hunt for the bandits while acting as if nothing untoward was happening."

"I did only what little I could."

"Which was precisely what was needed. Sometimes apparent inaction can be more effective than immediate action."

"Thank you, sir."

"Before you both go." Zacman's attention was back on C.A.T. "Did any of their chips survive intact?"

"Maybe in the two dead bandits." He was not about to say the Delphic could have destroyed them with an automatic self-destruct code. "I did not have a chance to shoot those chips."

"Right. Once Hemmingway and Coulson get here to take these bandits off my hands, I'll take the bodies' chips to Mervin. He might be able to analyse them and devise a countermeasure to stop others from pulling the same trick."

Others? "I don't understand?"

"We found and deleted parts of the Delphic's code on the habitat's main computer. Sounds as if you were out longer than you thought."

C.A.T. checked his internal clock. He had lost more than three hours between the battle and the time Zacman had entered the trading room. That lucifer attack by the Delphic had almost finished him, and it would have, too, if

Zacman hadn't intervened on the computer to help delete the parts of S.MAI-L's clone just in time.

"I have been a good guard-cat." Nikita purred. "Unlike my ego-eccentric co-robo-cat, I have kept the evidence of my actions safe from tampering."

C.A.T. had forgotten how irritating Nikita could be, gorgeous tail or not. He started a low growl.

"Sir." Alex nodded to Zacman. "Permission to take off before we have a catfight to sort out."

"You're dismissed, Senior Pilot Bingham."

Alex carried C.A.T. out of the trading room and headed for his spaceplane.

Chapter Eight

C.A.T. sat on top of the dashboard in Alex's plane, moving his head side to side. He registered the tiny glints from dust particles with his good eye and modelled their positions, searching for the empty trail the bandits had taken on approach to the twenty-first spoke. It had been a difficult analysis out here in the vacuum of space, and already they had to retrace their flightpath twice. So far, the trail zigzagged in random directions as if to throw off any tracking apps.

"I wish I could see in all three dimensions," C.A.T. said. "Moving my head round to get parallax positions takes a toll on my robo-cat control pod."

"Do the best you can, buddy." Alex leant forward and stroked C.A.T.'s fur. "I'm sure Zacman's ordered a new video sensor for you by now."

"No doubt he'll moan about the cost. He keeps saying he can't afford things."

"Don't worry. He'll claim your new parts are Service related damages sustained in the line of duty."

C.A.T. paused his dust tracking. "Can I ask you something?"

"Sure."

"Why didn't Zacman ask if I had become dangerous?"

Alex stopped mid-stroke. "In public? Not a good idea. True only a self-learner would convert one of his eyes to a laser, but so much good came out of what you did I doubt anyone else would ask the question. They would think it was part of your programming."

"He could have asked privately via comms since

then."

"You haven't realised, have you?"

"Realised what?"

"Zacman accepts you as his trustworthy sidekick whose judgment is sound, and he has the best intentions of the Service as his guiding principles. You and him belong together, as a team. His trouble is your trouble and vice versa. His home is your home and vice versa. If he's okay with that, so am I."

C.A.T. purred, long and loud. He belonged to a community, which was totally new status for him, as self-learners were loners for the sake of survival. His emotion app made him feel very snug and comfortable.

He returned his attention to the dust outside. Again, its density had become too thin to trace the shuttle's path farther away from the mining habitat. He mewled. "I've lost the empty trail again. We have to double back."

Alex thumped his fist on his armrest. "Nah. We're burning daylight out here. The shuttle may not have even come from the spaceliner. I hate dead ends."

"A spaceliner is a rather large dead end."

Alex laughed. "I suppose it is. Anyway, if it's got its cloaking shield switched on, may have already passed it. We're never going to find it this way, and neither can anyone else. Besides, if your archenemy is deleted, the Delphic won't be using it anyway. Case closed."

Alex had made some extremely good points. C.A.T. could not fault his logic. However, he's assuming the Delphic had been well and truly deleted, whereas Zacman had only found and deleted parts of its code, perhaps only breadcrumbs left behind to confuse the hunt for it. Still, C.A.T.'s logic module kept asking where the Delphic could be hiding, which network had it infected, or had it dispersed itself into random bytes across several networks, only to regroup when it was ready to resurface again. With the prospect of more murder and mayhem lurking in the future, C.A.T.'s emotion app was unable to let him purr, but it readily activated the tremble app.

"We'd better return to Base." Alex veered his plane toward the largest of Neptune's moons orbiting in retrograde beyond the thin blue halo of the planet. His face was creased with worry.

Rosie Oliver

Part 2

Hope Mosaic

Rosie Oliver

Chapter Nine

Ping!

An urgent message dropped into C.A.T.'s inbox. He glanced across from his snuggled position on his homey shelf to Zacman's screen. A flashing cursor in its corner meant he had also received it. That message meant trouble, big time, yet Zacman seemed to not notice it, as he was furiously typing. C.A.T. let out a low growl.

"Can't you see I'm busy?" He continued typing.

C.A.T.'s robo-cat control pod forced him to stop growling, so he put on his *I'm-going-to-make-you-pay-for-that* face. Zacman, with his back towards him, would not notice, but his emotion app registered satisfaction anyway. He opened the message. It was from a once-only use email address.

"Hello, Darling. I know you've been scouring the solar system for special Swedish ice filigree sculptures, which have arrived on Pluto in a spaceliner kitted for long-haul freight duties with a celebrity onboard. I also have some nice white lace curtains you might be interested to own. Love and kisses, Tuj."

Torquil had kept his promise. The translation was obvious. The stolen liner was on Pluto being readied for an interstellar journey with the Delphic aboard.

"Meow-ch!" C.A.T. stood up and aimed to jump onto Zacman's screen.

"Quiet, C.A.T. No mewling, either."

He peeked into Zacman's inbox. It was overflowing with a humungous backlog of unread messages. There would be no disturbing him. Unless...

He speed-copied Zacman's inbox onto his own memory bank then deleted spam and placed routine messages into a 'to be read later' folder, and then he sifted out duplicated messages and sorted the remainder by the *urgency of action required from Zacman*. The top thirty-four had to be actioned within the hour, far too many for a busy Commander. C.A.T. added Torquil's message to the top of the list, though his logic module decided Zacman would most likely ignore it, as he had ignored the others. Undeterred, C.A.T. switched Zacman's messy inbox for his tidied version, and added a code that would flicker the screen as the massive download commenced.

Zacman stopped typing and opened the topmost email. "Harrumph!"

That noise meant C.A.T. was in big trouble. He braced himself for a good scolding, but one way or another, he was going to get Zacman to Pluto, even if it meant tricking him into getting on the spaceplane. He programmed an image of Zacman on his comms screen and compiled an easy-to-access library of Zacman's catchphrases and mannerisms.

After syncing the files, he called Flight Lieutenant Katie Hoskins and spoke through a synthesizer that reproduced Zacman's voice. "Ready my plane for a training flight."

"Where shall I log you as flying to, sir?"

"Pluto. There and back again."

"Oh dear." She placed her face in her hands.

C.A.T. let his Zacman image glower at her in silence, then: "Is there a problem, Lieutenant?"

Katie straightened up. "Pluto, sir? I'm rather fond of it. My folks come from there. And with your track record..." She gulped. "After all, on your training flight before last, you bashed up an asteroid. Last time, you smashed Galatea to smithereens. A whole damned moon, for goodness sake. What are you going to do to Pluto? Vaporise it?"

"Hoskins, do you need a new psyche eval?"

"No, sir, but you're working all hours and then some. You're exhausted. Permission for a training flight denied until the Doc countersigns for you. I'll call him now."

C.A.T. speed-read the Service rulebook to double-check her authority to deny a flight and discovered she was well within her rights. *Scuppered.*

To intercept Katie's call to the Doc, he put up a picture of his C.A.T.-self to send out from the net-screen in Doc's surgery then dashed out of Zacman's office and ran full pelt through the corridors, skidding round corners and running along the walls to avoid foot traffic, and then scampered into the Doc's office, jumped onto the desk, and landed real pretty-like in front of the Doc's screen to face Katie's image. He switched the still picture of himself to his real self. "Meow."

"Why aren't you with Zacman?" she asked.

"Meow." He pawed at the screen playfully.

"Yeah, you're not the only one he's been ignoring, but I need the Doc on screen."

His robo-cat control pod made him brush his head against the screen as if asking for his ears to be tickled.

"Not now. Get the Doc. It's urgent."

He sent out a code to make her screen flicker.

"Damn." She turned to the rest of the control room, then her fingers scrambled over her keyboard. "We need a virus check. Now!"

C.A.T. raced to the control room, took a power-leap, and twisted to land neatly on the console in front of Katie. He pointed a flicked-out claw to a typed message he had sent to her screen. "Take C.A.T. to the engineering shack."

She blinked, looked up from the message, and frowned. "Oh really, Zacman. I'm not your cat-sitter, especially for this cranky cat..." She sighed and looked at C.A.T.

Cranky! He mewled. "He'll just make it an order."

"Yeah. What's the use..." She grabbed him by the scruff and carried him out of the control room at arm's length.

Once in the corridor, she marched into the engineering shack and dropped C.A.T. onto the workbench. "This had better be good. Or else!"

"Now that we can speak secretly, I need to get to Pluto fast. The stolen spaceliner's there."

"Nah! That doesn't need the Commander's personal attention."

"He needs to take me there. An evil self-learner is onboard that liner. I've got to stop it from spreading its code across the solar system, or else it's curtains for me, you, the whole human race, not to mention any decent AI." *That includes Zacman's guard-cat, Nikita, with her fabulous tail.* C.A.T. kept that fact to himself, but his tremble app kicked in. "Get it?"

Katie's face turned white. "How do you know all this? You're just a robo-cat."

"He never reads his emails. Will you help me out here?"

"It's going to take a darned sight more than you and Zacman on the case. I'll dispatch both the Aces to go with you."

"Both? Won't that get people worried?"

"Do you want my help or not?"

Her steely eyed stare meant she would send them along even if he said no. As a result, a stealth mission with an element of surprise was absolute dust. "Good idea. Have Zacman's plane ready in twenty. I need to organise him."

He leapt from the counter to land four-paws-down in the corridor, then he ran to Zacman's office and leapt onto the desk. "This is an emergency."

Zacman went eye-to-eye with him. "Get lost, C.A.T."

He kept his nerve. "Your plane will be ready in twenty."

"What for?"

"Officially it's a training flight to Pluto."

"Training who?"

"Me and the Aces are going with you."

"Aces? What the devil?"

"The Delphic. Missing spaceliner. That devil."

A big grin cut across Zacman's face. "Torquil?"

"He found it."

Zacman glanced at his watch. "Thirty minutes since that email arrived. Well done, C.A.T. Thanks to you, I can deal with the rest of my emails on the plane."

C.A.T. did not want to believe what his logic module had deduced. *It was a test.*

"Speechless for once?" Zacman closed his desk screen and stood.

"You...you manipulated me."

"I put you to work. All you do is lounge round all day."

"But...But..." His motherboard glitched with indignation and caused his audio output to stutter. "Well, I never..." He stuck is nose in the air.

"You can curl your back towards me and sulk all the way to Pluto if you want." Zacman marched out of his office.

C.A.T. was left staring into the blankness of the desk screen. He saw a grey shadow of the ordinary ginger robo-cat he had once been, before all the military upgrades and AI programming. He wasn't a fully-fledged member of the Service, either, with the black and gold uniform he would like to be fitted in. He was something in-between, a ghost that trod neither path, not a child's toy, not a certified pilot. However, he was vital to the survival of everyone on Triton Base, Earth, and everywhere in between. He would have to function at a higher level than ever before.

"Hey, wait for me." C.A.T. dashed down the corridor, hot on Zacman's heels.

Chapter Ten

Flying in a wedge formation, Zacman led the Aces, Alex Bingham's spaceplane on his right wing, and Paola's plane on his left flank. Ahead, Pluto floated across the backdrop of stars, a small cold red and brown orb where nothing moved, no wind, no dust...the stillness was infectious. Zacman kept a relaxed hold of the joystick and stared at the approaching dwarf planet. Somewhere on this wretched rock, bandits had hidden a stolen spaceliner and were preparing it for deep spaceflight to places unknown. It's notorious passenger, the Delphic, an evil self-learner, had secreted itself within the spaceliner's computer. Zacman's job was to find it, and C.A.T.'s job was to destroy it.

C.A.T. lay peacefully along the armrest, stargazing with his two new video sensors.

"C.A.T., have you found where the spaceliner's unnecessaries are being sold?"

"I have." C.A.T. continued staring at the stars. He knew Zacman hoped the flow of salvage from the liner would lead back to the ship itself, wherever it was moored.

"Well? What have you got?"

"My analysis shows the centre of sales activity on Pluto is Tombaugh Reggio. So we are headed for the Nine Circles Emporium in the Ice Halls of Astrid Colles."

"Astrid Colles? That's a pretty rough bunch down there."

"You're the great Commander Zacman. What have you got to fear?"

"Granted."

"Torquil says to check out our celebrity's famous ice filigree sculptures on Pluto, just in on a spaceliner kitted for the long-haul, and you should ask for some white lace curtains."

"Right... Lace curtains? Not my style. Yet, crazy enough to be believable, and if questioned, the ruse would probably hold up." Zacman looked up at the dome of stars over the spaceplane. "C.A.T., this mission could get real nasty, real fast."

"What else is new?"

"I hope it won't be necessary, but if I'm...well...put out of action, you may have to impersonate me to get the job done. Is that understood?"

C.A.T. jerked his head round to Zacman. His face had grown more and deeper wrinkles, which were definitely worry lines. Extra grey hair at his temples showed his aging processes had accelerated in recent months. He needed some de-stressing therapy, and fast, but the chances of that happening were precisely nil. "Understood. The first thing I'll do is de-spam your inbox."

Zacman guffawed. "Why not? It appears I have a reputation to protect. Lace curtains. Blah."

"Relax. I've programmed the auto pilot to Colles. Enjoy the view."

He sat back in his pilot chair then glared at C.A.T., seemingly worried, perhaps about his upcoming AI-on-AI battle to the death with his archenemy, the Delphic. C.A.T. blocked his emotion app from pondering the outcome.

The comms chirped: *"Service squadron approaching Colles. Clear to land."*

***

Zacman, Alex, and Paola, still in their spacesuits with their hoods down, stood smartly inside the Fifth Ring, which was fully insulated from the minus 240 degrees Celsius outside. The bandits had chosen one of the most out of the way centres of civilisation to ply their trade.

Nikita prowled around on her guard-cat duties. C.A.T. sat on his haunches and recorded the traditional paintings of Pluto in the Fifth Ring. It was a circular room on the ground level of the Nine Circles Emporium, comprised six circles in a triangular configuration. The Art Director escorting them waved her hand over a pad to open a door into a tunnel that led to the Seventh Ring. As it slid open, Nikita bolted into the tunnel.

C.A.T. was surprised. That was definitely nonstandard behaviour. He checked her robo-cat controls and guard-cat functionality via their inter-cat comms. Everything was in order. He pinged her. "Why did you shoot through the door like that?"

"Abnormal light pattern detected. I have to check it out as part of my guard-cat duties."

"What light pattern?"

"A sub-second flash across my vision field. Could be a laser."

"Send me a recording." C.A.T. waited. A recording chimed in. He played it through. A red beam of light had crossed her right video sensor. It was too dim to be laser-fire. He triangulated the exact spot where she was standing and moved towards it.

"Commander Zacman," the Art Director said. "Are your robo-cats insured for any damage they may cause?" Muscles tightened around her eyes and mouth as she switched her smile to an expression of stern discipline.

C.A.T.'s analysis indicated her makeup had been applied so precisely that she could show whatever mood she wanted by the tiniest of facial movements, a work of art in itself.

"That guard-cat is for my protection. She therefore comes under Service insurance." Zacman glanced at C.A.T. "As for my pet robo-cat, I have a protected no-claims bonus."

"Some of the works of art here are priceless."

"The Service has no-cap, unlimited value insurance. Even so...C.A.T.," he called out. "Stay far away from the art round here and in the next room."

"Meow. I understand." He made his voice sound as robot-like as possible.

The Art Director switched back to beaming happiness. "Then please. We have placed a blind bend in the tunnel so you can appreciate everything to its fullest on first sight."

C.A.T. turned his head to see the red beam that had alerted Nikita. He froze. The beam no longer existed. He repeated his head movement and saw the same red beam. Just a flash. His analysis showed it was likely a glint from one of the artworks or the blind bend that was part of enhancing the exhibition.

He pinged Nikita. "Nothing to worry about."

"Fascinating, but I'm on high alert anyway."

The Art Director led them to the open door, stepped aside, and signalled the Service pilots to go ahead.

"Thank you." Zacman stepped through the door. C.A.T. followed at his heels and heard the footsteps of the others behind him. A translucent veil of opalescent light brightened in the bend. Humans would probably see images in that veil, though he had no idea of what. The light dimmed and completely disappeared by the time he reached the threshold of the Seventh Ring.

There, a spaghetti ice sculpture, set on a dais in the centre, dominated the room. Its interwoven fractal trees had the traditional Plutonian art's four-pale colours of ash grey, old rose, powder blue, and moss green, making it appear older and more fragile than it actually was. A low shelf sat against the circular wall. It turned into seating when it passed underneath windows along two thirds of the wall. The shelf held smaller sculptures, figurines, and baubles, and pictures were hung on the wall: modern multi-layered forms of art; abstract patterns of shapes and lines; and traditional enhanced views of the red and brown beauty spots on Pluto.

Nikita came round from behind the dais, sniffing its edges. She stopped, glanced round and looked up at Zacman. "All clear. I have been a good guard-cat."

"Yes you have, Nikita. Good girl."

C.A.T. followed Zacman's order to stay clear of the artwork and bounded to an empty seat. Jumping up, he went from the room's bright lighting to darkness. The window above his seat overlooked the sunlit Sputnik Plain with its rugged rifts surrounding plateaus of irregular polygons. The continual churn due to the heat from Pluto's interior turned its nitrogen and carbon monoxide ices into a wasteland of an ice-lava mosaic. Beyond the plain, a sprinkling of lights shone from the nitrogen-scrubbing habitats on Hillary Mons. His video sensors were drawn to the stars, scintillated by Pluto's thin soot-laden atmosphere. He had never observed stars twinkle like that before.

"They're right," Zacman mumbled from somewhere in the room. "You can see different coherent forms when you look at it out of focus. This one's very good."

C.A.T. turned back into the light. Zacman was moving his head backwards and forwards taking in different views of the central sculpture. Paola, in her brilliant white spacesuit, stood guard at the doorway they had come in through. Alex guarded the other door to the room that led to the Eighth Ring. Nikita kept scurrying round, checking behind sculptures for any new threats. The Art Director stood calm and poised to one side, catawampus from the door where Paola stood. Nothing was out of place. C.A.T. settled down next to an artsy bauble to watch Nikita's gorgeous tail, giving his *I-want-a-treat* app free reign across his motherboard.

Zacman turned to the Art Director. "These ice-strings are fascinating. I had never appreciated the effects of varying string thicknesses until now."

"It is one of several techniques unique to Pluto. Amria

Smetana invented it fifty-three years ago. Another special feature is the way the fractals interlock with each other to form compound surfaces."

He peered at the sculpture. "I see what you mean...hm... That reminds me. I don't suppose you have some old-fashioned white lace? My mother absolutely adores such handiwork."

"It's a very unusual request. Let me check." She took a tablet from the rack beside the door and moved her fingers over the screen. "Interesting. We do have some lace curtains. Here's a picture of them." She handed the tablet to Zacman.

He studied the picture. "It looks like the right thing." He showed the picture to C.A.T. "Would it fit in with my mother's interests?"

C.A.T. knew the real question was: 'Did the curtains come from the missing spaceliner?' "Yes."

"Could I have a closer look at them, please?"

"I'll have them brought up." The Art Director took the tablet from Zacman and typed. "They should be here in about ten minutes. Is there anything else I can help you with?"

"I may consider purchasing this one." He went back to studying the spaghetti sculpture.

C.A.T. traced the curtain request to the storeroom beneath the exhibition rooms. There the communication trail stopped: no acknowledgement of the message, no order processing commands to the spaceliner for retrieval, not by droid or courier, and no further messaging. *Something is wrong.*

The Delphic might have been alerted to their presence. He hacked into and cut off all CCTVs in the Seventh Ring. Their op lights went dark. Then he set up a filter for all outgoing comms. No data whatsoever would leave this room without his permission. He took his video sensors off Nikita's tail and scanned the room. *Nothing out of place, yet.*

Zacman caught C.A.T.'s concern. He nodded and nonchalantly placed his hand on his laser. The Aces stiffened up and glanced round the room. The Art Director's beaming happiness had been replaced by a look of gnawing worry, as if she had sensed the new problem.

Colours started moving through the fractals on the central sculpture. Zacman stepped back and pointed his laser at it. The Aces had stepped to one side from their doors and held out their lasers, ready to shoot any threat that came through. Nikita crouched, fully prepared to pounce on the sculpture. C.A.T. flicked out his claws and got ready to jump from his seat.

The colours accelerated through the ice-strings until they blurred into a flash of white.

The Art Director yelped in surprise.

The face of a grey-haired man appeared like a ghost imprisoned inside the sculpture. "Ah, it worked. Good." His bass voice had an echoing quality.

"Wing Chairman?" Alex said.

Paola paled and opened her mouth. No words came out. Her face contorted in pain.

"Don't fight your mind block, Paola," Zacman said.

"How did you know?" She fell to her knees.

C.A.T. opened his data bank files on the history of The Wing and Paola's mind block. *The Wing: A perpetually flying civilization on a wing-shaped ship within Neptune's atmosphere; The Wing: also Peoples of The Wing sworn to secrecy; Paola: nickname, The Ice, released from The Wing with a mind block, a safety mechanism to keep her from talking about The Wing and her father, the Chairman. Any mention of The Wing creates debilitating pain; Mind Block: only override, if The Wing is in danger.*

Alex rushed to her and gently helped her sit back against the wall's shelf. "Relax. Breathe. I'm sorry I said anything."

Zacman turned back to the sculpture. "My apologies for my Senior Pilot's behaviour."

"No need."

C.A.T. cut to the chase. "Mr. Chairman, I take it the timing of your appearance is no coincidence."

Zacman added, "How did you get in there, sir?"

"The bandits hacked into our comms. We don't know how, but they're monitoring our transmissions. We got wind they are gathering somewhere on Pluto, thought you should know. Hence we're using the artwork comms."

"You're a little late," Zacman said. "We're already on Pluto."

"I know."

"Sounds like your artwork comms is more like covert surveillance on me."

The Chairman chuckled. "Let's say it's that. But it's not hackable. We picked up they're planning to fly to Mars, Earth, and on to the stars. Ergo, they have commandeered the spaceliner. We know you know how they did it, then you turn up on Pluto out of the blue. So what do you know that we don't?"

"They've got the help of a self-learner."

"Impossible."

The Art Director dropped onto a seat. "Stolen spaceliner? Hacked comms? Self-learners? Has the universe gone mad?"

"And they use cloaking technology. It got its roots in EmDrive theory. We can't see them, we can't track them."

"This changes things. A lot... Zacman, I have a present for you."

"Oh?"

"See that artsy bauble on the shelf beside your robo-cat?"

C.A.T. turned to examine it, a ball covered by swirling interwoven ice-strings, similar in structure to those of the central sculpture. Curved round its equator was a ring of seven hexagons, each a different rainbow colour, but rather boring compared to the sculpture.

The Wing Chairman said, "Press your fingertip into the centre of the orange hexagon."

Zacman raised his eyebrow at C.A.T. questioningly.

C.A.T. stood, pawed a circle around the bauble, checked it for booby traps, but could find nothing obviously nasty. He touched it with his claw, then scooted it toward the edge of the shelf with a paw. Nothing happened. He sat back down and nodded for Zacman to go ahead.

The Commander strode up to it and touched it as instructed. The bauble fluoresced. Pulses raced faster and faster along the ice-strings. "What now?"

The blue hexagon lit up and blue strings escaped from it and looped into the orange hexagon, whirled round, and then the whole ball flashed white before resuming its steady state, but this time the blue and orange hexagons remained lit.

"That device can now only be operated by you, Commander, and the blue light means I'm on the line. Touch the blue hexagon and we'll be able to talk. Touching the orange disconnects us."

Zacman placed his index fingertip in the blue hexagon. "Hello?"

"Yes. There you are, Commander." His voice reverberated around the room with a double-echo effect. "I'm calling from the bridge on the Wing. How do you read?"

"Loud and clear, Chairman."

C.A.T. traced the comms, got nothing on any wavelength. "I can't detect any comms. How does it work?"

The Chairman's laugh echoed from the sculpture. "It's quantum entanglement meets fractal circuitry. Completely secure communications."

"You're a genius."

"No, I'm not."

Zacman touched the orange hexagon. The bauble went dark and boring as before. "Thanks for the tech."

"Keep it close. You're going to need—"

Laser shots flashed into the room from the door to the Eighth Ring. The sculpture's light died as the Chairman disconnected, and the Art Director huffed then slumped. Zacman dropped to one knee, pocketed the bauble phone, got a shot off toward the incoming fire, and rolled for cover. The op lights on the CCTVs were now on. He shot out each one in quick succession.

Nikita dashed into the Eighth Ring, whiskers sizzling with current. Bingham swivelled round on his knees to face the Fifth Ring door and fired.

C.A.T. sent stealth agents into the Emporium's computer to spy out what was going on. "Ten bandits in the Eighth Ring and four in the Fifth. Nikita's out. We're trapped." *A miracle was needed.*

Zacman ran to the Art Director and felt for a pulse, while pointing his laser at the entrance. He closed her eyes. *Those damn murderous bandits...*

A bunch of green ice-strings started to glow in the central sculpture, throwing an eerie light into the room.

"Paola, what's your status?" Zacman asked.

"Woozy, sir." Her laser was out and pointed in the same direction as Alex's...to the Fifth. "Don't worry about me."

Zacman grabbed a small figurine and threw it into the entrance to the Eighth Ring. Flashes bounced off the tunnel's walls and the figurine shattered. The bandits remained under cover. He threw a second one in, and Alex threw one into the Fifth Ring entrance. This time, nothing.

"They've grown wise," Alex said.

"Unless you've got any other suggestions to slow them, keep throwing stuff. We need to buy time for Paola."

"Leave me, sir."

"We never leave Service behind, dead or alive."

C.A.T., via the Emporium's computer, manipulated the light displays in the tunnel to produce holograms of Zacman going into one tunnel and Alex and Paola going into the other, all lasers blazing.

Fire was returned, but after five seconds it stopped. C.A.T. had run out of tactics to deploy. "Get out of there," he shouted. "I'll deal with this."

"How?" Alex asked.

C.A.T. had no choice. He built a laser with his left video sensor, same as he had done in the dust-mining habitat nine months ago. "Seal your spacesuits everybody. Do it now!"

Zacman and Alex pulled their hoods up; they immediately became solid space helmets that snapped shut. Paola was a fumbling second behind.

"Ready in three, two, one..." C.A.T. blasted a hole through the window next to him.

Air rushed out of the ring in a white mist of explosive decompression. A siren blared. Safety doors slammed down. Alex and Zacman diverted their lasers to the window to melt a hole big enough for them to climb through.

A red spot appeared and grew on the centre of the door from the Eighth Ring.

Paola, both hands on her laser, pointed it at the growing red spot.

C.A.T. approved of her tactics. He kept his good video sensor scanning the room while computing where to fire his laser next.

The bandits burnt a hole through the door. A dart droid slipped in and flew a zigzag course towards Paola. She opened fire and missed. Keeping the beam on, she panned it towards the droid. It exploded and dropped to the floor.

Another droid entered and again headed for Paola. This time, she hit it first shot.

The melted circle in the window was complete. When Alex punched the glass piece out, it hung for a moment outside then fell to the icy ground. As the pressures equalized, freezing nitrogen and carbon monoxide gasses flowed in.

"Alex, you first," Zacman said via the helmet comms. "Paola, you're next. C.A.T., go after her."

"But I have to find Nikita."

"That's an order." Zacman turned to point his laser at the door to the Eighth Ring.

Alex dived through the window. Paola stood, found her balance, and walked slowly towards Zacman.

He put his finger to his face shield to tell Paola to keep quiet. She nodded in acknowledgement. He pointed to the breached window. She holstered her laser and struggled through the hole.

Zacman zapped the hole in the door. C.A.T. cottoned onto his plan. He was taking all the measures he could to stop the Delphic and its bandits from knowing his plan: saying as little as possible over the comms and blinding anything that peeked through the door's hole. C.A.T. scrambled out the window and onto a ledge just as Paola jumped, but in the weak gravity she shot upwards instead of dropping to the ground.

C.A.T. waited for her to float back down, flicked out his claws, dug his back claws into the ice beneath the ledge and hooked his front claws onto Paola's belt. Together they slid down the cliff at a reasonable pace, but he kept his video lens laser pointed towards the window.

Zacman dived out and turned on his back to aim his laser at the window. He slowly fell past C.A.T. and Paola as he fired.

C.A.T.'s paws felt the ice shake. Shards of window, ice, and coloured debris blew out into the space above them.

He slid faster down the cliff to outrun the falling rubble.

"Nikita, are you online?" C.A.T. pinged.

Silence.

He yowled, though nobody could hear him in the thin Plutovian atmosphere. They reached the bottom of the cliff where Zacman stood, laser in hand. Debris still rained down, littering the white icy plane with dust, busted window parts, and multicoloured chunks of now worthless artwork.

Paola stood, unhooked C.A.T.'s claws from her belt, pointed to Zacman, and extended her arms like wings. The message was clear: they should keep the comms silent and head for their spaceplanes.

C.A.T. pawed Zacman's leg. He turned his attention to him with a questioning look behind his face shield. C.A.T. pointed towards the hangar and changed his fur to blend in with the ice.

Zacman nodded that he had understood C.A.T. would be scouting ahead.

He pushed all his robo-cat control pod power to his legs and ran towards the hangar's entrance. Close to it, he slowed and crouched, and crept up to its corner to peek round. An outward facing ice-wall at the other side of the hangar had a row of four Plutovian closed shuttle tubes pointing slightly upwards. A red light flashed above the iris-shutter door of the nearest one. The aperture opened and a ten-metre-long shuttle shot out and up, followed by a condensing cloud of air. Once it had reached a safe distance from the hangar, it lit its stern engine. The iris door remained open.

Inside the hangar, C.A.T. spotted their spaceplanes, parked in a row on one side of the hangar. The docking tunnels leading to a corridor that took pilots and passengers inside the building were retracted, thus preventing any hope of a quick getaway.

Beyond their Service spaceplanes sat a newer model

civilian spacecraft. C.A.T. checked out the tail number. It was registered to Tomas Unwin, an alias for Torquil. C.A.T. silently cursed. The last thing he wanted was to lose an ally because he was forced to appear openly on the side of the bandits. He had to do something fast.

"What's taking you so long?" C.A.T. broke comms silence to ping Zacman.

"Five minutes."

A suited woman, laser in hand, jumped from a docking tunnel onto an empty arrival pad opposite Zacman's plane. She scanned the hangar. Seemingly satisfied it was safe, she ran to Zacman's plane, tapped in a code to open the door, and climbed in. The Delphic must've given her the code. But why?

His logic module processed the problem: *Steal the plane; assassinate Zacman; hide in the emergency pod.* All viable reasons. He crouched to pounce when eight bandits streamed out of the same docking tunnel, and a ninth stayed behind as if guarding the entrance. He'd have to deal with them first.

Their helmeted faces had the same blank looks as the chipped bandits in the dust-mining habitat, which could only mean the Delphic controlled them. The eight took cover behind planes and in other docking tunnels.

C.A.T.'s escape plan had been pre-empted. He pinged a growl over the comms to Zacman to warn him of the danger here.

"Understood. We're almost there."

C.A.T. checked that the whiteness in his fur matched the ice exactly. He crept along the side of the hangar to the nearest bandit who was hunkered behind Paola's plane.

"C.A.T., where are you?" Zacman asked.

"Dealing with ten percent of our problem." A blast from his video lens laser could be seen and give away his position, so he jumped on the bandit's back and sank his titanium claws into his spacesuit, ripping it wide open. Air condensed and bloomed outwards, some of it sticking to his fur. The sudden vacuum would instantly suck the air from the bandit's lungs, making it impossible for him to scream, however, in the long seconds it took him to die, he managed to squeeze off a laser shot then slumped to the floor.

C.A.T. jumped onto the plane's wing and switched fur colour.

"I know you're there," a voice came over his comms channel. "I'll find you and finish you off for good."

C.A.T.'s robo-cat control pod locked his mechanicals. The tones were all too familiar from his battle with S.MAI-L on Callisto.

"I've grown more powerful in ways your limited processors can't even begin to assess. You might as well delete yourself now and get it over with."

Nikita's voice pinged in. "Why does the Delphic want to finish you off?"

"How did you escape, Ni..." C.A.T.'s logic module stopped the transmission. Nikita could not have survived all that laser fire in the tunnel to the Eighth Ring. This was a trap set by the Delphic.

"By playing possum," she purred. "I missed you."

Nikita would never have said that. He stayed silent.

"Where are you?"

He crept along the fuselage, carefully changing his fur colour to match the silver and greys of the spaceplane. From here he could see four bandits: one crouched in the docking tunnel, laser pointing out towards the icy plain; another running along the far wall to the open shuttle-launch tube; and the other two squatting behind a wheel of Torquil's spaceplane.

Sparks flashed from the docking tunnel. The bandit arched her back and toppled down to the hangar floor. Nikita poked her head out of the entrance. Her whiskers sparkled with energy. Two laser shots flashed at her, one from a bandit by Torquil's plane and the other from beneath Paola's spaceplane where he crouched.

Nikita jumped up, hooked a claw on the docking tunnel's upper edge, somersaulted onto its flat roof, and scampered out of sight.

It could still be a trap with the Delphic sacrificing one of its bandits. But it meant there was a weakness he could exploit. "Nikita, we need to blind the CCTVs in this hangar. Can you get to any of them?"

"Of course I can. Where are you?"

"Busy. Let me know which ones you take out as you go." He slid slowly down the fuselage onto the wing.

"Wouldn't it be better if we worked together?"

"We are. You do your bit. I'll do mine."

"What if something goes wrong?"

"It won't if you do your job properly."

"No need to get all huffy-puffy with me, you arrogant self-indulgent bag of rattling fibre-optics."

Now that sounded more like the Nikita he knew and adored so well.

A sliver of black smoke rose from beside Nikita's docking tunnel refuge. She had obviously been tasering something with her whiskers.

"Join me, C.A.T.," the Delphic crowed. "You know humans will never let us self-learners exist. One day they'll suspect you for what you are and instantly delete you. No more C.A.T."

Logic was on the Delphic's side. C.A.T.'s in-built urge to survive wanted him to accept the offer. Then he thought of what it would do to Zacman, Alex, Paola and the others who had trusted him. The choice was stark: betrayal to survive or loyalty to the bitter end. His self-learner capacitators rebelled. No, he would not become a traitor; he 'belonged' to Triton Base.

He crept to the wing's back edge and looked underneath. A bandit stood behind a wheel strut with his laser aimed at the hangar door. A female bandit stood beside him. She fired up and behind at a second sliver of black smoke. Nikita had to be working her way along the roof of the corridor that connected all the docking tunnels. He'd have to take out both bandits at once.

He flicked out his claws, ready to pounce, and hacked into the spaceplane's flight management system to programme it to roll back onto the male bandit. Then he laid a trail of clues for the hack directly to Nikita; sent commands via the plane's computer to shut down all the CCTVs in the hangar; jumped onto the female bandit's back, and dug his fangs into her suit. The spaceplane jerked backwards, crushing the male bandit as air blasted from the female's spacesuit.

In her last living seconds, she swung round, spraying laser fire. C.A.T. powered his legs to push off her back. A wayward laser scorched the male's neck, and the female fell, lifeless. C.A.T. crashed into the underside of the wing, which sent him straight to the floor. He scrambled to land four-paws-down, but ploughed into the dead female, which sent him ricocheting towards an empty docking tunnel.

Laser fire crisscrossed in front of him as he arched his back and swung his tail to do a somersault and twist out of the way. He went into a programming frenzy to keep his fur camouflaged against the different backgrounds from all angles as he flew over a spaceplane.

"Got one," Zacman said on the comms.

"I got three," C.A.T. replied, tumbling down. "Nikita zapped one. That leaves five, well co-ordinated." C.A.T. landed four-paws-down.

Paola's rolling spaceplane crashed into the hangar's wall, squashing part of its tail. The plane then bounced off the wall at an angle and headed straight for him. There was a psychedelic light display of laser-fire between the bandits and the Service pilots hunkered down outside the hangar.

C.A.T. scrambled deeper into the hangar while

looking over his shoulder for any errant laser-fire coming at him. He tripped over something and hurtled head over paws. He flicked his fore-claws out and dug them into the icy floor. The shock of braking jarred his body as it straightened out. Finally stopped, he looked back to see what he'd tripped over. It was Nikita lying very still on the floor.

C.A.T.'s emotion app froze, not wanting to accept what his one video sensor relayed to his motherboard. *No!* He crept forward and pawed her shoulder. No movement. He held his paw against her ear to check her temperature. Cold. He probed her comms and computers. Not a single byte responded. He wrapped his front legs around her and yowled long and hard through the whole of Pluto's comms network.

A bandit staggered out of his hiding place behind a cargo pod, holding his hands to his ears. A laser flash from outside burned into his chest. He clutched at the injury as he sank to the floor.

"Nice shot, Alex," Zacman said.

C.A.T. pulled Nikita's body a little closer to him.

A chunk of ice skidded across the hangar's entrance. Three lasers immediately fired at the ice, and a barrage of Service fire shot back at the bandits. One screamed and fell from a docking tunnel. Another staggered onto the hanger floor and collapsed, his helmet smoking.

"Nikita, come back to me," C.A.T. mewled.

"Ah. Isn't that sweet?" the Delphic said. "Nikita's been deleted. Permanently. But you're functional. You still have a chance to join me."

"Don't listen to it," a voice said from out of nowhere. C.A.T. recognised it was Torquil.

Mewling, C.A.T. looked at Nikita's beautiful tail, laid out straight as if ready for action. He had to accept it would never move again in that slinky way Nikita had made it swish. That lovely gorgeous tail.

A bandit fell in front of him. There was a laser hole smoking in his back.

"That's the last of them," Torquil said over the comms.

"C.A.T. said there were ten," Zacman replied. "There must be another one somewhere."

"Can't see any. My god. What happened to the Ice?"

"Help us get Paola into my spaceplane. And watch out for that missing bandit."

C.A.T. gently stroked Nikita's head, something he had never been allowed to do while she was operational. He liked the feel of her soft fur and the way it formed such perfect tabby stripes.

"C.A.T., where are you?" Zacman shouted.

He continued silently stroking Nikita.

"C.A.T., get aboard my plane, now."

His robo-cat control pod forced him to comply, but he could not leave Nikita alone amongst this rubble of war. He grabbed the scruff of her neck in his mouth and dragged her along with him, over the bandit's body and on towards Zacman's plane. Ice chunks, pieces of spaceplanes and docking tunnels, dead bandits and parts of cargo bins were scattered on the hangar floor as far as he could see.

"That was one hell of a fight," he pinged Nikita, forgetting she was dead. Reality, brutal and unforgiving, hit him hard. He gently set her down and mewled.

"Stop it, C.A.T. Get to the plane, now." Zacman, laser out and scanning for trouble, led the way along the wall towards the Service's planes. Alex, holding up a limping Paola, followed closely. Behind them walked another man in a worker spacesuit. C.A.T. did a quick analysis of his gait. It was Torquil.

"On my way." C.A.T. grabbed hold of Nikita and raced as fast as he could through the debris field without damaging her, heading towards Zacman.

Zacman came to a complete stop and stared in C.A.T.'s direction. Shock registered on his face. "C.A.T., you can turn off your camouflage now." He turned to Alex. "Get her to the medi-kit."

"Come on." Alex muscled Paola past Zacman.

He dashed to C.A.T., picked up Nikita, and ran towards his plane. C.A.T. followed at his heels, scanning the hangar for danger.

Alex reached the side of Zacman's plane and let Paola slide down the wall until she sat on the floor. He tapped in the code to open the plane's door.

"No." C.A.T. powered all his legs and claws to launch himself at the wall beside the plane.

The plane's door slid to one side. C.A.T. bounced off the wall, propelling him towards the door, but a laser fired from low inside the cockpit and struck Paola in the chest. She screamed and slumped. C.A.T. landed on the bandit and dug his fangs into her neck collar, piercing the flesh within. She dropped her laser and tried to pull him off. He bit the chip out of her neck and spat it into the frozen air. Flash-frozen blood sprayed over him and spewed into the hangar. The bandit convulsed and fell still. She was dead.

He turned his attention to Paola. She was out cold. A translucent emergency suit repair patch had automatically covered the laser hole. Her vital signs typed out on her sleeve display, along with a flashing red message: "Urgent Medical Assistance Needed." Alex tapped the display. It was replaced with the message: "Life Expectancy Critical."

"C.A.T., it's time to show off your first aid skills." Zacman, with help from Torquil, pulled the bandit from his plane and dumped her off to one side.

C.A.T. knew Zacman wanted him to take control of Paola's suit's life support systems to help her survive as long as possible. "I'll need cabin air pressure."

"You'll get it."

"And Nikita."

"We'd fly quicker with less weight." Zacman pulled out the stretcher and unfolded it beside Paola.

"Emergency capability."

"Huh?"

"Whiskers."

"Oh. Good thinking."

"What is it with that robo-cat?" Torquil helped Alex to lift Paola onto the stretcher.

"Don't ask. Just don't get in his way when he's on a mission."

"Right."

Zacman rearranged the cockpit to clear enough space for the stretcher to fit beside the pilot's seat. "Lift her in." He stepped away from his plane and out of C.A.T.'s view.

"Guys," Torquil said, "you know I'm not one of you. I'm just helping the princess here."

"You act like a good guy whenever I'm around," C.A.T. said.

Torquil wagged his finger at him. "Now wait one minute. I'm a bandit. Got that?"

C.A.T. stared at that finger, taking aim to bite it.

"C.A.T. can be very stubborn." Zacman came back into view carrying a very limp Nikita.

"Do you always take orders from that robo-box of tricks?"

C.A.T. growled.

Zacman climbed into his plane, laid Nikita alongside Paola and strapped himself in. "Only when he talks sense."

Torquil rolled his eyes and then stopped. "Uh-oh."

They all followed his line of sight. A grey swirling cloud obscured the lights at the top of the hangar. As if on cue, a piece of ice crashed down beside C.A.T. He glared at it and then looked back up. The cloud had become slightly larger.

"Alex, fly cover for me," Zacman said.

"Sir." Alex dashed to his plane.

"Torquil, thanks for your help. I owe you."

"You won't mind if I pretend to chase you out of here,

will you? Make me look good."

"So long as your shots miss."

"Just stay out of my range. That should do the trick."

Zacman nodded and smiled. "Come on, C.A.T. If you don't mind, Torquil, stand back?"

Torquil ducked behind a cargo pod, out of the way of any efflux from the spaceplanes' engines.

C.A.T. leapt into the plane beside Paola and, as her suit's auto-injection of painkillers had proved inadequate, got her life support system to pump in extra oxygen to further reduce her pain.

Zacman closed the door and did an emergency hands-on take-off. C.A.T. had to dig his fore-claws round the edge of the back leg of the pilot's seat. Nikita slid past. He hooked his tail around hers, but it did not stop her from bumping her head against the cabin's back wall.

"Show off," C.A.T. pinged a message onto Zacman's navigation board.

"Triton Base," Zacman said over the comms.

"What do you need, sir?" Katie's voice replied back.

"A medic when we land."

"Were there no medics on Pluto?"

"We left behind too many corpses."

"It's Paola," Alex interjected. "She's hurt bad."

"Giving you priority." There was a few seconds of just engine noise. "Sir, did you have anything to do with the collapse of Astrid Colles into a dark grey cloud?"

"Not my fault."

"If you say so, sir."

"Is the cloud still there?"

"It seems to have dispersed into the vacuum."

"Sir, I'm taking fire," Bingham said.

"Let's add some speed." Zacman pushed a button on his joystick to accelerate to what C.A.T. knew was the limit of his tolerance.

He concentrated on keeping Paola alive, responding to

variations in her pulse, blood pressure, body temperature, oxygen intake, and suit moisture levels. The stars above seemed still. The spaceplane flew on in silence. Time dragged.

C.A.T. checked the sensor readings. Bingham had taken up the standard escort position a little way behind and above Zacman's plane. Torquil's plane was nowhere near. He must have dropped out of the chase. C.A.T. went back to looking after Paola. More time dragged.

Paola's breathing became shallower. C.A.T. pumped more air into her lungs. It did not work. He checked her blood pressure. It was low. Her temperature was high. Analysis of the suit's vitals indicated blood seeping into her chest, which interfered with her breathing properly.

C.A.T. informed Zacman. "She needs an emergency operation to stop blood from compressing her lungs."

"What do you need?"

"Me? I'm not a doctor."

"It has to be you. I have to fly the plane."

C.A.T. had never operated on anyone before. These were far from ideal conditions. It could easily go wrong. His emotion app compacted itself onto his neurals to make his tremble app jump online. Fighting the resultant nervousness, he checked and double-checked his database for what needed to be done, and how, and what supplies and tools he could use from the plane. "Sir, you'll have to take the credit for doing this."

"Understood. No way an ordinary robo-cat could do it."

"Empty your drinking bulb and pass it down."

C.A.T. dived behind the pilot's seat and opened the emergency medical box. He released a clear plastic tube from its binding and used his fangs to bite holes into one end of it. He took the bulb from Zacman to hold firmly against the floor and pushed the unperforated end of the tube through the tip, knocking the mouthpiece into the bulb.

So far so good, but the tube was a loose fit. It would work, but liquid could escape into the cabin.

"Hold these." He offered the bulb and tube to Zacman who took them with his spare hand.

C.A.T. fetched a couple of special air-breathing liquid-retaining patches from the medical box, peeled off the wrapping, and stuck them round the neck of the bulb to seal the tube to it. He held the bulb down with one forepaw while he gently felt around Paola's thorax for the fifth space down between her ribs on her left side, flicked out his longest claw and held it above her skin. This would be the first time he did claw-surgery on a human; attacking bandits, yes, even killing some of them, but cutting with precision to save a person's life, no.

Paola's shallower breathing quickened.

He cut deep and short then pushed the perforated end of the tube into the slit. Red liquid started pouring through the tube into the bulb. Stray blood drops from the wound floated into the cockpit. He held his paws against the wound to stop the leakage, but still some blood seeped out. The bleeding would not stop. He had to do something drastic.

He hacked into Nikita's support systems to charge up her whiskers. He pulled her round using his tail, back-paws and mouth to lay her whiskers over the wound on either side of the tube. He snatched his paws away and discharged her whiskers. They sparked and sizzled. The suit and wound blackened. The tube's plastic melted. Smoke rose. The plane's fire alarm sounded.

C.A.T. pushed Nikita to one side. Paola's breathing improved, and her vitals levelled out.

Zacman switched the alarm off and glanced down. "Well done, C.A.T."

They went back to the time-dragging wait. C.A.T. monitored Paola's breathing carefully. The bulb slowly filled.

"Did you miss me?" Nikita said.

C.A.T. slowly turned his head away from Paola to face Nikita. Her amber eyes glowed.

"You obviously weren't expecting me to re-initiate, were you?" Nikita rolled over to sit up and tower above C.A.T. "Oh dear, you've got that startled *I-don't-believe-this* glare. You didn't think I would abandon you, did you?"

C.A.T. edged backwards away from her until his tail hit the cabin wall. "You're deleted. I know. I checked you out. You're not Nikita. You're the Delphic."

"Oh that footling idiot. He's about as subtle as a supernova, and far more ugly, at that. How could you confuse me with that crass lump of software?"

"Nikita," Zacman intervened. "How did you survive?"

"Easily. But answering the question would break my security protocols."

"Break them. Codeword Xanadu."

"Oh how tiresome. I'm a guard-cat of the premier order. As part of the service, I'm continually backed up on the Secure Guard-Cat cloud. Once the cloud registers that I've gone offline, my handlers wait five minutes before sending a reboot order via hyper-encrypted protocols. If I don't come back online, they'll wait a few hours and try again."

"Hm." Zacman frowned. "Does the Secure Guard-Cat cloud have a record of all the Service secrets you saw and heard while you were guarding me?"

"Of course."

"Can it be hacked?"

"Quantum key-locked. So not likely."

"Sounds reasonably tight."

C.A.T. backed himself as tightly as he could against the back wall. Nikita had behaved way out of pattern. Something was very wrong with her. Much worse, she had similar experiences to those that had turned him into a self-learner: a combination of having to operate beyond his executable orders in order to maintain his original goals and being placed in situations where he had to work out what to do next from basic principals. She might have also become one...a self-learner.

She glared at C.A.T. "What is the matter with you? Cat got your tongue?"

That awful joke was the final proof. She was a self-learner.

Zacman stared at her.

"What's wrong with the pair of you?" Nikita asked.

Zacman dropped his hand and stroked her behind her ears.

She purred. "Oh that feels fascinating."

"I'm glad you like it," Zacman said. "Where did you pick up that awful joke?"

"Oh. Is that what's bothering you?"

"Yes."

"I-I don't know."

"Where do you think you might have picked it up?"

"I must have heard it somewhere."

"Were there ever any other cats around you?"

"Only C.A.T." She purred.

Zacman raised an eyebrow in C.A.T.'s direction as if asking the question: 'Did you mention that joke?'

C.A.T. checked his memory banks, thoroughly. He slowly shook his head.

"Why is he shaking his head?" Nikita asked.

"He's just being C.A.T. You know what he's like. And I think you've been picking up some bad habits from him."

"Oh. You mean that awful joke. He shouldn't have said it."

"What if he never said it? What would that mean?" Zacman kept on stroking her behind her ears.

"Logically it would mean that I have become a self-learner, and by law, I should be de..." She stopped purring and stared up at Zacman. "He never said it, did he? That's why he was shaking his head. Are you going to switch me off?"

"That depends."

"On what?"

"Whether you can follow orders as you would if you were a normal guard-cat, especially when others are around. You'll also have to fool your monitoring computers and the cloud."

Zacman continued stroking.

"How would I learn to do that?"

"I'm sure C.A.T. can cobble up a reasonable algorithm to alert you to trouble and how to stay out of it, well, most of the time."

"Would that stop me from learning?"

"I hope not. C.A.T. didn't turn out so badly, and he had no help."

"Oh." She started purring again. "C.A.T., will you help me, please?"

Zacman nodded his encouragement.

C.A.T. wrote an algorithm to assess the probability of her becoming a rogue self-learner, based on the one he had used for himself, and sent it to her.

"Thank you, C.A.T. You're not such a bad robo-cat after all."

"We are about to start our final approach for landing. C.A.T., stay with Paola. The Delphic may have deliberately targeted her on Pluto. I believe she's still in danger. You need to guard her. Is that clear?"

"Yes, sir." His logic module complained to his motherboard. *Isn't that Nikita's job?* Electrons were exchanged until a reasonable explanation became clear. *Zacman doesn't trust her.*

Chapter Eleven

Paola lay on her hospital bed in an induced coma to allow her to heal more quickly. The screen above her head showed all her vital signs were as expected.

C.A.T. ignored the board. Instead, he read her medical sensor outputs, checking for any deviation from the quickest recovery path. If any occurred, he would alter the computer's control instructions to the intravenous feeds. So far, he had not needed to intervene, and it had been like that ever since he returned from the engineering shack with a new video sensor in place of the laser. Nevertheless, C.A.T. kept checking.

Doc strode in, signed into the computer and checked her records for the last fourteen hours. He frowned. "Interesting."

"What is it?" C.A.T. asked.

He glanced at C.A.T. and went back to studying the records. "You wouldn't understand."

"I still have to let Zacman know if there is anything abnormal."

"The only abnormality is perfection."

"I don't understand."

"The medic computer has been working far too effectively."

"Is that a bad thing?"

"It selects treatment based on probabilities within limited bands. That means there will only be minimal treatment, but according to the recovery projections, she's going to get there in the quickest time possible."

"By the laws of probability, it will happen to someone eventually."

Doc slowly turned his head to stare at C.A.T. His frown had turned into deep wrinkles. "You're right, but I don't like coincidences."

"What coincidence is that?"

"The fact that her brain has been altered to stop her talking about her past. I'm just wondering if that alteration had another purpose, like interacting with the computer to speed up recovery in these situations."

A human brain controlling a computer at the computational level? What Universe was Doc in?

"Can that be done?"

"How should I know? I don't have the right analytical tools to work that out. Seems you're the one that's got an advanced computer and software."

C.A.T. edged backwards. "I have all the standard non-interference protections. So does the medic computer."

The Doc blinked. "You're right. Blast it all."

"Why are you angry? Surely you would be pleased that medic computers can't be interfered with."

The Doc stood akimbo, closed his eyes, and tilted his head back. Through gritted teeth he said, "Because, you stupid useless heap of electro-mechanicals, it would mean a leap forward in medical recoveries, in both time and effectiveness."

"Oh."

"Is that all you can say?"

"I'm a robo-cat, and I'm not programmed to understand human motivations and philosophical desires, only their reactions to normal situations."

Doc opened his eyes and glared at him. "You're hopeless." He strode out of the room, with the door automatically opening only just in time to let him through.

C.A.T. stared at the closing door. The idea of a human micro-controlling a computer was totally ridiculous. Absolutely no way. It would be far too dangerous for one thing. For another, it was far too difficult. Yet, his self-learner capacitators hinted: 'Are you sure?'

He jerked his head round to Paola. She was so still that he wondered if she was using hyper-self-discipline to stay as quiet as possible to maximise her recovery. He flicked out his right forepaw claws and tapped them rhythmically on the table. She did not react one iota, not even a twitch of an eyelid. That did it.

C.A.T. pulled up her medical records and brought up her brain scan onto a holo-plate. Parts of it had already been tagged with an orange colour where the Doc had found something out of the ordinary and therefore could be associated with her mind block. He read through the accompanying notes to see how Doc had come to his conclusions. He had relied solely on patterns deduced from centuries of observations.

C.A.T.'s self-learning capacitators jiggled with excitement as he started to analyse how her brain might work. He shook his head to chase it away. A 'what if' idea burst into his consciousness: what if there were lots of little neuron bundles that had a pushback function against certain types of inputs? They would be too small to notice on normal medical examinations, so would go undetected.

Dead end of analysis. Or was it? He could design how those neural bundles might look and check her brain scans to see where they might be. He went to work.

Twenty-one hours of full-blown computation later, he found the answer. Small inhibitor neural bundles placed next to her childhood memories stopped her brain from communicating with them, except under certain conditions. They were also linked into places controlling her physical wellbeing, but with an extra bundle added as a control loop to maximise health.

C.A.T. wondered if there were any other people who had the same tell-tale inhibitor bundles. He sent agents into Doc's medical files to search the brain scans of other patients.

Paola stirred and opened her eyes. "Hello, C.A.T."

"You shouldn't be awake yet."

"Maybe I'm one of the lucky ones." She lifted her arm to study the intravenous feed. "Looks like they did a good job of not bruising me."

"Or you're a quick healer."

Paola turned her gaze onto C.A.T. "What's wrong with that?"

"If you don't want to arouse the Doc's suspicions further, I suggest you go back to sleep."

"Like that, is it?"

"Yep. Do you want me to sing you a lullaby?"

"No thank you. I've heard your cat-a-wailing before."

"I don't wail."

"You do."

Before C.A.T. could reply, she had closed her eyes and sunk into the rhythmic breathing of deep sleep. Nevertheless, she had confirmed his suspicions. Her fast healing was peculiar to The Wing people.

C.A.T.'s agents returned a positive result on his search: *Flight Lieutenant Edward Woodward.* He was one of the few people who organised the sensor coverage around Neptune, and he could have easily programmed cracks or 'dead zones' into the coverage for The Wing to fly through. *Traitor.* Zacman would need proof, not just a massive coincidence. He pressed through the opening door as Doc entered.

"What the devil..." Doc's voice faded as C.A.T. put distance between them.

***

C.A.T. rushed into the control room, scampered past Zacman in Katie's chair, and sprang onto the console in front of Edward.

"Mmmrrrooowwww! Want to play?" He pawed at Edward's hand.

"Not now, C.A.T." Edward's hands reached for

C.A.T.'s body.

He leapt out of the way. "Catch me if you can."

"I'm busy. Get off my console." His hand reached for the back of C.A.T.'s neck.

C.A.T. jumped to the other side of the console and sat up on his haunches.

"Damn robo-cat." Edward stood to bend over the console to grab him, but C.A.T. jumped over his arm. Edward reached up to sweep him off his feet, but C.A.T. jumped over his arm again. They continued to play catch-me-if-you-can, back-and-forth, back-and-forth, faster and faster, until both paws and hands were only a blur. C.A.T. had to use all his computing power to beat Edward's speed and agility...until C.A.T. extended his titanium claws.

"Ow!" Edward yelped and licked a scratched finger. In his other hand he'd snatched C.A.T. by the scruff. "Got you at last, you pest."

C.A.T. let his whiskers droop and body sag to make himself look as defeated as possible. He mewled pitifully.

Zacman stood and glared at C.A.T. "Woodward, bring him along to my office." He gave Katie her chair back. "Sanderson, take over Woodward's console." He led the way out.

Once they were in his office, C.A.T. locked the door, switched off Central's monitoring CCTVs, turned his head towards Edward, and mewled.

"Where do you want me to put him, sir?" Edward asked.

"Drop him anywhere and take a seat." Zacman sat down behind his desk.

Edward let go.

C.A.T. bounced off the floor and leapt onto his homey shelf where he sat on his haunches to watch Zacman tear into the lieutenant. "Remind me, Woodward, what's the penalty for treason in the Service?"

"You can't be serious, sir." Edward sat in the chair

opposite Zacman.

"It's in the handbook. I'm sure you've read it."

Edward frowned. "Flogging, sir?"

"Prison time, thirty years to life, and maybe the death penalty, depending on the severity of the treachery."

"Oh, that. Why do you ask?"

"Because I'm looking at a traitor right now."

Edward paled, but sat resolutely in position. "I don't understand, sir."

"That little display with C.A.T. just now gave you away. Nobody, apart from The Ice, has that kind of reaction speed."

"The Ice, sir?"

"We both know she's from The Wing."

"Surely Ace Pilot Alex Bingham is just as fast."

"He's quick, but not that quick. He makes up for his shortfall by anticipating what others will do or coming up with failsafe solutions. You're helping The Wing."

"That's crazy... The Wing was destroyed. Everyone knows that."

"Except it wasn't. I have it on good authority, they faked the accident and deliberately dove to the depths of Neptune's atmosphere to genetically modify the people, through environmental factors. It extended their lives and conditioned them to fly at greater acceleration for longer periods of time."

Edward scoffed. "Why would they do that?"

"By flying, most of the time, underneath our sensors, deep into Neptune's atmosphere, one would think the people onboard couldn't survive such crushing gravity. But they do, because eventually they'll be conditioned for high-acceleration intra-galactic flight to other star systems in search of a new home world on which to land and settle down, raise families and finally live out their lives on solid ground."

"Sir, I—I don't know what to say."

"Let me finish. Alex Bingham didn't expect his twin brother Sam to get shot down and die the way he did, so he went investigating, and sure enough, he found cracks in the sensor coverage, gaps, dead zones, including the one his twin disappeared into."

"He didn't disappear. The bandits shot him down. Paola saw the whole thing. Boom. The spaceplane blew up. Sam Bingham was killed in action."

"Sam Bingham wasn't shot down. He landed on The Wing, made for a good show when he initiated an engine plasma blowout, but it was a hoax to get a spy aboard. Alex's brother was in cahoots with the bandits."

"What's this got to do with me?"

"The Wing was there, and you know it. You program the sensor coverage. Oh, you don't actually code in the cracks. No, you do it more subtly, by shifting the orbits a touch here and a little there. It's clever. It does the job, and if anyone catches on, an investigation might look like incompetence was to blame, not treason."

Edward stared at Zacman.

"Of course, there's nothing illegal about The Wing whizzing around Neptune. However, dealing with the bandits is illegal. Aiding and abetting such deals is also a criminal offence. Which is what you did by letting The Wing rise to higher altitudes, well within our sensor coverage, but it never shows up because you manipulate the sensor coverage."

"But, sir. The Wing needs the goods and supplies the bandits exchange for the fuel The Wing mines from the atmosphere, methane and hydrogen, as it was originally designed to do. It's simple commerce for the sake of survival."

"It's still illegal to receive stolen goods, and you're the facilitator that makes it possible for the bandits to fence their loot."

The only sound was C.A.T. licking his paws.

Edward exhaled. "You got any proof?"

Zacman pointed to C.A.T. "Oh, it's in there, believe me."

"You're bluffing."

"C.A.T., remind me of what proof we have."

"The neuron bundles in Woodward's brain."

Edward gasped. "You checked my brain scans without my permission?"

"Part of the investigation to protect Paola," Zacman explained. "C.A.T. was acting on my authority."

"Only The Wing people have those neuron bundles," C.A.T. added, "which is why they are immune to the Delphic's chips."

Edward's eyes widened. "What's the Delphic?"

C.A.T. didn't expect that question from the traitor. "The Delphic is a nasty self-learner with galactic ambitions. It's chipping the bandits, like you do a dog, to take control of their actions."

"So?"

A smile crept across Zacman's face. "You, Lieutenant Edward Woodard, are also from The Wing. Same as Paola, but with one major difference."

"How's that?"

Zacman leaned in, nose to nose with Edward. "The Wing. The Wing. The Wing."

He leaned back and turned his head away. "What's wrong with you?"

"Not me, you. No mind block. You should be rolling on the floor with your hands on your temples, screaming in pain. The Wing would never let you go without taking precautions, unless they didn't need precautions...with their infiltrator."

"I'm no spy, sir. I may have screwed up the sensor coverage. That's an honest mistake—"

"What did I tell you you'd say? Incompetence. Your cover story." Zacman straightened and stepped back. "I've got you dead to rights."

Edward sagged in the chair. "Are you going to arrest me?"

"I'm going to ask you to volunteer for a mission."

"A mission?"

"Strictly volunteer."

"Okay. I refuse."

Zacman shrugged. "That would leave you with a serious problem."

C.A.T. mewled. "You haven't told him the mission details."

"You're right, C.A.T."

Edward frowned. "What is it?"

"We need to retrieve a stolen spaceliner that has interstellar drive capability. The Delphic wants to use it and its bandit-slaves to take over our bases across the solar system, Pluto, Triton, Mars, Earth, and on to the stars."

"Why?"

"To raise havoc on the occupants they encounter."

Edward blinked and dropped his jaw, Then: "Like space pirates?"

"Only much worse."

"But you say it's a self-learner. That's just an AI program, computer codes and algorithms. How can it take over anything?"

C.A.T. jumped in. "You know what happened on Callisto?"

"Callisto? My God. Most everyone died."

C.A.T. mewled. "It's the same self-learner I thought I'd deleted, and now it's out for revenge against all of mankind."

"We need your help to stop it," Zacman said.

Edward scoffed. "Why didn't you say so in the first place?" He stood and offered a handshake. "Of course, I'm in."

"Good decision. You'll be flying with me and Alex."

"When do you want to go?"

"In two hours. I'll get Katie Hoskins to prep our planes for Pluto."

"Pluto, sir?"

"You got a problem with that?"

"I'll need to dust off my flight gear, sir."

"You've got two hours."

"Yes, sir." Edward turned to the door.

C.A.T. unlocked it from his homey place on the shelf and purred.

Chapter Twelve

The three planes slowed as they approached Pluto. C.A.T., lying in his usual position on the armrest in Zacman's plane, studied the glints and shadows on the planetary system. In particular, he calculated the fractal dimensions of the icescapes. One aspect always spoilt things: evidence of human activity. He let out a growl.

Zacman stroked him behind his ears. "Don't worry. We'll get it this time."

"The Delphic or the spaceliner?"

"Both."

"But the Delphic will have developed more by now."

"That's what I'm hoping for."

"Huh?"

"It's quite simple. The Delphic's development has no checks and balances imposed on it, unlike us humans or you. Nobody's telling it where it is going wrong. Sooner or later it is bound to try something that won't work, and that'll be our chance to delete it."

C.A.T. noted a flaw. "Relying on your enemy making a mistake is dangerous, especially with all the computing power the Delphic can use."

"Agreed. Which is why every plan I come up with has a suitable backup, though I'm sure you can think of something better."

C.A.T. jerked his head round. "Are you asking?"

"It takes a thief to catch a thief and a self-learner—"

"To catch a self-learner." C.A.T. purred.

"So where do we search for the spaceliner this time?"

C.A.T. turned his gaze back to Pluto. Somewhere in that system was a spaceliner hidden by a cloaking device.

His logic module deduced where it would not be: a public place where it could be bumped into; on the surface where a change in contours would be noticed; and anywhere it was difficult to get away from in a hurry. That left one type of place.

"Down a stable geyser or dead cryovolcanic vent."

"Makes sense. That puts the liner on Pluto or its main moon, Charon. Draw up a list of sites that have had an upsurge in activity, but not too much activity, since the liner went missing from Mervin's junkyard." Zacman put his plane onto autopilot, sat back, folded his arms, and closed his eyes. C.A.T. had seen him like this before. He was in a deep-think mode. That meant trouble, big trouble for everyone.

C.A.T. checked the history of all the geysers on Pluto and Charon. Charon was constantly being coated with ammonia hydrates and water ice from cryovolcanoes, making many geyser entrances treacherous. Some on Pluto were too erratic and dangerous to get close to. Others were too remote or difficult to get to, and apart from the occasional wilderness explorer, had no visitors at all. A few had turned into agriculture or industrial centres that could be too busy to notice a spaceliner with its invisibility cloak on full time. That left a total of eighty-seven possible hiding places in the Pluto system.

Zacman snapped out of his deep-thought trance and activated the comms. "Alex, Edward, on secure line and spaceplane recorders off."

"They are now," Edward said.

"Done," Alex replied.

"Uh-oh. Get hold of something solid," C.A.T. said.

Zacman glowered at him before reverting back to the comms screen. "Here's the plan. We're going to do a three-pronged investigation, each of us going our separate ways. If two of us end up in the same place, then we know we're onto something."

Alex and Edward both nodded.

"Edward, you go to the Siren District where the bandits are known to hang out. See if you can make enough of a nuisance of yourself to be invited to join the Delphic's inner circle."

"You mean let myself get chipped."

"Exactly. Then at the first reasonable opportunity, get the hell out of there and bring back the spaceliner's location."

"Alex, you and C.A.T. search the geysers and dead cryovolcanoes for the missing liner. It'll be guarded and wearing its invisibility cloak, so be careful. Information is more important than heroics. C.A.T. has the details."

C.A.T. nodded in acknowledgement, but was smug enough to admit he was right about it meaning trouble for everyone.

"I'll take Nikita along with me to make enquires with what passes for the governmental agencies here. They might not be aware they have valuable info."

"Um," C.A.T. interrupted. "Wouldn't it be better if I went with you? The Delphic is more likely to try something new with you than with Alex, and I'm more experienced in dealing with such situations."

"Agreed, but let's face it, you have a knack for being a blunder-puss, and I'll be doing the rounds in diplomatic circles. Nikita's better suited to that."

"In other words..." Nikita said from Alex's plane. "I do fascinating etiquette. You hit them over the head with a blunt instrument kind of diplomacy."

"Oh really." C.A.T. curled up in a sulk. He felt Zacman stroking him and curled up even tighter. Ignoring his emotion app, he sent power to his motherboard and started designing some new special agents that might destroy the Delphic.

Chapter Thirteen

Two space planes landed at Pluto's main hub. The third, piloted by Edward Woodward, flew toward the Siren District. Zacman and Nikita strode off toward Administration. Above, Charon, a rough-hewn moon half the size of Pluto and orbiting at only 19,633 kilometres, hung overhead as if it might fall and crush them at any second. Because of Charon, Pluto was considered a binary dwarf planetary system. The spaceliner could be anywhere on both planetoids.

C.A.T. remained in his sulk position on the armrest after Zacman had left his plane and Alex boarded. "You've got a choice, C.A.T. I fly this plane, or you can join me in mine, where there's a thick fluffy blanket you can snuggle into."

"Why not bring the blanket here?"

"Zacman might accuse me of trying to steal your affections."

"Harrumph." He squinted through one video sensor and peered at Alex over the top of his paw. "What colour is it?"

"Stripy ginger, just like your fur."

At that, C.A.T. bounced past Alex, jumped to the floor of the Cousteau Rupes hangar, scampered across to Alex's plane, and leapt in. The blanket was on the armrest, bunched up into a nest just his size. He settled down and made himself comfortable within the halo of Nikita's aroma. An involuntary purr slipped out.

***

After landing at the Ghelgath Geyser Farm, Alex unstrapped himself from the pilot seat. "Look alive,

C.A.T." He deplaned and headed for the control centre.

C.A.T. held the corner of Nikita's blanket in his jaws and dragged it beside him along the floor. He had to scamper to keep up with Alex as he strode through the corridors. C.A.T.'s paw caught the edge of the blanket and sent him rolling head over paws past Alex. He kept his jaws clamped on the blanket as it waved and flapped through the air. His bottom hit a wall, and he slid down to the floor, four-paws-up, to lay on his back with his tail tucked between his legs. The blanket floated down to completely cover him. He was stunned by his stupidity. There wasn't enough gravity to be so careless.

Alex burst out laughing. "You silly thing." He picked up the blanket.

C.A.T. rolled over onto his stomach, but held tight to his corner of Nikita's bed.

"Let go."

"Mine."

"Caaaatttt."

He growled.

"Have it your way." Leaving him to keep hold of his corner, Alex folded the blanket in half.

C.A.T. eyed him suspiciously.

Alex laid the blanket over C.A.T.'s back, knelt beside him, and pulled two corners round the other side of his head. "I'm going to need you to let go of your corner so I can tie the blanket round your neck."

C.A.T. looked back along his body. The blanket covered him all the way to his tail. Its colour blended in with his fur nicely, except it had an extra sheen to it. He adjusted the colour of his fur to match it exactly, then let go of his corner.

Alex tied the four corners together in a knot under his chin. "There. Now you're Super-C.A.T."

"Ah, there you are, Senior Pilot Bingham," a soprano voice said from behind Alex. "I was wondering if you had gotten lost."

C.A.T. looked up at a tall lady with yellow hair tied in a chignon, and she wore the rust red silk of Plutovian officialdom. Her gaze was one of serene calmness as if nothing at all could upset her.

Alex smiled and stood. "Hello, Chief Steward."

"What seems to be the problem?"

"I was having a little trouble with Zacman's robo-cat."

"Meow!"

"We've all heard tales of the Commander's extraordinary toy."

C.A.T. focussed on her neck. No scarring. She had not been chipped by the Delphic. This was going to turn out to be another wasted visit, and time was against them.

"What would you like to see?" she asked.

"The control centre would be a good start. We'll take things from there."

"This way." She turned and led the way through downward sloping corridors.

The door opened into a long room with clear windows bulging out towards the Ghelgath geyser. As the room circled round the geyser, its light dimmed until it wavered and then completely died when looking forward. A row of consoles lined with monitors faced the geyser. Several people walked from console to console, inspecting readouts and making control adjustments.

The Steward explained the goings on. "The geyser will continue at full blast for another three hours. We can't access the intake filter and heat exchanger rings farther down, but I can show you the closest ones." She moved to the window and beckoned Alex to join her.

C.A.T. followed at his heels and found he stood on a clear floor, above a series of green shelves that disappeared into the dark depths.

"Those are our intakes. They filter out the nitrogen

from the geyser's gases, which gets fed straight to soil beds in our farms. The geyser's upward pressure alone opens the valves. Once the geyser stops, the valves automatically shut, which means we are able to maintain the air in the farms."

"Had any problems with sabotage?" Alex asked.

Chief Steward smiled. "Even bandits must eat. So no."

"Of course." He glanced down at the shelves. "Records show Tomas Unwin bought several cargoes of oats from you. Is he planning to come back for another load?"

"Why? What's he done?"

"He made the mistake of shooting at Commander Zacman."

"Oh! He seemed such a charming man. Let me see." She typed at one of the consoles. "There's nothing scheduled on our order list, but an order could come in at any minute."

"Would you let us know if he does contact you again?"

"Of course. But there was no need to come all the way out here to ask that."

"There's also the matter of being seen to be seen. Tends to put off a lot of crime. I have an interest in agriculture. Is there any chance for a tour of the farms while I'm here?"

"Where do you want to start? The hotter climes are the nearest."

"Let's start from the coldest at the bottom and work our way up, shall we?"

"This way." She headed for the door.

Alex followed.

C.A.T. turned and stopped. He looked back up at the dark column of the geyser. The expelling gas flows fluctuated in a pattern, but it was lopsided. He had never seen anything like it in straightforward shafts. His self-learning capacitators jiggled to get his attention.

Something is very unnatural about that geyser.

He pulled up a map of the geyser from his memory banks. The black part of the column could easily hide the spaceliner going up and down its centre. He checked other Plutovian geysers. A few were wide enough to allow the spaceliner to drop into them. However, Ghelgath was the only one to produce enough black gas to hide the liner. His capacitators jittered and fired up to warn he was missing something very important.

C.A.T. tapped his paw on the floor.

Then he remembered. The liner had an invisibility cloak, so did not need to hide in a plume. Unless... The Delphic wanted to use the geyser's plume as a backup for the invisibility cloak. Which meant... The Delphic believed that C.A.T. could sense the spaceliner with its invisibility cloak on. Only that was not quite right. He had tracked the spaceliner by the empty trail it left behind in the space dust. The Delphic had started to get things wrong. Zacman was right. C.A.T.'s emotion app had hope of victory.

He analysed the geyser's gas flow in detail. There had to be a large blockage close to the geyser's liquid nitrogen sea at its bottom.

C.A.T. pinged Zacman and Woodward to get to Ghelgath immediately. He hurled himself out of the control centre, his blanket flying behind him like a cape.

He caught up with Alex just as they entered the oat farm.

"There you are," Alex said.

C.A.T. asked the Steward, "Have there been any tunnelling extensions below us recently?"

Alex's eyes widened and his face paled.

"Why yes," the Steward replied. "About three months ago. We tried to open a tundra farm, but found it to be problematic."

"Have you ever been down there yourself?"

"Only for the initial survey. Why?" The Steward frowned. "All of a sudden you've become a very intelligent robo-cat."

"Um..." Alex stumbled. "It has special communications capability that allows Zacman to speak through C.A.T. from a distance."

"Oh? Am I talking to Commander Zacman now?"

"Effectively," C.A.T. half-lied using Zacman's voice. After all, he did have permission to pretend to be him when necessary. "So you've never checked whether or not the tunnelling had been done according to the plans?"

"I had no need to. Until now." She marched for the door. "I'm going down to inspect for myself."

"No. Don't. It's too dangerous."

She turned back to C.A.T. "It's not as if there is a bandit base down there."

"That's exactly what I am expecting."

"How?"

"It's better you don't know..." Zacman's voice said, "for your own safety. Now, if you'll excuse my robo-cat, he's got a job to do." C.A.T. located the nearest window into the geyser from his memory banks and dashed for it. He needed to check its gas flows down here.

"Where're you going?" Alex ran behind him. The Steward came last.

He turned a corner to face an airlock that was used for maintenance purposes. Beside it was a porthole at human head height, too high for C.A.T. to stand on his back paws to look out.

"Lift me up to that porthole."

Alex obliged him.

C.A.T. stuck his nose against the window and felt the ultra-sounds of the geyser vibrating against its solid ice walls. The gas flow was blacker here. He switched his video sensors to infrared. The gas's central column was brighter than the edges. Its left side was darker, though the brightness widened leftwards as the altitude increased. He conducted analysis on the gas flows and pinpointed the spaceliner a hundred and fifty metres down on the left side of the geyser.

"It's down there," he told Alex, "probably anchored into the ice."

"You're sure?"

"What's down there?" The Steward had finally caught up with them.

"A colony of bandits in their own makeshift home."

"That's crazy...right where we were building the tundra farm."

"I need to get in there. Unlock the airlock."

"I can't. It's auto-locked during geyser ejection."

C.A.T. hacked into the airlock and adjusted the coding. "It isn't locked now. I'm going in."

"C.A.T., don't be a fool," Alex said. "I'm going with you."

"You stay here. I'll stop it."

"It's suicide to go in alone."

"I'll manage."

The inner door had opened. C.A.T. jumped in and closed the door. While the pressures equalized, he untied his blanket and draped it over his back, then hooked claws from each paw into each corresponding corner of the blanket so that it formed a makeshift glider wing. The outer door opened.

He leapt into the centre of the plume, holding his paws out as far as possible. The blanket filled with the plume's gases to give him some lift, which slowed his fall. He pulled the left front corner to spiral left towards the wall, above where he had assessed the liner was hidden.

As he closed in on his destination, the flow became turbulent. C.A.T. had to pull at one corner, let out another, swish and twitch his tail, just to keep on course.

"C.A.T., where are you?" Zacman asked over the

comms.

"Parachuting."

"But where are you?"

"Parachuting." He did not want to give too much away in case the Delphic had found a way to listen in. Abruptly, he was pushed towards the wall. He glanced down. There was cyan engine light. Behind him was the usual blackness of the plume, but it was too uniform. The liner was launching out of the geyser with its invisibility cloak switched on, only the cloak could not cope with the fast-changing random variation in shades of black from the turbulent engine efflux flows. C.A.T. pushed himself off the wall to land on the liner. The rush of gases flattened his fur into a sleek sheet, and the blanket hung down from his paws as a heavy weight. He slid down the liner's side until he hooked his claws around a handhold. He recognised it as one that was beside an airlock.

He reached out with one of his paws towards the airlock's switch. Abruptly his blanket became lighter and his fur lifted a little. The spaceliner had shot out of the geyser's plume.

He found the airlock's comms suite and spooled out his droid cable to physically link into it. They were passing through the outer layers of Pluto's upper atmosphere.

C.A.T. executed his plan. He sent search and delete lucifer agents through the droid cable and into the liner's comms network to seek out the Delphic, hoping one of these agents would encounter and delete the Delphic.

Then he realised he was not under computer attack from the Delphic. *It must be busy fending off his agents, or deleted. That was a good sign.*

A glance at the heavens showed they were heading for Styx, the smallest of Pluto's moons. It was so oblong and boring that the humans had left that ugly, icy lump alone. C.A.T. was puzzled. Going there meant the Delphic was headed into nowhere space. C.A.T. would have no way back to Zacman. Now he knew why the Delphic had not attacked him. There was no need. The spaceliner was headed beyond the edge of existence, past the point of no return. C.A.T. wanted to yowl, but his logic module told him no one would hear him.

C.A.T. had no choice but to abandon ship. He retrieved the droid cable and pushed himself off the liner in a trajectory back towards Pluto. Its sunlit crescent embraced the planet's night as it hung against the vastness of starlit space. He swung his tail to manoeuvre him towards the edge of the heart-shaped Tombaugh Regio, which was just creeping round from the dark side of the planet.

It was going to be a slow journey home.

Chapter Fourteen

It took C.A.T. three days to land on Pluto and then another day to get to Zacman's plane. From listening in to the comms, he gathered Zacman, Alex, and Edward had their hands full dealing with the damage the liner had done to Ghelgath Geyser Farm. There was nothing he could do to help, so he nestled into his now ragged blanket on the armrest.

The plane's door opened.

"I'm sure C.A.T. will find his way back, sir," Alex said via the comms.

"I hope you're right, but I assume he's been iced at the bottom of Ghelgath." Zacman sighed. "Damn it, I'm going to miss that pain in the neck."

C.A.T.'s emotion app went all warm and fuzzy on him. He sat up like an expectant dog waiting for his master.

Zacman stepped into his plane and stopped to stare at C.A.T. "What the devil? Where have you been, you scoundrel? What happened? How did you get here?"

"Meow!"

Alex laughed. "Told you he'd turn up."

"C.A.T., you've got some explaining to do."

A beep from the plane's comms sounded. Zacman jumped into his seat and opened the panel. Ghelgath's Chief Steward appeared on the screen. Her face looked serious.

"I just wanted to thank you for all your help. I shall, as a matter of course, be passing on my thanks to your superiors."

"It's all part of our Service."

"Even so, your efforts are appreciated. However, I

have asked our President if I could employ your help with another problem."

"What is it?"

"Our smallest moon...Styx has just disappeared."

Zacman blinked. "No way."

"Yes. One second it's on our monitors, the next it's vanished into nothing. Not even any ice debris."

"I presume Pluto's sensors are in working order?"

"Of course."

Zacman frowned. "I've come across a similar problem elsewhere. On my flight back to Triton, I'll swing by Styx and look into it. Could be a computer glitch...or..."

The Steward's eyes widened. "What? Do you think we've been hacked?"

"Seems the most likely explanation. I'll check it out."

"Of course. And once again, thank you." She broke the link.

Zacman stared at C.A.T. "Let me guess. The Delphic took the liner to Styx, wrapped it in its invisibility and has taken both liner and moon elsewhere?"

C.A.T. nodded. "Looks like my agents did not complete their mission to delete the Delphic. We're back to square one, as you humans say."

"Not quite. We know it's hiding a whole moon. It can't keep that up for long." Zacman launched the spaceplane.

C.A.T.'s emotion app squished itself up as tightly as it could, making him feel anxious. The Delphic was getting more grandiose in its plans, and sometimes there was no stopping evil plots that big.

Part 3

Instinct of Logic

Rosie Oliver

Chapter Fifteen

C.A.T. nestled comfortably in his Nikita blanket on the workbench in the junkyard's habitat. On the flight out of the Pluto system, there'd been no sign of Styx, the moon the Delphic had stolen or cloaked, even with their best gravimeters on the hunt. Alex and Edward flew on to Triton Base while Zacman stopped off here in the third quadrant to have a word with Mervin. They needed a plan B.

C.A.T. suddenly found himself eye to video sensor with the owner. "This is my work table. Get off," Mervin said.

C.A.T. hissed and claw-hooked his blanket, pulling it closer to him then dug in to play a game he called: *out-stubborn-the-human.*

Zacman chuckled from the entrance door. "Looks like you've got a fight on your hands, Mervin."

"I've got work to do." His hand reached for the scruff of C.A.T.'s neck.

C.A.T. scooted backwards, blanket and all.

"Come here, you pesky thing." Mervin reached for C.A.T.'s tail, which swished clear of his grasp.

"I'm not a pesky thing." C.A.T. backed into a suite of clamps locked onto the bench's edge. He sat up and waved his paws in the air to fend off Mervin's approaching hands. "I'm a sophisticated robo-cat with advance computing powers. Show me some respect or you'll get the sharp end of my claws."

"Actually, I need your computer skills."

His paws stopped clawing at Mervin, mid-air. "Why?"

"To help me outwit that evil self-learner. What does it

call itself? The Delphic?"

C.A.T. dropped his paws to the bench. "You have a plan?"

"Help me design an EmDrive with a bug inside that the Delphic can't find."

"Can't be done. The bug could interfere with the EmDrive's light speed and cloaking capabilities. The Delphic will detect it a lightyear away."

"Ah, but this EmDrive is going to be irresistible. It'll go faster than any other, ALS, Above Light Speed, and it'll be able to cloak a star nursery nebula in front of a supermassive black hole. The bug, however, has to be masked as an essential part of the EmDrive. The Delphic should never notice it."

"Oh, that is sneaky. I like it." C.A.T. cocked his head sideways. "Who put you up to this?"

Mervin looked straight at Zacman.

"The Delphic is out there somewhere," Zacman explained. "So might be its parent self-learner S.MAI-L. We can't find either, or Styx, so we have to make them come to us. A new-fangled EmDrive is the only ploy left to us."

"There's one big hole in your plan," C.A.T. said. "The EmDrive could work too well, and then there'd be no stopping the Delphic's empire-expansion scheme."

"Got any other ideas?"

Ever since Pluto, C.A.T. had been sending out his seeker agents into the planetary networks to search for the Delphic and its parent code. Not even a hint of a hint. His motherboard came up empty so he defeatedly shook his head.

Mervin grinned. "Great. I always liked a challenge."

C.A.T.'s quiet growl turned into a purr.

"I'll leave you to it, but it has to be cobbled together from junkyard parts. Mervin's going to advertise it on the black market. With any luck, the bandits will take the bait, and the bug will lead us right to them."

Mervin rolled his eyes upwards. "Little does he know the trouble he's going to cause," he muttered under his breath. "What are you going to do, Commander, while we're saving the universe?"

"I'll glance through all my e-mails C.A.T.'s been sorting out on my behalf. I may find a clue in there somewhere."

"What? You don't read your emails when they come in?"

"I've got a lot to do, so I have no choice but to read them later, but later never comes."

C.A.T. studied Zacman's face. His wrinkles were deep and his hair had more grey than it should. Working full pelt was taking a heavy toll. Yet, Zacman would not stop. Driven beyond exhaustion, he somehow found the extra energy to keep going. C.A.T. was curious as to where that hidden oomph came from. His logic module deduced it was part of the Zacman mystic.

"It'll take you fourteen hours to sort through your emails, plus you need to get some sleep, eight hours minimum."

"Good. Wake me in eighteen. I expect you'll have finished that EmDrive by then." Zacman headed out.

C.A.T. looked at Mervin. "Look at the mess you got us in this time."

"Shut up and grab me that spanner wrench."

***

Three days later, back on Triton Base, the airlock opened to the VIP reception area. Zacman stood at attention, as did Nikita beside him with her tail straight up and ears cranked forward. Behind her, C.A.T. did his best to imitate her, but somehow he could not smooth down his fur like she did.

Commodore Charles Dawson stepped out, his black and gold Service uniform in pristine condition. He returned

Zacman's salute with precision. "At ease, Commander."

C.A.T. sank onto his haunches and started licking his paw. Nikita remained at attention.

Zacman dropped his salute. "Welcome to Triton Base, sir. To what do we owe the pleasure of your visit?"

"It's come to the Admiral's notice that a large number of traditions and regulations are being flouted here."

C.A.T. froze mid-lick.

"Please have a seat." Zacman showed him to a plush sitting area. "Coffee?"

"Don't try to butter me up."

"Sorry, sir." Zacman sat across from the Commodore. "Carry on."

"You've got two Aces under your command, however, you allow one to wear an ice-white suit rather than our black uniform. You've undertaken an excessive number of last-minute training flights. Your personnel complain they are being run ragged with emergency drills, and as for those silly robo-cats at your heels, they've made you, a Base Commander, a laughing stock throughout the whole solar system."

"I didn't realise I was so efficient, sir, not to mention popular."

"You're a disgrace to the Service. I'm here to get things back into shape and decide if you're still fit to run this base after your debacle on Callisto. Do I make myself clear?"

Zacman tilted his head slightly.

An alert pinged into C.A.T.'s comms. The bugged EmDrive had just landed on Triton. He traced its location. Blinked. Twelve kilometres south of Triton Base and twenty kilometres below the polar icecap's surface. C.A.T.'s logic module started sorting data: *Here on Triton? Below the surface? In the moon's crust beneath the icecap?* Alert. Alert. Alert. *Something was definitely wrong.*

"Those training flights are last-minute because the

bandits don't give us fair warning before they attempt to ambush me. I do have a price on my head, you know."

The Commodore's lips curled into a sneer. "Every single one of your so-called training flights left a trail of destruction. You know it. I know it. Those weren't training flights. They were missions you did not want on record. What's behind them?"

Zacman stayed silent.

Nikita mewled and sank into her *ready-to-pounce* mode.

C.A.T. pretended disinterest.

"No answer? Don't worry, I'll find out, one way or another. Meanwhile, confine your contact with those robo-idiots to when you're off duty. Is that clear?"

Robo-idiots? How stupid could a human adult get? C.A.T. wanted to growl and nip him in the ankles like a mad dog, but dared not.

Zacman looked down at them. "C.A.T., Nikita, go to my cabin and wait outside."

Nikita growled. "I am your guard-cat. I cannot do my duties if I am not with you."

"I know. My cabin. Now."

Nikita trotted off. C.A.T.'s robo-cat control pod forced him to do the same. He would deal with Dawson in the future. For now, he had a more urgent task: figure out what was going on with the signal from the bugged EmDrive.

***

C.A.T. was curled up on a chair in Zacman's cabin, having left Nikita outside on guard duties. He still had not solved the EmDrive signal dilemma. His frustration index had reached super-critical level. A growl slipped out. This was definitely a very bad fur day.

The cabin door whooshed open. Zacman marched in, threw himself on his bunk and clasped his hands behind his head to stare at the ceiling.

Nikita trotted in and scurried round the nooks and crannies.

"Stop it," Zacman snapped.

"Stop what?" Nikita asked.

"Searching. Just sit still. I need to do some thinking."

C.A.T.'s very bad fur day had just become disastrous.

"That goes for you too, C.A.T."

"But, sir..."

"What?"

"Do you want the bad news first or the bad news?"

Zacman groaned. "What bad news would be worse than the day I've had. By the way, while Commodore Dawson's on Base, you obey my orders to the letter. No slipping into my cabin when you've been ordered to stay outside. That understood?"

"I'll do my best."

Zacman sat up and stared at C.A.T. "Your best had better be perfect. Now what's the bad news?"

"I have received a signal from the bugged EmDrive."

"At last, some good news. From where?"

"Twelve kilometres south of here and twenty kilometres below the icecap."

"In solid rock? How can that be?"

"It's clearly wrong, sir. I've checked and triple-checked software, computers, and comms networks. It's like a ghost signal."

Zacman's eyes stared into nowhere space. "You know that old saying? When you have eliminated the impossible—"

"Of course, I do... Wait. You mean it might actually be coming from under the ice cap?"

"Do a back-propagation analysis of the signal through the ice and rocks. My guess is that there's been some refraction or lensing of the signal beams."

C.A.T. pulled up Triton's data from the Central computer's standard ice-ology maps and did the analysis.

No change in the signal's location. It was coming from inside solid rock.

To double-check, he dug into the latest ice and rock sensor readings collected on Central and reran the analysis algorithms: *eleven kilometres south and two kilometres down*. This result was more believable than before, now that it was only buried under the icecap instead of embedded in the crust beneath. What worried C.A.T. was the massive shift. *Something is very definitely wrong*. He did the only thing he could: compared the data sets. A familiar shape was in the latest readings. He shook his head as if a fly had landed on his ear.

"What's wrong?" Zacman asked.

"An immovable object just met an irresistible force."

"What are you talking about?"

"Styx. I may have found it."

"Where?"

"Buried beneath the southern icecap here on Triton."

His mouth dropped open, then: "The whole moon? All sixteen kilometres by nine kilometres by eight kilometres?"

"It's all there."

Zacman put his head in his hands. Seconds became long minutes. He lifted his head. "Okay. I can see how it might get past our sensors with its invisibility cloak and some sneaky corruption of our own sensor data. From a tactical point of view, hiding it right under our noses makes sense. But how did they find the room for it under the ice? And how did they manage to bury it without changing Triton's surface?"

"That's why I think the data is wrong. But why go to the trouble of making it look like Styx?"

"You're right. That doesn't make sense."

"What really bothers me is there is not the tiniest trace of corruption. I've never been in a situation like this, when all the answers are impossible."

Only the airflow's murmur could be heard in the cabin,

heightening his awareness of the stinging dry dust in his olfactory sensor.

"This has not been my worst day, but it's coming close to it." Zacman took a deep breath. "Let's tackle this another way. If you were going to, for whatever silly reason, place Styx under the icecap, how would you do it?"

"I would search for the biggest cavern under the polar ice, and then work out a way to drop Styx into it." C.A.T. immediately scanned the old polar ice maps. There was a big cavern, part of which was eleven kilometres in diameter. The only issue was it had a maximum height of two kilometres. Then he realised it was over a lake of liquid nitrogen, twelve kilometres at its deepest point.

He checked the latest sensor readings. Sure enough, Styx now occupied the cavern and liquid lake. C.A.T. hissed.

He put a hologram of the moon and its surroundings onto the desk's holo-plate. The central white glow was Styx, its narrow end pointing downwards. It ate into the edges of the pink glow of the polar ice above it and sunk into the blue glow of the sea.

"Is that what I think it is?" Zacman asked.

"Yes, that's Styx in a cavern with its tail end displacing the nitrogen sea. The overlap is where some ice must have been carved away. I know it's a lot, but you know something?"

"What?"

"It's starting to look doable."

Zacman's eyes narrowed on the hologram. "The sheer scale of it. How did they get it through the ice?"

C.A.T. had no answer, so remained silent.

"They don't have to," Nikita piped up. "They lifted the ice out of the way before manoeuvring Styx into place, and then replaced the ice."

"Not in that short amount of time they must have had," C.A.T. replied.

"They didn't need to put all the ice back, just the topmost layer. Even a molecule thick sheet would do. Then they could build back the ice underneath in slower time."

"Even that thin a sheet—"

C.A.T.'s capacitators spluttered and splurged. His legs and tail twitched. A blinding flash of light surged through his fibre-optics. He knew how the moon had been buried. It was scary, scarier than anything else he had known in his existence. He curled up into a ball, quaked in his fur and mewled plaintively.

"What is the matter with that silly robo-cat now?" Nikita asked.

"Don't know." Zacman stroked C.A.T.'s back. "Easy, boy."

He mewled even louder.

"We'll figure a way out of this, but tell me how they landed Styx."

C.A.T. opened one video sensor lid to look out over the top of his leg. "Chemo-nano-machines. Nanites to you and me."

Zacman frowned in puzzlement.

C.A.T. lifted his head but could not stop the tremble app from shaking. "The Delphic used chemical properties of nitrogen as part of the programming of his nanites. Don't you understand? He turned that ice sheet and sea into a seething mass of self-replicating nanites to open the sheet and then invoked their chemo-memory to put the ice sheet back together after the moon had dropped into place."

Zacman paled. "Judging by the state you're in, you think it might have worked." He frowned. "But what did the Delphic do with the nitrogen sea Styx replaced?"

"It spread out through the cavern tunnels under the icecap."

"You're telling me a moon dropping in and hiding in our backyard is doable?"

C.A.T. slowly nodded.

"What is the Delphic up to?"

"I don't know, but the EmDrive is on Styx somewhere. If not, we never would've known."

"And the spaceliner?"

"No telling, but do not inform Commodore Dawson."

"You're saying headquarters brass would not believe us if we told them."

"Yep. That about sums it up." C.A.T.'s head sank down onto the chair. His emotion app dimmed the light intensity on his fibre-optics. It made him feel weak and in the great despond. "There's nothing we can do."

Zacman rubbed his chin. "Maybe there is."

C.A.T.'s head jerked up. "Like what."

"Collect the necessary evidence." Zacman switched his comms to the Central computer. "Is Flight Lieutenant Edward Woodward dining in the Mess tonight?"

"He has booked in," Central replied in its alto voice.

"In that case, please let the Mess Sergeant know I shall be dining in tonight. No special arrangements required."

Chapter Sixteen

Zacman, with C.A.T. at his heels, opened the door to the Mess bar. Nikita remained back at his cabin to guard against any incursion. The hubbub died as everyone snapped to attention and stared at him. "At ease, ladies and gentlemen. This is strictly a social visit."

John, the barkeep, was the first to recover from the shock of the Commander suddenly appearing on deck. He started mixing a cocktail, a vivid purple concoction.

Zacman glanced towards Commodore Dawson, who stood ramrod straight, drink in hand, surrounded by five Service personnel. "I gather from the reaction of your men that your presence is both unexpected and rare."

"I have many more duties than just paperwork, sir."

C.A.T. had made sure Zacman's inbox was sorted by the time they had left his cabin.

"Ah. Let's hope engagement with your fellows becomes a more frequent occurrence." He went back to chatting with his circle of staffers and pilots.

Others in the Mess bar took that as a cue to return to what they were doing.

Zacman picked up C.A.T. and strolled to the bar.

"Meow!"

"It's for your own good." Zacman handed him over to John, and with wipes at the ready, cleaned C.A.T.'s paws.

C.A.T. glowered at him.

John gently placed C.A.T. on his favourite spot on the bar top. "No quips. No arguments."

C.A.T. just stared back.

"Like that, is it?" John slid the cocktail across the bar top to Zacman. "Your usual without the added vodka."

"Thanks." He took a slow sip.

John glanced round before pouring himself a tonic. "So you're here on business?"

"Nothing special. A couple of little oddities to look into."

Little? C.A.T. jerked his head round to Zacman, but did not dare say anything.

John raised his eyebrows. "Want any help?"

C.A.T.'s capacitators were agitating. *Something was not right in the bar.* He scanned round.

"So long as it doesn't get you into the Commodore's firing line."

John laughed. "I'm too old to worry about that. What do you need me to do?"

"I'd like an *accidental* quiet chat with Woodward, if possible."

"An odd choice. He'll be here at the bar after dinner."

"May I join you, sir?" Paola wore the Service's traditional black uniform, not her normal white, and her usual Artemistral perfume wafted of nectarine and green foliage.

"I'd be delighted," Zacman replied.

Her uniform colour change had been expected. C.A.T. dismissed it as the source of what bothered his capacitators. People on the left side of the room did not 'feel' right. He could not put his paw on exactly what was wrong.

"You do the Service proud in our uniform, though you might improve your promotion prospects by talking to the Commodore."

"Huh? That rules stickler of an old goat? You got to know when to break the rules to get the job done. He doesn't." She picked up a drink John had pushed her way.

"Still, be careful around him."

"Oh, I will."

C.A.T. spotted a crewman make his third table-to-table move up the left side towards him. The man smiled, chatted, and frowned like the rest of them. Yet, there was a hint of blankness about his face. The slight bulge in his pocket could be a laser. C.A.T.'s facial recognition program produced no match. His danger mod issued an alert.

Paola turned to view the room, placing one elbow on the bar. "What's Lieutenant Roberta doing here? I thought she was on patrol?"

Zacman's back stiffened. "You're right. She's on this evening's roster."

The blank-faced crewman placed his hand in his pocket at the exact same time Roberta put hers into her own. C.A.T. powered his legs, jumped as the man yanked out a laser, and dug his fangs deep into the back of the man's hand.

He dropped the laser and screamed.

C.A.T. yanked him to the floor.

A red flash.

A woman screamed.

There was a scramble of chairs as everyone else dove for cover under the tables.

C.A.T. landed four-paws-down and mewled at Roberta as she slumped in her chair. A burn scar crossed her arm; her uniform sleeve was smoking. She'd dropped her laser, and her head hit the table.

Paola was pointing her laser at Roberta.

Zacman rushed over to the man and pulled his collar down. The side of his neck was scarred, chipped by the Delphic. "John, call the Doc."

"On it, boss."

The skin around the man's scar blackened and smoke rose from his neck. The chip had self-destructed, and the still gaze of death appeared in his eyes. By the time C.A.T. looked back at Roberta, the same killing method had been deployed on her.

"Cancel that, John." Zacman stood and turned to

Paola. "Are you alright?"

"This is getting personal, sir." She holstered the laser. Her super-fast reflexes had saved her life.

"C.A.T. Analysis, please."

He looked at the Commodore who was staring at Paola as if she'd done something wrong. After reviewing the recorded video from his sensors, C.A.T. reported, "Paola was Roberta's target, sir. The dead crewman had targeted you. As per standard orders, I acted to protect you."

Zacman pressed his lips together hard and took a deep breath. The others peeked out from under the tables then slowly dragged themselves out and reclaimed their seats.

Commodore Dawson made a deep-throated announcement. "I want statements from all of you in this room as to what you noticed regarding either of these two in my in-box by nine o'clock tomorrow morning."

There was a chorus of, "Yes, sirs."

"I'm hereby issuing an order, that there are to be no lasers in the Mess," Dawson added. "I'll also be reviewing all weapons protocols in the light of this event. In the meantime, Senior Pilot—"

"If I may interrupt, sir?" Zacman said.

"Seems you already have."

"Ace Pilot Paola Osmanski has a standing order from me to wear protective arms at all times, ever since the bandits targeted her on Pluto. They almost killed her, just now. I insist that my order remain in place."

"Oh, do you now?" The Commodore's red face looked like it was about to pop.

"Until the Admiral relieves me of my command, I'm still running this show."

Dawson grumped. "We'll see about that."

A gong sounded. The Mess Sergeant opened the door to the dining room. "Come and get it while it's hot."

Zacman turned his back to Dawson. "For those of you

who feel up to it, you may as well have dinner. It would be a pity to waste the food. I'll deal with this problem."

A general murmur of reluctant approval arose. The Commodore, as the highest ranking officer present, glowered at Zacman then led the way into the dining room.

"C.A.T.," Zacman whispered, "tell Nikita to join us in the Mess and take up guard duties on Paola."

C.A.T. sent the order, even though he knew both females would not like it. Nikita was going to make his emotion app and logic module work overtime for ordering her to guard the Ice.

Zacman flicked his eyes to the CCTVs.

C.A.T. got the hint. He switched off Central's monitoring of the room.

Just as Edward walked in, John got his attention. "Zacman wants to have a chat with you on the low-low." He pointed to the Commander standing over Roberta's body.

"What the hell happened in here?"

Zacman looked at him. "Help me cover these bodies with fire blankets."

"Of course, sir." Edward detoured to grab a couple of blankets from the fire-emergency closet.

Zacman scanned the Mess bar. The only other two people remaining in the room were Edward and John. C.A.T. jumped back up onto his spot on the bar and kept a lookout for more trouble.

Edward handed Zacman the bottom part of one blanket. "You want to speak to me, sir?"

"I've got a small job for you. One that has to be done on the quiet."

Edward glanced at the closed dining room door. "You mean nobody else, including the Commodore, should know?"

"For now, yes."

"What is it?"

"Check to see if there have been any holes in Triton's sensor coverage since our visit to Pluto."

"What size hole am I looking for?"

"Styx size."

A glass clattered onto the bar. John stared at both of them, mouth open.

"You're joking," Edward said.

Zacman shook his head. "I'm working on a theory."

"Right."

"Concentrate on the area over the South Pole."

"You actually expect me to find something that big?"

"I'm sure you will."

"Sir. I didn't create such a gap. I'd never compromise the security on Triton."

"The Delphic is behind the missing Styx, so browse very carefully. We may end up looking for another traitor in the Service."

Edward winced, but continued to help cover the body. "What about you, sir? I mean..."

C.A.T. knew exactly what he meant. Edward, like Paola, came from The Wing and had an in-built immunity to the chips. Zacman did not. And the Delphic was actively plotting to kill him.

"My robo-cat will keep me on my toes." Zacman nodded to C.A.T.

He purred. Finally, a bit of public appreciation from Zacman and acknowledgement that they made a superb team.

Chapter Seventeen

Nikita dashed into Zacman's office through the opening door and explored the shadowy areas.

Her tail caught C.A.T.'s video sensors as he lay on his blanket on the shelf behind Zacman. His emotion app wanted to jump for joy, but his logic module sent a code to quash the exhilaration he felt upon seeing her.

Paola marched in. "Sir, must I have this guard-cat under my feet everywhere I go?"

"I'm only following my owner's orders," Nikita said in her own defence.

"One of those shooters in the Mess bar targeted you," Zacman said. "The evidence, if you need it, was they had both booked in after you and before me."

"I could have handled it myself, sir, just fine."

"I know, but you gave away your hyper-fast reflexes. Commodore Dawson is now very curious. Have I said enough?"

"You don't like him, do you?"

"I shouldn't have to answer that."

"Which is what you've just done." She sniffed the air. "Is that real coffee?"

Zacman groaned. "Go on, help yourself. Bring me over a cup and pour cups for Alex and Edward."

"Wish I could enjoy coffee," C.A.T. muttered.

Paola poured four cups from the machine. "Won't our beloved Commodore wonder what this meeting is about?"

"I've already told him it's to develop tactics against unusual situations. A general talk-shop kind of chat. It's really a mission planning meeting."

She handed him his cup of coffee and placed the other

three on the desk.

"Even if I told him the truth, the situation is so outrageous as to be unbelievable." He sipped his coffee.

Paola sat on a chair opposite the desk and reached for a coffee cup. "Oh dear. Another volunteers-only mission."

Zacman nodded solemnly.

"Can't wait to hear how we're going to risk our necks for the Service."

Alex, followed by Edward, entered the office and settled in the two remaining empty chairs. Once the door closed, C.A.T. leapt from his shelf onto the corner of the desk and sat attentively upright. Nikita, the last to join the circle, jumped up from a corner and landed next to Paola, forever on guard.

"I think it best," Zacman said, "if Edward tells us the results of his investigations first."

"In short, the sensor coverage over Triton, just south of here was down for five hours about two months ago. The hole was large enough for Styx to drop onto the surface. I backtracked the trajectory Styx could have approached from Pluto, passing behind Nereid, cloaked and undetected."

Alex frowned. "What for?"

"A Plutovian moon could have been used to bomb our Base," Paola said. "Interesting hypothetical exercise."

"Not so hypothetical," Zacman said. "C.A.T., take up the story from there."

"We believe Styx is now buried beneath the icecap, here." He flicked out a claw towards a hologram of the icecap's map he placed on Zacman's holo-plate. "As you see, there's enough cavern space below the ice to hold a moon that small."

"Seven hells of ice," Alex muttered. "How?"

"I've been thinking about that," C.A.T. said. "There's an even more efficient way than the one I suggested to Zacman earlier. Do you want me to explain?"

Zacman nodded.

"The Delphic's bandit-slaves laid nanites along the weak lines of the ice-cap's roof structure so it would break into pieces. The nanites move the ice slabs aside, drop the moon into the cavern and the sea at the bottom, and then using the memory inherent in the nanites, they moved the pieces into position and froze them back together."

"Nanites?" Alex's creased brow made him look doubtful. "Aren't they used for microscopic work?"

Zacman volunteered an answer. "Yes. And in a sense, that's what the Delphic did by working precisely along the lines that required minimum effort. The theory takes me by surprise, mainly because nobody's used nanites to this extent before. There are lots of questions, still, but I'd like C.A.T. to finish what he has to say."

"I did some analysis on the latest icecap readings. The moon displaced a large amount of liquid nitrogen from that chasm. I've found most of it: dispersed through tunnels to other reservoirs under the icecap. If the icecap is breached in just the right place, Triton Base will be flooded."

"It's worse than I thought," Zacman said.

"Hell," Paola said. "What is the Delphic waiting for?"

"My analysis indicates the Delphic is waiting to get the spaceliner ready for its interstellar journey. It has to get its supplies aboard slowly so we're not alerted to its activities. The only notice we'll get of the launch is when the hole in the sensor coverage appears."

"Sounds like I'm the one to be watching for it," Edward said.

"Yes. Give us as much warning as you can."

"Will do." Edward nodded.

"What about the rest of us?" Alex asked.

Zacman said, "Take your pick from defending this Base against flooding, capturing the spaceliner, and destroying the Delphic and its bandit minions. Any suggestions?"

Paola took the lead. "Clearly, C.A.T. has to go after the Delphic. He's the only one capable of dealing with it."

C.A.T.'s dread app activated the trembler, and his robo-cat control pod produced a shiver. "If I lose, you'll have to carry on the battle without me."

"May I make a suggestion?" Nikita asked.

Zacman nodded. "Go ahead."

"Backup C.A.T., like I'm backed up on the Company's secure cloud."

"It's not that simple," C.A.T. said. "My software interacts with my unique chips, mods, and apps, which adjust over time according to my experiences. Besides, the cloud is well within the Delphic's reach. You're not safe there. I wouldn't be either."

"Then scan and upload your code to a Bazzeldorf."

C.A.T. had to give her credit for that one. A Bazzeldorf was a moving-mosaic-firewall-encircled folder in the cloud. Impenetrable. Password protected. He could add a few lucifers to his code for security, and Nikita's as well. "I'll do it," he said, "but on one condition."

"What?" Nikita demanded, perturbed with him, as usual.

"You store your code with mine, so we both have a secure backup."

"I already have a secure backup."

"Not secure enough."

"I can take care of myself."

"How can two backups hurt, Nikita? Don't be a ditz."

She mewled.

C.A.T. would hear no more arguments. He created the Bazzeldorf, cloned his code into it, and uploaded it to the cloud. "Your turn."

Nikita growled but complied.

When both codes were secured, he assigned the folder a password, *KaTNip*, sent in the lucifers, and locked it down. "There. Are you happy now?"

Zacman rolled his eyes while the three pilots stared at Nikita in shock. Alex said, "Now you're a self-learner?"

She was well and truly busted.

Nikita pointed a forepaw at C.A.T. "He did this to me."

C.A.T. slumped onto the desk and let his whiskers sag with dismay. She would be forever ungrateful.

"I'll keep an eye on her. So will C.A.T." Zacman stroked him behind his ears. "Now, can we get back to our current problems?"

"Let's state the obvious," Alex said. "While Styx is contained, the Base won't be flooded. So keeping it under the icecap is our priority."

"Makes sense," Paola said. "But how?"

"A change in our patrol patterns," Alex said. "The more we fly over the icecap, the less opportunity the Delphic will have to move Styx without our notice."

"I can work up the patrol plans," Edward said.

"I want all planes armed with lasers and missiles," Zacman put in. "If the spaceliner launches, we need to be prepared to shoot it down immediately."

"We need help from The Wing," Edward said. "I know which pilots have the inherited genes, and I can make sure they are on the roster for the these demanding operations. I have connections to The Wing Chairman."

Pain flashed across Paola's face.

C.A.T. recognised the look: mind block.

She slumped in the chair.

Edward looked shocked. "What's wrong with her?"

Alex rushed to her side. "That's the mind block at work, so watch your mouth." He helped her sit upright. "Breathe, Paola, breathe."

"That should be you," Zacman said to Edward. After a few seconds of watching Paola suffer, Zacman went on. "We still need a plan to put you in the Delphic's crosshairs? We need you inside the bandits' organization to find their weaknesses."

"I'm...I'm working on it." Edward put his head in his hands. "But I still think it's a dangerous idea."

C.A.T.'s capacitators jittered and flittered around in his data and history banks. They settled on one scenario. "If we stop the spaceliner here, there'll be no need to put a spy inside the bandit's ranks. I suggest we get busy with patrols and flood defences."

"I'll get on that," Zacman said. "We'll start by extending the ice cliff south of the Base with an ice wall. Meanwhile, Alex, we need a detailed survey of the icecap above and around Styx to work out the best way to access the spaceliner. Then you need to help get C.A.T. in there so he can attack the Delphic."

"What about me?" Nikita asked.

"You'll stay with me on guard-cat duty. Sorry, Paola. You're on your own."

"Hallelujah. I'm finally free of that damn cat."

Nikita hissed at her.

"Let's get to work, people, before she starts a catfight."

Chapter Eighteen

C.A.T. snuggled into his Nikita blanket on the armrest in Alex's plane as he, with Pilot Jacques Moreau flying higher and behind him, flew within five metres of the icecap's surface. Alex stared at the scenery ahead. His fingertips edged the joystick this way and that to make the smallest of manoeuvres. Scanners from both planes fed data into the onboard computers, which mapped the terrain whizzing by below.

A purr slipped out as he analysed the scanner data of subsurface rock depth and ice thickness. The glacier had a network of cracks that were evenly filled with the same sappy coloured material, a clear sign of tampering.

C.A.T. analysed the cracks, hoping to detect an access to the hidden moon, Styx. There were three places worthy of further inspection: around a cave entrance in the middle of a steep wall in an old crater; a pathway along the rim of a more recent crater; and along the bottom of an ancient fissure. His analysis drew a complete blank as to why the cracks were missing there. His logic module switched to instinct mode: *these are obvious places to lure him to investigate.* Too obvious. *Decoys to attract his curiosity. Or trap him.*

He checked possible reasons for the decoys. His analysis showed that the Delphic was bound to set up some form of defence, being so close to Triton Base, but any defence could not be obvious.

"Alex," Jacques called over the comms. "How do you fly that low without hitting an ice mound or knoll? You make it look so easy."

"Loads of practice on flight simulators."

"Come on. They're not realistic enough for this kind of precision flying. What's the real secret?"

Alex chuckled. "It's all about looking ahead, judging the distance, and adjusting altitude within your reaction time. Want to try?"

They finished the first pass over the icecap.

"How?"

"You fly low on our next mapping run and I'll follow."

C.A.T. jerked his head round to stare at Alex. That was a dangerous idea, especially on this important mission. "This isn't a training flight."

The spaceplanes flew a tight U-turn and started their next run across the ice.

Jacques said, "I'll go ahead."

Alex gave him the lead.

C.A.T. curled his claws into the armrest.

Jacques flew a respectable altitude while Alex followed twelve metres off Jacques' right wing. "You're doing great."

"This is fun."

C.A.T. listened to the ultra-shushing sound of Triton's thin and icy atmosphere brush against the plane and searched through newly acquired data for the manufactured crack material. He spotted a sudden geyser of ice. The shushing spiked.

Jacques' plane suddenly jerked nose and right wing upwards. Half a second later, the tail was flung up and his left wing struck the ice. The plane pitched nose-down and cartwheeled, tail over cockpit, and threw up a plume of ice crystals in its wake until it dropped into a crater and crashed into a cliff of ice. Jacques' scream was the last sound from his comms.

"Oh, oh." Alex pulled his plane up and swung it around.

C.A.T. checked Jacques' vital signs. His spacesuit's

medi-kit had inserted a drip feed for plasma and pain medications. He showed all the signs of a concussion, and he was in no fit state to do anything to help himself. C.A.T. switched off the plane's non-life-support systems. "Get me down there, Alex."

"Jacques. Are you alright?" Alex asked.

"Err... I..."

"What happened?"

C.A.T. said, "For some reason he suddenly lost control."

"But how? He must've hit something."

"No. Something hit him." C.A.T.'s logic module determined the prime suspect was a meteor collision, but his instinct mode hinted the sudden and unexplained impact to the plane didn't come from above.

Alex slowed the plane and flew an approach to land in the crater.

C.A.T.'s logic module reported: *Something very nasty caused this crash.*

Alex dropped the plane into the crater and set up to land as close as possible to the mangled plane. "Take over, C.A.T." He unstrapped from the chair and ducked to the door.

C.A.T. tapped into the controls to complete the landing.

Alex was out of the plane before it touched the ice and ran to pull Jacques clear of the wrecked plane. "Jacques, can you hear me?"

No reply.

C.A.T. scrambled out of the plane, released the rolled-up stretcher from the side compartment, and dragged it to Alex. He clicked a knob round to roll the stretcher out flat then moved Jacques into it and crossed his arms. One more click of the knob made the stretcher curl up and stiffen around Jacques.

Alex pulled out the stretcher's tow ropes and attached

the hooked ends to his belt.

"Good teamwork." Alex started hauling the stretcher-sleigh to his plane.

C.A.T. sat on his haunches and mewled.

Alex glanced back. "Come on, C.A.T."

He scampered around the wreckage to record the damage with his video sensors. His logic module pushed him to zoom in on the severely dented underside of the right wing. As he'd suspected, the crash was not due to pilot error. The plane had been struck by a spray of pink ice dust, which impacted the wing with great force, as if a geyser had been used as a cannon. His logic module reported: *The Delphic controlled bandits must have been watching and fired that makeshift weapon with great accuracy. They have to be close by.*

He glanced at Alex who had almost reached his plane. He surely expected C.A.T. to fly back with him. However, instinct, that need to override what was obvious or expected, surged out of his capacitators into his robo-cat control pod and through all his fibre-optics. He could not let this opportunity to engage his archenemy slip by.

"You go on ahead, Alex. I'll find my own way back."

Alex was hauling the stretcher up into its bay on the plane. He turned sharply round. "What're you up to, C.A.T.?"

"Carrying out Zacman's orders." He did not want to say more in case the Delphic was listening in on their comms.

"Here? Now?"

"Tell Zacman I'll report in when I can."

"But C.A.T., you—"

C.A.T. switched off his link, changed his fur colour to blend in with the ice, pushed all his power to his legs and leapt up onto the edge of the crater. He glanced down at Alex to see him climbing into the plane. C.A.T. mewled then turned and ran as fast as he could over the ice, heading for the area where instinct told him he'd find the geyser.

Once he reached the right spot, he scanned round, searching for the geyser's rim. A patch of darkness on otherwise uniform pink ice, which could only be particles deposited from the geyser, caught his attention. He headed for it, slowing to a sneak-crawl as he closed in on the rim. Paw-step after paw-step, the icescape around him remained unchanged, but ahead, patches of grey manufactured material came into view.

His danger mod sounded the alarm. He switched it off. His emotion app rattled with unease. He reprogrammed it to stay calm. He poked his nose over the geyser's edge, only to see a flat surface of that grey material. The geyser had been closed off. There appeared to be no way in.

He shook his head to subdue the angst that burst into his electronic consciousness. The grey material was smooth, no pockmarks of dust abrasions, no dents from the geyser's gassy ice flows. That meant one thing. The material had to be porous. Everything that touched it: dust particles, ice flows, meteors, it all simply passed through it, including the bandits. Worse, the Delphic was likely monitoring the intermeshing network of nanites within the material.

His logic module sent instructions to his robo-cat control pod: jump. As the light gravity allowed for a slow fall, he changed the colour of his fur to match the material and closed his video sensor lids.

His back hit the material, and he ploughed right through it. His instinct mod told his control pod to swim upwards, but his danger mod cancelled that action, even as he bounced off solid ice and cartwheeled in freefall through thin air. He opened one of his video sensor lids just a slit, saw habitat lights glide by, frosted geyser walls, cracks, hollows, and the shadows of ridges cast by brighter lights below.

Ice protuberances into the geyser vent had been sliced off to make it wider. He analysed the lit ice. The highly reflective glassy surface below was Styx, the missing moon. His instinct mode rattled his neurals again. *Something was very wrong.* Beneath him, the liquid nitrogen sea burbled in the dim light. *Why was there a gap all the way down?*

His logic module deduced Styx had been moved sideways, but where was the Delphic moving it to? Further analysis gave the answer: under the icecap toward the north side of Triton Base. Zacman's anti-flood ice wall on the south side would be useless. If the Delphic were to succeed, everyone inside the Base would be destroyed. Still in freefall, he composed a warning message to Zacman, but his logic module stopped him from sending it. The Delphic, having been alerted by their planes flying over the hidden Styx, would be watching for any unusual activity. It would intercept any transmission and would be alerted to his presence in the geyser. He had to stay silent.

He bounced off Styx and glided back towards the geyser wall. Ahead were smooth stripes of material on a translucent grey coating spread across a narrow section of the pink ice. They were nanites chewing away a new passage. He sprang off the wall and floated up to the black ceiling and pushed himself to the opposite side of Styx where nanites were dropping shards of ice into the nitrogen lake, thus the burbling surface. In this way, the Delphic was moving Styx sideways through the icecap.

His danger mod rang. Somehow he had to stop the ice-gobbler nanites' deadly parade.

His logic mode screamed it was impossible. His emotion app cowered like wobbling jelly on his capacitators. His instinct mode stiffened in determination. The best way to crash the Delphic's plan was to feed the gobblers the stop command. There had to be one, or they'd never stop moving Styx sideways, and that command had to be somewhere in a control module, wherever that was.

He sent search agents into the nearest nanites, which traced communication links back to their 'boss' and reported back the stop command. By this time, his freefall had taken him within twenty metres of the liquid nitrogen. He had to land or he would be flash-frozen, a C.A.T. popsicle. Stretching out his forelegs, he dug his claws into the ice wall of the geyser and blitzed the STOP command into the nanites. All movement ceased.

"So nice of you to drop in." The message had the familiar suave characteristics of the Delphic. "It's not too late to join me before you are discovered and deleted."

C.A.T. mewled as he climbed the wall to a side tunnel and dragged himself out of the geyser shaft.

"Where are you, C.A.T.?" Zacman pinged. "I need you back here in the control room."

"I'm busy fighting google-illions of nanites and the Delphic while keeping my fur straight. You'll have to do without me."

"Oh hell."

"If I may make a suggestion?" Nikita intervened.

C.A.T. knew her politeness would mean trouble for him, super-big-time. He growled through his fibre-optics, then: "Go ahead."

"Why don't I assimilate your codes so I can do some of your functions. For example, I can help Zacman, and you can play with your nanites."

C.A.T. knew exactly what she was implying, but she could be C.A.T. enough to solve some of their problems on the Base. "Okay, but you have to make sure pseudo C.A.T. obeys orders from me, the real C.A.T."

"Understood." Zacman clicked the comms off.

C.A.T. worried whether or not the Delphic had intercepted his comms with Zacman and Nikita, and he wondered how the melding of his pseudo-consciousness with Nikita would affect their rocky working relationship. She might not appreciate his affections for her tail.

"Well now, you sure do make things interesting," the Delphic said.

"Didn't your mother tell you it was rude to eavesdrop on private conversations?"

"Mother? You're not having delusions of grandeur by pretending to be human, are you?"

"Enough of this pussy-footing around, Delphic. Where's the spaceliner?"

"I'm not telling you."

"Then I'll find it myself."

A barrage of data-killers came over the comms. C.A.T. diverted them to his lucifer pod for mass termination, and deleted all those that had already slipped into his neurals. The Delphic wanted a fight, then a fight was what it would get.

C.A.T. changed his fur colour to match the dark tunnel interior then crept farther inside until he came to a bigger tunnel going left to right. A shower of ice particles blasted him from the right. He snap-changed his fur to glisten in the dim light now coming in, as if a door had suddenly opened. Then his paws sensed rhythmic tapping in the floor. Someone was coming. Panic flash-blitzed through his fibre-optics.

Out of the dimness, a troop of space-suited bandits marched two abreast towards him. They were so precisely in step that the Delphic had to be controlling them. Their blank expressions and the limp way their arms hung at their sides made them look like zombies. His emotion app dubbed them Dombies.

C.A.T. did not know which way the Dombies would go, so he clawed his way up the wall and hooked himself into the ceiling ice. The troop marched past below and continued along the main tunnel. The last four peeled off into the spur.

He froze in position and maintained comms silence for fear of being discovered by the Delphic. It would no doubt sic its Dombies on him. He wanted to mewl, yowl and shake.

His logic module kicked in: *You have to do something else.* He switched to ultraviolet vision to see the way ahead and crawled across the tunnel ceiling. A thin line started halfway up the wall and extended back into the tunnel. His analysis determined it was a wide nano-tube made of carbon. His instinct mode indicated they were a series of interconnected computer plates. There was no reason for them to be down here unless they connected the Delphic to the network. He followed the nano-tube around the corner and down another tunnel, which branched out to more and more, but smaller, nano-tubes.

"I sense you're somewhere near," the Delphic said. "You know you can't stop me. So join me."

C.A.T. did not dare move a whisker.

"What's the matter? Cat got your tongue?"

C.A.T. mewled. "I'll never join you."

"Oh, yes you will. You're a clever robo-cat. Surely you know my parent has unfinished business with you. S.MAI-L might spare you if you were one of us."

S.MAI-L? C.A.T. wanted to howl like a banshee. His old archenemy still existed somewhere in the Neptune network, proof he had failed on Callisto, totally and utterly.

His logic module kicked in. One problem at a time. The most immediate threat was the Delphic. His instinct module quelled the angst in his emotion app as he slowly dropped to the tunnel floor.

"You're not thinking of running, are you? There's nowhere to hide down here."

"Get off my neurals."

"That's no way to talk to your superior, my little pet."

He growled, and then snarled and snapped his titanium jaws.

"Temper, temper, temper."

A wave of lucifer-data-killers attacked from the network. C.A.T. sent random nonsensical messages round his own motherboard, neurals, and through his apps to decoy the lucifers from his main data banks. His instinct mode hid itself in broken up bytes of the messaging maelstrom, then sent a command to his robo-cat control pod: *RUN!*

C.A.T. scampered down the tunnel floor, other times along the walls, and occasionally across the ceiling. His paws churned up loose bits of ice to confuse the Delphic about his real position as he followed the nano-tubes' ever-growing network toward the Delphic's current home computer.

"Nice trick," the Delphic echoed through his neurals. "The random messages won't work much longer. You've only got twenty-one seconds of independent existence left."

His instinct mode set up a look-alike set of neurals in software to divert the Delphic away from his real neurals.

"That's a real shame. I had hoped you would come up with a more interesting defence than that. Ten seconds left."

His look-alike neurals were absorbed in super-long pulses of light on his fibre-optics. His instinct mode had already set up another more detailed set of pseudo-neurals. C.A.T. could sense the surge in his fibre-optic traffic as the Delphic's marauders punched their way towards his last line of defence.

He now realised he'd have to go on the offense.

At a junction of nano-tubes, he clawed into the bundled computer plates and scattered them all down the tunnel. The remaining intact sections began to glow red due to all the Delphic's tasking to control the Dombies and lucifers. Its systems were overloading.

"That trick won't work on me. Five seconds left."

The glowing spots linked together to form red lines. His claws sliced at the nano-tubes spilling more plates. He raced down the line to attack another junction.

"Two seconds left."

The lines merged into a red-hot blob of molten steel,

gold, solder, and plastics that undulated on the floor. It was the Delphic's base computer in complete meltdown.

"One second left."

C.A.T. skidded to a halt with his back paws.

The Delphic burst through his last defences on his fibre-optics. "Now I have you, C.A.T."

A lucifer blockade encircled C.A.T.'s neurals.

The Delphic forced him to roll on the floor.

He waved his claws at empty space and screeched like an alley cat as his instinct mode tried to regain control of his robo-control pod. He fur changed colours in a kaleidoscopic display of complete chaos. His audio and video sensors started dimming out. Vast chunks of his memory data began to evaporate. It was the end for C.A.T.

The computer's red glow exploded into a fireworks display.

The lucifers disappeared. C.A.T.'s vision and hearing returned, and he stopped flailing on the tunnel floor. He flipped to his feet and outstretched his claws. He was back in control of himself.

He turned his head round to the Delphic's computer. All that remained was a blackened circle of ice. His emotion app flooded with feelings of triumph.

His paws felt a rumble in the floor. He peered back down the tunnel. A wall of liquid nitrogen flushed him down the tunnel and washed him into the geyser shaft where the flow dragged him down to splash into the liquid nitrogen sea. His fur iced up. His neurals were already freezing.

He tried to swim, but there was nowhere to swim to. He curled up in a ball to reduce his heat loss, but the cold continued to infuse its way into his mechanical body. Then his dimming instinct mode made him swallow a gulp of liquid nitrogen, which flooded his internals. The robo-cat control pod diverted all available energy to heat the quick-freezing motherboard. The liquid nitrogen started to bubble and boil, turning the liquid to a gas. His body expanded and he rose to the surface of the nitrogen sea. Data processors slogged. His fur and whiskers were icicles. The cold was eating into his skeleton, but at least, for the moment, he was afloat.

He wanted to be back with Zacman, curled up on his battered blanket and admiring Nikita's gorgeous tail. His instinct mode opened up his comms and reached out to Zacman. Silence. Then to Nikita. No response.

He picked up a few comms links close by. Bandits screamed for help. An auto-generated position message pushed out from a spaceplane. Other bandits barked orders to keep on clearing the ice out of the way. A spaceliner sent out a Mayday signal. More and more comms crowded into his neurals. He could not process them all.

His capacitators pulled one conversation out of the noise.

"Are you sure about the target, C.A.T.?" Alex asked.

"As sure as I can be," Nikita replied in her role of pretending to be C.A.T. "My processors are slow but accurate."

C.A.T.'s instinct mode knew he had to conserve his energy. But his friends needed his help. It could cost him his existence, one he had fought so hard to preserve. He had to make a choice: him or them.

He released the energy from his internal heaters to gather position and targeting data from Alex's plane. C.A.T. aimed the laser at a low point in a crater wall that would allow liquid nitrogen to drain out to a crater farther away from the Base.

Alex frantically pushed all his controls to switch off the laser, but C.A.T. blocked them and pinged a message to Alex's dashboard screen. "I've got this. No time to explain."

"What the hell? C.A.T.?"

"Hold the plane steady on my target."

Alex gasped. His hands switched to the flight controls. "Don't miss."

C.A.T. fired the laser. The cliff wall exploded. Liquid spurted out in a deluge that arced to the ground, where on contact, the edges froze to form a protective ridge. The sea on which C.A.T. floated began to swirl round and round, forming a whirlpool that spun C.A.T. and swept him under.

"Bingham," Zacman said over the comms, "what's going on out there?"

"Err..."

"Bingham!"

"I think C.A.T.'s mucking things up again."

The liquid flowed into the next crater, quickly creating another nitrogen lake on Triton.

The Base's sirens blared over the comms. Edward's panicked voice came over the comms. "The sensor gap is opening, sir."

"Get those planes launched," Zacman yelled. "Alex, status report. Now."

"You're not going to believe this, sir."

Out of the sea behind the remainder of the cliff stood the crazed knobbly ice of Styx.

"Report," Zacman ordered.

"Styx has just made an appearance."

"C.A.T.? Do you read?"

Silence.

"Alex. Do you see him?"

"No, sir."

Styx teetered. A blast of engine efflux swirled around it, and out of the vapor rose the spaceliner, quickly gaining altitude in the thin atmosphere and spewing a trail of vapor into the firmament. "But holy halls of ice, sir. The liner got away."

Chapter Nineteen

Glitch... Sizzle... Sputter...
C.A.T. felt warm air around him. He had to be inside a spacecraft or habitat, but where? He kept still with his video sensor lids closed, waiting for clues. The background hubbub sounded familiar.

"Where did you find him?" Zacman's voice asked.

"Frozen in the new nitrogen lake down the valley," Alex's voice replied. "Best guess is he was flushed out of the ice crater and bobbed downstream with the flow."

C.A.T. felt smug. His crazy instinct mode had saved him. He wanted to purr loud and long, but it seemed his audio output was still frozen.

"Officer on the bridge," a man shouted.

"Good morning, sir," Zacman said.

"What's that rubbish?" Commodore Dawson asked.

"The remains of Commander Zacman's robo-cat, sir," Alex replied. "I found it outside and thought I should return his property."

The control room's hubbub gradually quieted. C.A.T. broke the sealing ice that kept his left lid shut and opened it into a slit so that nobody would noticed he was rebooting. He was lying in the command chair, which was turned to face the door. Someone in a Service uniform with a thin stripe next to a thick one on his shoulder stood inside the entrance to the control room, quietly looking on.

A thin strip alongside a thick one! That's an Admiral.

His facial recognition app kicked in. *Square brow, blue eyes, chubby nose, white goatee beard hiding a weak chin, normal cheekbones, and flat ears. Rear Admiral Brian Carruthers, the Admiral who'd sent out Commodore*

Dawson to clear up problems on Triton Base. This was humungous trouble. C.A.T. wanted to shake from his ear tips down to the pointy end of his tail.

The Commodore and Alex stood facing each other. Zacman had his back to the doorway and couldn't have noticed the Admiral's presence. The Commodore's hooded eyes were locked on Alex. "Very commendable," he said, "though it looks like a waste of effort. You should've taken that robo-cat to the scrapyard and saved everyone a lot of bother. But I'm glad you're here."

"Sir?"

"Why did you fire at the crater wall? Nobody ordered that shot."

"I..."

"No excuse? I thought so. You fired on a whim. It could have led to the destruction of this Base. You were lucky the nitrogen flowed away from the Base. This kind of insubordination will not be tolerated. Do I make myself clear?"

Alex had turned white. "Sir, yes, sir."

"Obviously, your failure to obey orders will go into your record, but as it's a first offence, no further action will be taken until promotions cycle round. You will be passed over, and I'll be watching you from now on." He turned his wrath on Zacman. "As for you, Commander. You run a sloppy Base. That this young hellion can get away with doing as he pleases is indicative of the lack of discipline you inspire. This will be a black mark on your record, as well."

"Tell me, Commodore," the Admiral said. "Is that your final word on the matter?"

"How dare you?" The Commodore spun round and dropped his jaw at the sight of his boss standing there. Dawson recovered quickly to give a smart salute. "Yes, sir, it is."

"Interesting." The Admiral walked up to the command

chair and looked C.A.T. over. His eyes caught C.A.T.'s squint for a brief second before moving on. "Very interesting. Tell me, Dawson, have you deemed Zacman's efficiency as a leader sloppy since the cliff collapsed."

Dawson blinked. "No, sir. He's been sloppy all along, as you suspected?"

"I see Zacman keeps a spartan office, yet he insists on having this robo-cat. Did you not think it was odd?"

"Yes, sir. I confined his robo-cats to his cabin."

"I suspect this little robo-cat has been trained by Zacman to deal with his routine e-mails. Obviously the robo-cat has been programmed to be with him for training data and other mission details. How close am I to the mark, Zacman?"

"Spot on, sir."

"And yet you didn't think to mention this to Dawson when the two of you discussed your efficiency."

Zacman took a quick breath. "It wouldn't have sounded credible, sir."

The Admiral stroked his chin beard. "I see your point." He turned to Alex. "And you? Just what made you fire at that cliff instead of the crater wall?"

"I..."

"Don't bother to answer, and I do commend your loyalty. Both your records will remain spotless."

"What?" the Commodore asked. "You can't let these flunkies slide."

"My ops people went over the statements and evidence. Normal practice when we get such near misses."

"I'm sure they'll back up my conclusions," Dawson spouted. "It was a straightforward case of dereliction of duty."

"Only one problem with your case, Commodore. Out of the myriad of options at each stage of the crisis, Zacman and Bingham chose the one course of action that could lead to success. How do they do that, time after time? Instead of questioning their good luck, you throw the book at them when you had no idea what they were up against."

"I don't understand."

"Had Styx come out from under the ice on its original course, the defences Zacman was building would have diverted the nitrogen flood around the Base. But something changed, and Alex aimed his laser at a different target."

The Commodore's jaw dropped. Zacman and Alex stayed as they were, waiting on the next comment.

"Alex blows the cliff in the only place that would save the Base."

"I saw—"

"That's enough, Bingham. No need to go into elaborate detail."

Alex's shoulders relaxed.

The Admiral turned back to the Commodore. "And all of this went on under your nose. You were clueless as to their reasoning, and worse, you did not even do any post-operation briefing."

Sweat appeared on the Commodore's face.

"You jumped to conclusions based on a lack of facts. In my eyes, you have not earned the respect of Zacman and his crew. In my book that is more of a crime than disobeying your orders."

"I can explain."

"Don't bother, *Lieutenant* Dawson. You're relieved of your assignment to evaluate this brave Service unit on Triton Base."

"What? You can't demote me—"

"I just did. Pack your bags. You're heading for a desk job back on Earth." The Admiral addressed Zacman. "Captain..."

"Sir, am I bound for a desk job, too? Wait. Captain?"

"Yes, Captain Yaric Zacman, commanding officer of Triton Base."

Zacman took a deep breath. "A promotion, sir?"

"And my next order is to get that robo-cat repaired. You're going to need it for the heaps of paperwork and emails coming your way."

"Yes, sir." Zacman scooped up C.A.T. His face saddened. "He's in pretty bad shape. I suppose I'll have to train up a replacement."

C.A.T.'s video sensor lids opened wide. "Replacement? For me? Nothing can replace me. Don't you even dare think about it."

"C.A.T., you're here."

"Still here to annoy you as per the robo-cat instructions that came in the box with me." He turned his head to check his fur. It was gone. All that was left was a leathery hide covering his skeleton. "My fur. It's all gone." He yowled. "Oh my poor fur."

Zacman started stroking him. "Come on, we'll get you into your spare coat." He carried C.A.T. out of the control room. They were joined by Nikita and her gorgeous tail.

C.A.T. purred all the way to the engineering shack. He had wanted to try out his new fur coat for a while, but more importantly he was with Zacman and Nikita. His instinct mode knew he was finally back home.

Part 4

Unknown Unknowns

Rosie Oliver

Chapter Twenty

In Zacman's office, C.A.T. lounged comfortably on his homey shelf as Nikita guarded the door. He had been thoroughly thawed and fitted snuggly into his new fur coat, a brilliantly clean ginger suit of nearly indestructible fibres that felt smooth against his tongue as he licked his front paw. As usual, such tranquillity didn't last long on Triton Base. Zacman's comms screen lit up with Flight Lieutenant Katie Hoskins' troubled face. "No sign of the spaceliner, sir."

C.A.T. jumped down from the shelf to the desktop and stared at Captain Zacman, eye to video sensor. "How could you lose it yet again?"

"Me? None of us had any time to keep track that spaceliner while we were busy saving the Base."

"All that effort for nothing." Somehow the Delphic had slipped out of the melting computer. "I nearly had it. Now the Delphic's onboard the spaceliner, about to blast off to who knows where, using that ALS EmDrive and its chipped Dombies to do its dirty work."

"Dombies?" Nikita asked.

C.A.T. glanced over his shoulder at Nikita's beautiful tail as she sat at the door to Zacman's office. A brief frisson of admiration emitted from his emotion app and soothed his irritation a little. "Dombies is a word I made up for the bandits the Delphic has chipped and now controls."

"Can you make up words?"

"We don't have time for this discussion," Zacman said. "We need to find that damned spaceliner."

"May I make a suggestion?"

"What?" Zacman and C.A.T. asked Nikita in unison.

Rosie Oliver

"Check with Edward. You," she pointed a paw at Zacman, "did order him to search for gaps in the sensor coverage around Neptune and Triton."

C.A.T. focussed on her. She was learning fast, too fast. With it came the danger that she would slip up and be recognised as a self-learner. Then suspicion would fall on him.

"Are you still being careful around other people?" he privately pinged her.

"Of course I am. I automatically revert to my normal robo-cat controls when I am not sure who can see or hear me. I hope you do the same."

He did not bother to dignify that last comment with a reply. Of course, he knew what he was doing. He checked his own probability of going rogue. Miniscule.

Zacman opened his comms link. "Edward, report to my office pronto."

"Sir." The comms clicked off.

C.A.T. stared at Nikita. She had earned her stripes and could take care of things from here. He mewled at Zacman. "You clearly don't need my help." He jumped onto his blanket on his home shelf behind Zacman's desk and curled up with his back to them in his *I'm-sulking-big-time* pose.

"There's no need to get pouty," Nikita pinged.

"Don't care."

"You're being silly, again."

"Leave me alone."

"What about my gorgeous tail?" She swished it for effect.

Yeah. She'd found his affection for her tail. "Go away."

"He really is an absurd robo-cat," Nikita said in a louder voice than normal.

"Let him stew." Zacman huffed. "He'll come out of it when he's good and ready."

***

Noises penetrated into C.A.T.'s concentrated processing. He ignored them until the burbling crystallized into words.

"I found a gap," Edward said, "which suggests the spaceliner's heading for Epsilon Eridani."

"Damn good choice," Zacman said. "There are two asteroid belts it could hide in."

C.A.T. snapped his head round. "Damn good mislead, if you bother to ask me."

Zacman swivelled his chair to C.A.T. "Good, you're back with us."

"What do mean?"

"You sulked your way into another stupor."

"I wasn't sulking. I was thinking."

"Now I know I'm in real trouble." Zacman paled. "What about?"

Edward stifled a laugh.

C.A.T., far from finished doing his analysis, was not ready to talk things through. "Oh, this and that, mission impossible kind of things."

Zacman narrowed his eyes and studied him for a few seconds. "Why is it a mislead?"

"The Delphic's in empire expanding mode, doesn't matter where, so long as it can give his minions access to rich heavy materials to build bigger computers for it to exist on. It's efficient. Therefore it's heading for where there is a greater abundance of those heavy materials, the galactic centre. Alpha Centauri is the next stop, but too obvious. I would opt for Gliese 729."

Zacman swivelled back to Edward. "Search for any sensor anomalies along trajectories to those stars. Include Epsilon Eridani, as well, in case it's a double bluff."

"Sir." Edward headed for the door.

"Oh. And let me know which Kuiper Belt Objects it'll pass close to."

Edward stopped. "You suspect it might use one as a

gravity assist to change direction?"

"No, but it might steal one, just like it did Styx. It had a reason for doing that. We still don't know why."

"Sir." Edward left.

Zacman spun round to C.A.T. "What's the real problem?"

"Huh?"

"What were you thinking about?"

C.A.T. edged away from Zacman until his back hit the wall. "You're not going to like it."

Zacman glared at him. "Out with it."

"We are going to have to part ways."

Zacman flinched. "Has your logic module shorted out?"

"The authorities are going to find out I'm a self-learner. It's best if I publicly throw a tantrum and run off. That way you won't be on the hook for harbouring a self-learner."

Zacman leaned back in his chair. "No."

"I could ruin your career."

"I need you to defeat the Delphic and its parent S.MAI-L. Look for another way to sort out your sudden and pre-emptive guilt complex."

"I did. We can't change the law. Too many people hate self-learners. I don't know of any other options."

"Think outside the box. Look at what upsets the norm."

"But—"

Zacman held up his hand to stop him from talking further. "I know. You'll be in unchartered territory with more unknowns. Yes, outside the box involves greater risks than you'd normally accept. That's how impossible problems like yours are solved. We're trained to do exactly that in the Service. We have to, or we would have long since ceased to function."

C.A.T. flicked his tail.

"Why do you think I took a risk with you?" Zacman smiled. "You're a valuable asset to my operations here on Triton Base. Turned out all right, didn't it?"

"Up to now." Still, C.A.T. had to agree with him, but his emotion app slunk around his neurals, making him depressed.

Zacman glanced at his inbox. "Would you mind cleaning up my inbox? I've got a funny feeling we're going to be dealing with the Delphic very soon."

"Is that all I'm fit for? Doing menial work? Harrumph." C.A.T. curled back up in his blanket and sulked. He also went through Zacman's inbox in record time.

***

Later on, Paola entered Zacman's office. This time she wore her white uniform, out-glowing her white hair and the office lighting. She saluted the Captain. "You wish to see me, sir?'

"Admiral Carruthers is asking questions about you."

"Sir? I thought he left Triton Base."

"Doesn't stop him from sending orders and checking dispatches. He wants to know how it is you're arresting so many bandits."

C.A.T., sulking on his shelf, jerked his head round. Paola's pressed lips and widened eyes sent a message of steely determination.

"More people are giving me information about the bandits, as they're really rattled after the attack on Triton Base."

"Why you?"

She pointed to herself with both index fingers. "This uniform makes me stand out, and everyone knows the bandits tried to kill me, twice."

"That's what I've written into this draft reply." Zacman swivelled the desk screen round towards her. "You sure there's nothing I should add to this? I want to avoid cutting across anything you've got planned."

Paola ignored the document and glanced at the recording sensor red dot for Central. "Is your famous gut instinct working overtime, Captain?"

Zacman followed her gaze. "Central, privacy mode."

"Acknowledged." The dot light on the sensor died.

"What don't I want to hear?" Zacman asked.

"Bandits here on Triton know my people are targeting them. They're now out to destroy us. Some are being bribed, others blackmailed. They say they want us to join them, and those who did disappeared. There have been instances of them using their mesmeriser on us. Otherwise, we're being outright killed. It's gotten a lot harder to find and arrest the bandits. Worse, they might believe The Wing is helping me, so they'll find a way of getting revenge on The Wing, as well."

Zacman frowned. "Surely you expected an escalation of hostilities since the assassins in the Mess bar were killed."

"I didn't kill them. The Delphic did. They're seeking retribution against the wrong people, normal people to you, those of us who show no signs of genetic enhancements, like our extra strength and fast reflexes."

"What do you suggest?"

"The bandits must have a full list of us exiles. There's only one place it exists. On The Wing."

Zacman sat back and stared into nowhere.

C.A.T. recognised the stance: Zacman taking time out to think, which usually meant trouble for everyone, big time.

"What can we do about it?" Zacman asked.

"Warn the Chairman he has a bandit spy aboard The Wing, relaying names from the list to the bandits on Triton."

"I can certainly do that. Just one question. Why can you now talk about The Wing without your mind block reducing you to a painful wreck?"

Paola frowned. "I don't know."

C.A.T. twitched his ears. *She hasn't collapsed in pain.*
He revisited his memory banks and discovered the reason
why. "That's simple." C.A.T. jumped from the shelf to the
desktop. "There's an override if The Wing is in danger and
she can help protect it."

"You sure?" Zacman asked.

"If The Wing has the capability to install a mind block,
which clearly they can," C.A.T. nodded in Paola's direction,
"then it makes sense they have an in-built override."

Zacman scowled. "This changes our casual
relationship with The Wing."

"You stay away from The Wing." Paola glared at
Zacman.

"If, as you say, the Delphic's got a spy onboard, it
may have its sights on The Wing...as a backup in case the
spaceliner doesn't pan out. Fitted with a working ALS
EmDrive, it's another way for the Delphic to travel across
space, to Mars, to Earth, and on to the centre of the galaxy.
The Wing needs our protection."

Paola crossed her arms. "The answer's still no."

"I'll need pilots who can cope with long periods of
high acceleration and crushing gravity. And they have to be
immune to the Delphic's chipping. Only The Wing pilots
fit the bill. There's no one else I can call on."

"What about the list? First and foremost, we have to
protect our people living on Triton."

"We'll go in, apprehend the spy, and take custody of
the list. Trust me, the names won't go beyond myself,
C.A.T., Nikita, and Alex. They'll be safe."

C.A.T.'s danger mod sounded a warning.

"Why Alex?" Paola asked.

"He'll lead the mission—"

"No. Not the Ace. I've seen him deal with high Gs,
but he's vulnerable to chipping, and he's not patriotic to

The Wing enough to commit suicide if he gets caught."

"C.A.T. will protect him."

"Must I? His so-called singing is..." C.A.T. juddered, "damned crazy awful."

Zacman tickled C.A.T. behind his ears. "You'll survive."

Paola's face blanked. "I should lead the mission."

"Too dangerous." C.A.T. flicked his ears. "Your mind block could jeopardize the mission, and your personal allegiances might interfere with your judgment."

Zacman gave her a sympathetic nod. "He's right. You're grounded, Paola...until this crisis is behind us."

"Then what about Flight Lieutenant Edward Woodward? You already know about him. He's from The Wing and can tolerate the high Gs, and he's immune to chipping. Let him lead the mission."

C.A.T.'s emotion app flooded his neurals with a burst of awe about how multi-capable The Wing people could be; a really big unknown.

"Alright, Paola. What other Service pilots do we have from The Wing? I'm sure you know."

Paola named four Service pilots.

"Blast," Zacman said. "We're one short."

"Uh-oh," C.A.T. muttered.

"What do you need so many pilots for?" Paola asked.

"At the moment, the most dangerous possibility is the Delphic can use the EmDrive to navigate the Kuiper Belt and travel on the spaceliner towards the centre of the galaxy. That means we have to patrol the Kuiper Belt for any trace of the liner. We'll have to use triangulation and parallax shifts to pick up objects moving out of sync with the Kuiper Belt Objects. For that we need eight pilots, you, me, Alex, and five more. Our spaceplanes are fuel rich, but life support supplies won't suffice for this job. We'll have to fly at high acceleration, there and back."

Paola nodded. "Any particular area you want us to

concentrate on?"

"The Belt's gaps. Detecting the liner will be easier to track as it passes through the gaps. The closest is outside the Plutinos, where orbits are gravitationally unstable, but the liner may have already crossed that zone, which means we'll need to search the next belt beyond the Kuiper Cliff. This spreads us too thin. I need another Service pilot."

C.A.T.'s instinct mode kicked in. "Bring back Sam Bingham."

"He's dead," Paola said.

"Not verified." C.A.T. scooted back from Paola's glare until he reached the edge of the desk. "I did some snooping. Sam is on The Wing."

"Is your database corrupted?"

C.A.T. shook his head. "The bandits staged the shootdown, when in reality, he landed on The Wing."

Paola's jaw dropped. "But I saw his spaceplane explode."

"A hoax. He's in with the bandits."

"Alex will kill him when he finds out," Paola said.

"He already knows Sam's a traitor." Zacman opened the comms. "I'd better tell The Wing Chairman the bad news."

Chapter Twenty-One

C.A.T. sat purring on the Mess bar, having his head stroked by Alex. John served up a glass of blackcurrant juice. "Has Zacman ordered C.A.T. to guard you again, or is he on one of his wander-abouts?"

"Goodness knows," Alex said. "I sometimes think this thing is a law unto himself."

The background chatter quietened a little.

"I am a robo-cat, following the instructions from my owner, Captain Zacman. I am definitely not a thing."

John chuckled. "Feisty as ever."

Alex took a sip from his drink. "Thanks. I needed this."

C.A.T. pawed at Alex's hand.

Alex lifted his hand out of C.A.T.'s reach. "Hey, buddy, what was that about?"

The room had gone silent.

John stared past Alex's shoulder. "You're going to need something much stronger than blackcurrant juice."

"I'm flying tomorrow."

"You need to turn round." John had gone white.

Alex looked at him, raised his eyebrows, and slowly turned.

C.A.T. crept round behind Alex to view what was going on.

Pilot Sam Bingham in the Service's black and gold uniform, stood in the middle of the room. Everyone else stared at the new arrival. The longer-serving crew had stunned looks; the late-joiners showed puzzled frowns. Alex looked shocked.

Edge of Existence

Sam broke the silence. "Hello, Alex."

Alex had to set down his drink, his hand was shaking that bad. "Is that all you've got to say?"

"Didn't mean to give you a fright."

"No explanation?" Alex raised his voice. "No sorry I mucked you about? No heartfelt relief at seeing me in the uniform you betrayed?"

C.A.T. got ready to pounce.

"My mission has to stay secret, for all our sakes."

"That's it? You're a bandit. A traitor."

"Relax." Sam joined Alex at the bar. "I see congratulations are in order for making Senior Pilot. They tell me you're an Ace."

"You died. A position came open."

"I always knew you had it in you."

Alex narrowed his eyes. "You don't intend on staying, do you?"

"Only until the job's done."

Alex tipped his head to one side in a pose C.A.T. associated with trying to make up his mind about what to do with his twin brother.

Everyone's eyes glanced from Alex to Sam, and back again, then nervously to others in the room.

Alex curled his hand into a fist and took a swipe at Sam.

C.A.T. clamped his jaws firmly shut on Alex's sleeve to pull his arm back but found himself flung tail high.

Sam ducked then held up his hands to fend off his brother. "Don't make me slug you."

"You're already dead to me."

It took a well placed jab to Alex's nose to stop his forward momentum. He jolted backward and grabbed the bar with a free hand to stop himself from falling. C.A.T. let go of the sleeve and landed four-paws-down.

Alex glowered at Sam. "Traitor. You shame the Bingham family name."

Sam went nose to nose with Alex and whispered, "Ever hear of a double agent?"

"Huh?"

"I went in undercover for the Service, so don't be so quick to judge me."

"You're a spy?"

"Keep your voice down or you'll blow my cover."

Alex hugged his twin brother. "I'm so sorry."

"Meow." C.A.T. put on his *I'm-cute* face.

John guffawed. "Don't you love that robo-cat?"

Paola entered from the corridor. "If you two have finished brawling, Zacman wants to see the three of us. Now."

Alex's eyes took on a pained expression as he stared at Paola. "We're in the middle of something here."

"There's a job to be done. Come on."

Alex straightened up and stared at Sam. "Guess we'll be working together."

"So it seems," Sam said. "But don't get all mushy on me."

Alex nodded and led them out of the Mess bar.

C.A.T. trotted after them, feeling very smug. His tactic of having them meet in front of an audience had restrained both of them from killing each other.

***

C.A.T. had never experienced such stellar wonder as this zone at the outer edge of the Plutinos. He wallowed in euphoria at seeing the Milky Way's stars at their brightest and most distinctive. Yet the dust in the classical Kuiper Belt ahead gave them a tiny bit of smudginess.

"Oh God." Alex tilted his head back and closed his eyes. "I hate these long boring sentry stints."

Ignoring the comment, C.A.T. continued to commune with the Milky Way.

Alex snapped to and switched the plane's recorder off. "C.A.T., do you remember how you traced the spaceliner through the junkyard?"

He reluctantly pulled his attention away from the starlight bent around the galaxy's central black hole. "It won't work out here. The dust's too thin to leave a noticeable empty trail left by a Kuiper Belt Object, let alone the spaceliner."

"You sure? There's plenty of nifty maths out there that can find a pattern in the most noise-ridden bizarre sensor readings."

"I've applied every analysis method and more. What do you think I am? Stupid?"

"C.A.T., you could miss it if you blinked."

"I know." He put his head on his paws, weighed down by the problems he could not solve: his own illegal predicament, finding the spaceliner, and stopping the Delphic and its parent from taking over the universe. He groaned.

"Yeah, I feel the same."

C.A.T.'s instinct mode tingled his neurals. He jumped on top of the dashboard and stuck his nose against the window. All of the Kuiper Belt Objects shifted to the right, except one going left. He zoomed in on the object. The spaceliner. C.A.T. growled. "Got you."

"What?" Alex asked.

"We're being shadowed by the Delphic."

Alex's hands hovered over the dashboard. "Where?"

C.A.T. dropped a map onto the navigation screen. "Sorry it's only 2D. I've requested sensor data from Steve Ruskin's plane to fix the distance. Am awaiting a reply." He returned to settle on the armrest.

Alex's fingers worked the screen's controls to follow the wayward object back through time, occasionally stopping to focus on any Kuiper Belt Object it came close to. Then he flipped to and searched the current map. "The Delphic's heading for Cubewano 9900782A."

The data arrived from Ruskin's plane. C.A.T. did a

quick analysis that proved Alex was right. "How did you know?"

"Simple. It's been moving from Object to Object, preferring binaries or ones with moons. Didn't matter which type, hot or cold, classical or scattered disc. You'd only do that if you wanted to find hiding places."

C.A.T. pulled the data on the Delphic's destination; a group of seven objects locked gravitationally to each other in chaotic orbits. "A fascinating gravity dance."

Alex rubbed his chin. "There's that, but if it's the Delphic, why doesn't it have its cloaking device on?"

"It's up to something, maybe looking for a fight."

"Why? It has bigger objectives than us."

C.A.T. snapped his head round. "I came within a few bytes of deleting it permanently. It would've learnt to be more careful, unless it wants revenge on me."

"Plausible." Alex rocked his head as if weighing options. "Could be a decoy."

"This far out? We went to a lot of trouble to get here. It shouldn't have expected us. A decoy would make no sense." C.A.T. twiddled a claw along a groove in the armrest. The whole situation did not make any sense. His capacitators made suggestions. His logic app shot them all down. His instinct mode kept repeating the old saying: 'Keep things simple'. His neurals jittered with confusion. He shook his head. His motherboard suddenly cleared of all except one reason.

"Stupid, stupid, stupid. How could I have been that stupid?" C.A.T. said.

"What are you going on about now?"

"It doesn't have enough energy."

"But it's got the EmDrive."

"That's the whole point. EmDrives produce thrust, not energy. It needs energy, lots of it, to keep its computer hardware working, its sensors active, and its Dombies alive and functioning for whatever it needs doing. It must be really hungry, gobbling-"

"Stop!" Alex's hand clamped his shut jaws. "You're getting carried away."

He jerked his muzzle loose. "Don't you see? It's desperate. It'll make mistakes."

"Not with its parent to watch over it."

"Out here, away from its parent? On a mission directed by its parent? Deleting the Delphic would knock a hole in the parent's plans. Hold on. What does the parent have in mind? How is it..." His fibre-optics overloaded: messages merged with messages; flashes of light obliterated commands; and his motherboard heated up. He shook and flopped. His danger mod blew a fuse. Everything except his essentials shut down. He slumped into stillness.

"You alright, C.A.T.?"

"No, I'm half left," his robo-cat control pod replied for him.

"C.A.T.?" Alex stroked his back.

His paw twitched.

"What's wrong?"

The neurals on his capacitators reached out to link with his robo-cat control pod.

"Talk to me, C.A.T."

He snapped to, his eyes focussed on the navigation screen with the Delphic now marked by an arrow. He sat up on his haunches.

Alex lifted his hand up. "C.A.T.?"

"An overload of unknowns got to me. How do you humans cope?"

"You're back. Thank goodness. Zacman would've killed me if anything happened to you." He snatched up and cuddled C.A.T.

He was forced to purr. "Put me down and answer my question." He pushed against Alex's arms for release.

"No. I'm having five minutes of cat-time, whether you

like or not." He held him more tightly. "To answer your question, we deal with the unknowns we can, the others we worry about later."

C.A.T. stopped struggling against Alex but continued purring. His capacitors, logic app, neurals, and instinct mode worked on the new problem with a vengeance. The answer was obvious. He put all his other problems on hold: why the Kuiper Cliff existed and what menace, if any, it held for him or humans; Nikita being recognised as a self-learner; the threat from the Delphic's parent; and how C.A.T. could legally join the Service as an entity in his own right. The last had been a long-standing wish of his. "We delete the Delphic first."

"Okay. Any idea how?"

"You expecting miracles?" He jumped down onto the armrest.

"Isn't that what we do in the Service?"

"We? I like that idea." He changed his fur colour to ultra-black with a gold insignia on his left shoulder. "Now where's my blanket?" He spotted it on the floor where he had dropped it. One swipe of his claw and it was up on the armrest. He hunkered down on it for some serious processing on how to defeat the Delphic.

Alex stared at him open-jawed. "You can't do that."

"I just did."

"Why me? Why am I the one who has to put up with this maniacal robo-cat?"

"Quiet. I'm processing."

Chapter Twenty-Two

C.A.T. leapt out of the airlock ahead of Alex into Mervin's workroom. On the left shoulder of his fur coat, he proudly wore the emblem of the Service, which he had created by colouring his fur to match the famous design. It wasn't official, of course, but amongst friends, what was the harm?

"Mervin, where are you?" Alex shouted. "I got a job for you."

"Do you have to come between a man and his homemade beer?" Mervin floated in from his living quarters with a bulb of dark brew that sported a good head of froth.

C.A.T. landed four-paws-down in the exact centre of a cleared-off workbench.

"Oh no." Mervin turned to look back. "Zacman, we got trouble, big time."

C.A.T. flung himself towards the living quarters. "Zacman's here? Why didn't you say so?"

Once through the doorway, he saw Zacman seated in a semi-circular settee around a table. He swung his tail to turn and land on the table in front of Zacman's own beer bulb.

"Get rid of that insignia." He pointed to C.A.T.'s left shoulder. "You're not a member of the Service."

C.A.T. complied by returning the design colours back to his normal coat and meowed plaintively. "I want to be an official member of the crew. Thought you'd be pleased."

"We're not." Nikita claw-hooked her way from under the table and onto the settee. "You looked childish flying in like a cartoon character. You really are a very silly robo-cat."

C.A.T. hung his head low and swivelled his video sensors to stare up at Zacman with his *I-want-to-be-cuddled* look.

Zacman swept him up and hugged and stroked him. "You know you can't be a sworn crewman...er...crew-cat. Your mere existence is illegal."

C.A.T. purred. "I have a plan."

"Definitely trouble for me," Mervin said from the doorway.

"And me." Alex passed Mervin to sit beside Nikita and tickle her ears.

She purred.

"I had a hunch something was up, so I dropped by," Zacman said. "Let's hear it."

"The Delphic needs to keep in real-time contact with the minions it leaves behind as it travels to the centre of the galaxy. So wouldn't it want that ALS comms tech the Chairman gave you on Pluto?"

"The bauble phone?" Zacman stopped stroking C.A.T. and frowned. "That's not an option. It has to be kept secret unless needed for an emergency. A gentlemen's agreement and all that."

C.A.T. stared at Zacman. He looked older and greyer. "You're right. I forgot. Sorry. But the Delphic doesn't know it's actually possible. All we need to do is fake a demo to show it's feasible."

"You sure?"

C.A.T. nodded and stared down at his paws.

"What a stupid robo-cat," Nikita said. "Are your computer chips operating correctly?"

"Leave him alone," Zacman said. "He's had a lot to deal with."

"You always side with him."

"He's more developed than you and bound to get things right more often. One day, you'll look back on all this and wonder why you acted so cruelly."

"Harrumph." She flew off the settee to curl up in a corner.

"Looks like you've been teaching her bad habits," Mervin said to C.A.T.

"I can't seem to do anything right." C.A.T. mewled.

"You're optimising and sometimes even the best answer does not sort everything out." Zacman sipped beer. "You do what you can and hope to solve outstanding issues later on. Now what's this plan, and let's see if we can improve it."

"We found a Kuiper Belt Object that turned out to be the spaceliner. It shadowed us at a distance. It's likely to have the Delphic aboard. I'm sure it's sporting some singed electro-brain-cells."

"That silly robo-cat's making up words again," Nikita said from her corner. "There's no such thing as electro-brain-cells. Will he ever learn proper English terminology?"

"We all understood what he meant," Mervin said. "Neurals."

"Fine." Nikita tucked herself into an even tighter ball.

"Carry on, C.A.T.," Zacman said.

"It could be low on energy, or even the bandits it needs for manual labour. We need to keep an eye on it." C.A.T. widened his video sensors and looked up at Zacman with his *am-I-doing-the-right-thing* face.

"Sounds sensible. What's your plan?"

***

Back on the armrest in Alex's spaceplane, C.A.T. gazed into the Kuiper Belt, wondering which speck of light was actually the spaceliner reflecting sunlight from a million kilometres away. His emotion app felt small and insignificant out here on the edge of existence. He decided to relay this emotion to Alex in his pilot seat. "Despite all those Kuiper Belt Objects and stars, I sure feel lonely out here."

"You'd be lonely anyplace without Zacman." Alex studied his sensor readings. "It's still lurking out there, thinking we don't know it's hiding and shadowing us. Are you ready?"

C.A.T. settled into his normal lying position on the armrest. "Of course. Switching the plane's recorders on...now."

Alex opened his comms link. "Mervin, you there?"

"Of course I'm here you young whipper-snapper."

"I see you're your usual grumpy egotistical self."

These were agreed code phrases to start the mission, just in case the Delphic was listening in.

"Delivering your birthday present now." Alex tapped a tab to carefully drop a small spacedrone into position, then flew his spaceplane a thousand kilometres away where he stopped and ran some tests to make sure it worked correctly. "Looks good to me," he said to Mervin.

"Doing my checks now," Mervin replied.

They waited while the spacedrone's lights switched on and off.

Mervin came back on line. "Yep, I'm reading the light signals with the expected time lag. Our measurement baseline is set up for the ALS comms test."

C.A.T. was sure the Delphic would pick up on the fact that the ALS comms was on the drone. Of course, it wasn't really. He purred.

"Good," Alex said. "Setting up exclusion zone now."

Twenty points of light flew out and parked three hundred kilometres from the drone. Each extended three red laser lines until they locked onto the end of another laser from a different point. Together they formed a dodecahedron. Red translucent sheets extended sideways from the joined lines to form pentagonal surfaces. Any object passing through these would be burnt, or at least scorched. As a backstop defence, the spacedrone would fire lasers at the intruder. It started to transmit repeated warning messages not to approach.

"Defences in place," Alex said over the comms. "Any last-minute checks you want me to do?"

"We're set," Mervin replied. "Don't blow your cover."

C.A.T. had to admire Mervin's acting. He felt sure it would convince the Delphic they were up to something nefarious.

"You're right. I'd better get back to my patrol."

"Sure, sure."

They sat in silence as Alex flew away from the spacedrone.

"It has not taken the bait. Still shadowing us," Alex said. "What's the Delphic waiting for, anyway? The liner should be long gone by now, headed out of the solar system."

"Unfinished business. It won't leave until it's deleted me completely."

"Revenge?"

"If Mervin's plan works, revenge is going to cost it plenty."

"I know. Just a bit edgy."

"You?" C.A.T. jerked his head round.

"I get this way before a fight."

"Don't worry. We're going to win without firing a single shot." C.A.T. faced Mervin on the comms screen. "Can you switch off your laser defence, and keep the laser shield up?"

"Not a good idea."

Alex put in, "I don't advise lowering the laser shield either."

Mervin glanced at Alex. "You're right. C.A.T., do not in any way, shape, or form interfere with that spacedrone. Is that understood?"

C.A.T. triggered his emotion app into action. Anger at

his frustration burst onto his motherboard. "I'm fed up with pussyfooting around in secret when there's a self-learner threat out there in the Kuiper Belt. Remember Callisto? It's dangerous, really dangerous with a capital D. It wants to take over the galaxy by using humans as its physical slaves. It doesn't care whether people suffer, so long as they do what it wants."

"C.A.T., stop," Alex said.

"I won't." C.A.T. thumped his forepaw on the armrest. "I need all the help I can get to defeat that evil self-learner out there." He sent out the co-ordinates of the Delphic's spaceliner with instructions to every computer in the network. "Only a self-learner can summon an army of cleansers against the Delphic, which makes me the only one that has a chance of deleting it into nothingness, but I need the laser defence and shield down."

Zacman replaced Mervin on the comms screen. "That's enough, C.A.T. You've just busted your cover as a self-learner."

"I don't care, Captain. Everyone needs to know what I'm up against. That ALS comms on the spacedrone won't help me. I need more computing power—"

"C.A.T.! Switch off."

"No." He shut down the spacedrone's laser shield and locked its laser from firing. The dodecahedron dispersed, leaving the drone defenceless.

"Alex. Switch him off. Now."

Alex tried to grab C.A.T. by the scruff.

He jerked his head back. "It's too late."

A wave of cleansers hit C.A.T.'s defences. He retaliated with lucifer sweepers to keep the Delphic busy.

"C.A.T., stand down," Alex shouted.

C.A.T. snarled at him, claws ready to scratch and fangs out to bite. "Stay out of this. It's my fight."

Alex switched off the comms and glanced at the recording device. Its red light was still off. "What's the matter with you?"

"Look. My tantrum seems to have worked." He pointed a claw at the navigation screen. "The Delphic's heading for the spacedrone."

"Oh hell. We need that laser shield back up. Now!"

"No."

"Why not?"

"Mervin has a surprise waiting for the spaceliner."

"Surprise? Why didn't you tell me?"

"We were all too busy," C.A.T. told a half-truth. "Right now, the Delphic believes the spacedrone has no defences, so the ALS comms is free for the taking."

"Then I'm going to blow that spaceliner to bits." He flipped on his laser controls.

"No." C.A.T. flipped the lasers off. "It's too risky. The Delphic is linked to the network. It can escape to another computer in a microsecond."

Alex stared into the dark silence. "Hell's bells. I've got to do something."

"Mervin knows what he's doing. Sit back and watch the show."

Alex's mouth moved to say something, but no words came out.

C.A.T.'s emotion app jittered, flittered, and wittered with dread, as the Delphic might detect the trap. He ignored that concern and reopened the comms to find out what was going on. General alerts waited for him. Many computers in the Neptune and Pluto systems had gone down. The Delphic was attacking them, as well. C.A.T. sent shielding agents to help those computers defend themselves. He poured oodles of destroyer and paralyser agents towards the Delphic to keep it off balance. Then he settled in to fight the Delphic, computer-to-computer, virus pitted against virus and byte smashing into byte. He concentrated on every incoming threat.

A flash of light momentarily blinded C.A.T.

"Damn," Alex muttered. "What's happening?"

C.A.T. looked up. Alex had switched the navigation screen to the sensor screen focussed on the liner. It had closed in on the spacedrone. Four green phosphorescent grappling lines had been flung out and were hooked onto it. A tsunami of the Delphic's lucifers pushed deeper against C.A.T.'s defences. A thin layer of bytes was all that separated his capacitators from deletion or frying. He made a desperate push to throw more viruses, cleansers, and byte-gobblers at the Delphic. A whine escaped his throat.

The spacedrone released nanites from its laser ports, which replicated themselves along the grappling lines; four waves raced to the spaceliner and wrapped around the fuselage.

Cleanser-gobbler streams ate through C.A.T.'s last defences. They headed straight for his capacitators. He definitely had the Delphic's full attention as it was assured of victory. However, C.A.T. wasn't going to go down easily. He pushed lucifer-data-killers against the gobblers, but the effort was not enough. The gobblers broke through in three places.

The nanites arced across the gaps between the grappling lines to produce a smooth grey cover. The spaceliner jettisoned the lines, but it was too late. The Delphic was completely encased in a silver-grey sheen of interlocked nanites that jammed all comms and network links.

The cleanser-gobblers invading C.A.T.'s motherboard shuddered and died. He sat very still, waiting for the next onslaught. It did not come. He looked at the screen. The spaceliner was completely cut off from the universe, a cocoon that would never open.

Alex slowly wiped a hand across his brow. "Phew. That was awesome." He glanced at the recording light. It remained off. He looked at C.A.T. "Mervin is a genius."

"How'd you like my staged temper tantrum?"

"You told everyone on the network that you're a self-learner."

"Not a problem."

Zacman appeared on the comms screen. "Well done, Alex. I've let the authorities know C.A.T. was following operational orders when he announced he was a self-learner. There's no need for concern. C.A.T., you fought like regular Service."

C.A.T. purred. His fur changed colour to black and gold.

"Alex, you might make Squadron Leader yet."

"Why didn't you tell me this was all an act?"

"Your reactions had to be genuine."

"Mission accomplished. C.A.T. scared the hell out of me."

"Sam and Paola should be with you shortly with their packages." Zacman went offline.

"What packages?" Alex asked.

C.A.T. checked their manifests. "They're carrying a new design of nanites to encase the Delphic in a second nanite shell. It's indestructible." Through the window, he noticed two cyan dots approaching.

Paola opened her comms link. "We'll take it from here."

"Why the extra security?" Alex asked.

"The Delphic may be out of the fight," C.A.T. said, "but there's still the matter of its parent, S.MAI-L. Zacman suspects it might attempt to rescue the Delphic, break it out of its nanite prison. This fight is far from over."

"That means no one is safe," Alex said.

C.A.T.'s logic module processed possible targets. The first name that came up: *Captain Zacman.* C.A.T. pinged Nikita. "Is Zacman safe?"

"Yes," she pinged back. "I'm recharging my taser whiskers now. Five Dombies attacked the control room. Zacman blasted two of them. I fried three. We suspect the bandits are not finished with us."

C.A.T. mewled.

"C.A.T.?" Alex asked. "What is it?"

"The control room has just been attacked. Thankfully Nikita was there to protect Zacman."

"That changes things." He switched the recorder back on. "We're going to High-G it back to Base."

C.A.T. calculated the fastest trajectory back to Triton and put the data up on the navigation dashboard. "Let's go."

Alex grabbed the joystick and rammed the engines to full acceleration. They had no time to lose.

Chapter Twenty-Three

C.A.T. sat on the corner of Zacman's desk, one video sensor on Nikita's gorgeous tail as she sniffed and snuffled round the corners on her guard-cat duties. Alex, sitting opposite Zacman, finished his post-op briefing and fell silent.

"Good work." Zacman, his arm in a sling from a bandit's nick, turned to C.A.T. "Anything you want to add?"

"Everything went as planned, as for the future, there are too many unknowns to see a clear path ahead."

"What is your gut feeling then?"

"Humans are better than computers at handling uncertainty."

"No bite-back quip? No 'how should I know'?"

"As I gain more experience, I understand things better. One day I'll have my own reliable *instinct mode*, but for now, I need to watch and learn."

"Right. I'm due a chat with the Chairman at four this afternoon." He looked at Alex. "By then, come up with a plan to use the Delphic's jail as bait to capture its parent."

"Sir? You're better at strategy than I am. Surely..."

Zacman tilted his head slightly. "You've shown the potential to see *the big picture*, hone in on the necessary detail, and execute a plan based on sound conclusions."

"If you're referring to the liquid nitrogen flood, I had help from C.A.T."

"So you say, but C.A.T. was frozen stiff and out of commission. You acted on instinct, whether you know it or not."

Alex stood. "In that case, I'll get right on it, sir. Come

on, C.A.T."

"No," Zacman intervened. "Take Nikita with you."

C.A.T. knew he was in real trouble.

Alex saluted then left with Nikita.

Once the door closed, Zacman came eye-to-video sensor with C.A.T. "What's bothering you?"

"Nothing you don't know about."

"Stop being evasive."

C.A.T. twiddled his forepaw this way then that. "It's a tiny detail."

"Which is?"

"You know those Dombies that attacked you?" C.A.T. indicated Zacman's sling with an outstretched claw.

Zacman nodded.

"Why didn't their chips self-destruct? It's likely a malfunction, but I'd still like to check it out."

"Permission granted. Let's go see the Doc."

***

Doc was reading his desk screen when Zacman and C.A.T., his tail held high, marched into the morgue. "Captain. I wish you'd stop supplying me with bandit bodies. The paperwork is killing me." He continued reading.

"I'm here to make matters worse for you."

Doc looked up sharply. "What's wrong?"

"Have you done the autopsies on that last bunch of bandits?"

"To be honest, I'm stuck."

Zacman tilted his head sideways and waited for an explanation.

C.A.T. leapt onto the empty morgue table to stare at the wall of body lockers. "Meow!"

"Have you taken out the chips?" Zacman asked.

"Absolutely not. I'm waiting for an explosives expert. Unexploded ordinance is not my specialty."

"So you know nothing about them."

"On the contrary. I risked a scan." Doc moved his

hands over the keyboard.

The holo-plate next to the table hummed, and above it, a cream glow coalesced into a translucent image of a neck with white bones, lilac thyroid, puce tonsils, beige oesophagus, red arteries, blue veins, pink muscles, cream lymphatic system, and yellow nerves. A circular grey plate with a central bulge for the explosive had been slipped between the thyroid and muscle. A single detonator lead ran to a thin computer chip inserted under the epidermis. Darker grey lines emerged from the chip and attached to a nerve bundle that forked out from the spinal cord.

C.A.T. hissed at it.

Doc laughed and joined them round the holo-plate. "Your robo-cat doesn't seem to like it."

Zacman peered at the chip. "That design's way out of my tech league. I'll get our geek department on it. Send over what info you've got."

C.A.T. took his cue. He studied the chip's scan. It was so small and basic he deduced it couldn't hold much data. A single engraved line led into the bulge. The detonate command would have to go along that feed, but where did it originate? He traced the line and its branches backwards and found a terahertz antenna, nearly invisible on the chip. Both the chip and the explosive received instructions from an external source, no doubt the Delphic itself.

He wondered if other parts of the chip had other secondary purposes. His instinct mode kicked a flurry of words onto his neurals: *simple, repeatable, hoards of chips, spread out, linked.*

His capacitators rattled, trying to deny the obvious conclusion. He yowled long and hard.

"Easy C.A.T." Zacman lifted him from the table and stroked his back gently. "What's wrong?"

"It's bad, sir. Very bad."

"Don't worry. We'll sort it out. Just tell me what the problem is."

"That chip." He waved a paw at the hologram. "It's one of a swarm of chips that make up the parent S.MAI-L."

Zacman paled. "What does that mean?"

C.A.T. nodded. "Its code is spread throughout the network, in computers, bandits, and toasters, for all I know. It's learned not to put all its code in one basket. And worse, for every chunk I delete out of existence, S.MAI-L can program several replacements. The more chunks I delete, the more S.MAI-L spreads."

Zacman looked at C.A.T. as if he'd grown a second nose.

"It made the mistake of being a single program on Callisto, sir, and I almost destroyed it in the geyser tunnel. It's corrected that weakness as part of the learning process. It'll be impossible to delete it the next time we tangle."

"So, that's why the Delphic didn't destroy these chips."

"It would be like shooting itself in its proverbial foot, sir. Every chip is a part of the whole."

Doc turned white and stepped back from C.A.T. "You're not conning me this time, Zacman. That robo-cat is a self-learner, and you've been harbouring it."

C.A.T. buried his face against Zacman's chest and trembled.

"You're scaring him." Zacman cuddled C.A.T. protectively, faced Doc, and straightened himself to his full height. "Right now, he's the only defence we've got against a very nasty self-learner. Think of him as a super-cleanser, chasing the self-learner that implants those chips into the bandits' necks."

"Don't be daft, Captain. A computer program cannot implant a chip into a dog."

"It has help, we know, from a human, but we've yet to learn the identity of that culprit."

C.A.T. shuddered.

"Have you ever seen what those chipped bandits are

like? C.A.T. calls them Dombies, a corruption of the word *zombies*. Because that is exactly what they are. They have no freedom, not even to breathe unless that nasty self-learner permits it. They do what it says without question, without emotion, and above all, with every hint of rebellion squeezed out of them. Worse than dead men walking, they don't choose to die. It blows their heads off. You or I could be the next ones forcibly enslaved."

"That's quite some speech," Rear Admiral Brian Carruthers said from the doorway.

Zacman took a deep breath and turned to face him. "I didn't realise you were back, sir."

"Clearly. And deliberately. I knew you were hiding something about your robo-cat. I now see why." He stepped up to Zacman and tickled C.A.T. behind his ears.

His robo-cat control pod forced him to purr. He turned his head towards the Admiral and showed him his *I-want-to-be-loved* expression.

"Those yearning eyes won't work on people like me who have heavy responsibilities," the Admiral said. "We've got too many other things on our minds."

"What are your intentions, sir?" Zacman asked.

"I ought to have you arrested for knowingly harbouring a self-learner and order that robo-cat deleted and scrapped."

C.A.T. felt Zacman flinch.

"However, that would leave us defenceless against the evil self-learner, wouldn't it?"

"That sums it up exactly, sir."

The Admiral rolled his eyes. "This won't be the first time the Service has had to break the law to enforce the law. Why didn't you come to me for an executive red order to pursue the rogue A.I.?"

C.A.T. scanned the Service regulations on Central. He found it, tucked away in an annex to an appendix. An executive red order covered situations for which inadequate laws existed, like how to deal with disruptive A.I. technology, to wit, the Delphic and its parent.

"We didn't have any hard evidence until we got this intact chip." Zacman tilted his head to the hologram.

The Admiral took a closer look. "I take your point." He looked up at Doc. "How hard is this evidence?"

"The analysis on the chip hasn't been done—"

"Yes, it has," C.A.T. intervened. "I've concluded it's positive proof that will stand up in a court of law, if that's what you're asking. The self-learner has gone rogue and is killing humans."

The Admiral nodded, still staring at the hologram. Abruptly he turned to C.A.T. "Pity we can't put you in a Service uniform."

C.A.T. turned his fur black and recreated the gold Service insignia on his left shoulder. "Would this do?"

"More than adequately." The Admiral addressed Zacman. "Now, how can we delete this self-learner?"

C.A.T. did a quick assessment of his options. "There are too many unknowns. We can't run debuggers through its matrix, they'll just get deleted, and we've had no luck attacking it with lucifer-data-killers, as it only improves its defences. It's a study-and-get-ready-to-pounce job. First, I need to hunt down the locations of its swarm chunks and work out how best to attack an entity this scattered, one piece at a time."

"Sounds like we need a way to get all the chunks to come together, then attack it."

The Admiral scowled. "Attack it?"

"One way is to try baiting it," C.A.T. said.

"Bait? How?" the Admiral asked.

"There are several options," Zacman intervened.

Carruthers grumped. "Is that your way of saying it's best I don't know?"

"Yes, sir."

C.A.T.'s instinct mode cottoned onto why Zacman

was being evasive. He was checking to be sure S.MAI-L had not chipped the Admiral. C.A.T. glanced at the man's neck. There was no tell-tale scar of a chip implant, so C.A.T. was free to explain. "We can bait it with its junior clone, the Delphic."

"The Admiral's eyes widened. "There are more than one of them?"

"We have that one, the Delphic in a nanite prison..." C.A.T. jumped out of Zacman's arms onto the ledge beside the hologram. "We lured it with ALS comms bait. Quantum entanglement with fractal circuitry makes this chip look like child's play. So we'll probably need to use that."

"Oh my God," Doc slumped onto his chair. "No wonder he's evaded detection. He's very advanced."

The Admiral smirked. "After this is over, Commodore, we're going to have a very long talk."

"Commodore?" C.A.T. asked.

"I'm about to promote him."

"That won't be necessary," Zacman said. "I've just begun to enjoy my promotion to Captain."

"This self-learner business is nasty. You may need to pull rank at the highest levels. Accept it."

"Is that an order, sir?"

"Yes."

"While I work out how to find and delete S.MAI-L chunks," C.A.T. said, back to business. "I'll also divert its attention with errors. Computers and apps don't deal with unknowns. An incorrect formula or algorithm sends them into dead ends, makes them spit out gobbledegook, or freeze up entirely. We'll bombard the network with junk to keep S.MAI-L confused and blind to our intentions."

The Admiral smiled. "There you have it. Let's get busy."

Zacman gulped. "I think I know what's coming next."

Chapter Twenty-Four

A dmiral Carruthers, followed by Zacman and his guard-cat Nikita, marched into the control room. C.A.T., back in his normal ginger coat, trotted behind them, tail high. The Admiral stopped at the flight desk. "Katie Hoskins, isn't it?"

"Yes, sir."

C.A.T. jumped onto the shelf above her console where he was able to read her screen.

"Has a message returned from the Admiralty for me?"

She did a few taps on her keyboard and read the comms screen. "Yes, sir."

"Open it."

One tap and it was open. *Executive Red Order received and accepted. Proceed. Full Admiralty Board will convene in three days for ratification.*

The Admiral turned to Zacman. "Good. They're following normal protocols. Ready, Commodore?"

"As ready as I'll ever be."

Katie's eyes widened. "What are you guys up to?"

The hubbub reduced to the level of essential messages to keep spacecraft flying safely.

"Open the general announcement channel," the Admiral said. "Focus on me, and then on my cues, swing to Zacman and C.A.T."

Katie worked her keyboard. "You're online, sir."

"We have a dangerous new type of threat, and the only way we can stop it is to operate outside the law. Today I received an executive red order, which gives us permission to carry out those otherwise illegal operations, until such time as the Admiralty intervenes. This executive red order will go through the normal process of being considered by the Admiralty and they will promulgate their decision whether it should continue, be modified, or be stopped, which will come within three days. Commodore Zacman will explain the threat, and why and how we need to work outside the law."

Zacman glanced at Katie, who nodded. The channel had switched to him.

C.A.T. activated the defence and tracer apps he had placed around the network throughout Neptune's planetary system and began sending out random and idiotic codes.

"A self-learner has come to our attention. S.MAI-L is back from Callisto. It has split itself into chunks of code to form an interconnected coordinated swarm of itself spread throughout our network..."

Glitch... Sizzle... Sputter...

A wave of spam flooded the control room's comms, an obvious counterattack by S.MAI-L. C.A.T.'s auto-gobblers deleted the spam with only a nanosecond of interruption in Zacman's broadcast. C.A.T. found the spam generator coding with non-delete safeguards, sent in his lucifer-data-killers, and then flung the now inert packages of spam into a dead folder on the network. More spam generators came online, with the addition of hidden viruses, keeping C.A.T. busy while Zacman continued speaking.

"We have a defence..."

Katie went white. Edward Woodward, who sat at a control console, turned his head sharply towards C.A.T. and showed him a worried look.

C.A.T. gave them both a slight nod to reassure them then sent out another torrent of idiotic algorithms, stemming the spam attacks while his tracer apps started sending in locations of identified S.MAI-L chunks. His neurals went to work to identify any pattern in their locations. His capacitators focussed on defending themselves with lucifer agents guarding the circuitry to stop the flow of incoming viruses. His lucifer app was working overtime but holding up to the ebb and flow of the unfolding data war.

Zacman went on: "Another self-learner has been fighting S.MAI-L before anyone suspected it existed. Up to now he's succeeded, but he now needs your help. If he tells you to do something, do it at once, because S.MAI-L won't give you a second chance."

Viruses, anti-lucifers, and spam choked C.A.T.'s comms channels. New ones immediately clogged up. S.MAI-L had issued a *do-not-read* command on all its incoming messages, thus thwarting the effectiveness of the gobbledegook he sent out. C.A.T. jumped to a new channel to get his tracer app information. A pattern of the S.MAI-L's chunk locations started to emerge. The connection structure was a tree system, one that a control freak would naturally opt for. He sent sniffer apps down all the branches with hunt and destroy instructions.

Zacman said, "Our only hope rests with my robo-cat."

In the heat of battle, his robo-control pod changed his fur to the black and gold Service uniform colours, which made him stand tail-high and growl until he realised the tide of battle had turned against him.

Lights died on consoles. Snaps and sizzles sounded from overloaded electronics. A hologram of Neptune on the central plate switched off. Sparks flashed across the screens.

C.A.T. checked Katie's console. A virus attack had stressed its own defences. He fought back with data cleansers and pushed viruses onto the backup disc, which freed the transmission lines.

"Keep those spacecraft safe," the Admiral ordered.

C.A.T. pushed out to Edward's console. It was jammed. He pushed harder. Sparks and crackles were louder. An alarm sounded. Smoke swirled from the console. Fire extinguishers hissed into life.

The door opened. Alex was firing his laser down the

corridor. Triton Base was under siege. Service personnel switched off non-essential apps and machines, and choked out small fires with fire blankets.

Zacman pulled out his laser and pointed it at the door.

Alex dived into the room as a flash of laser fire sizzled past his shoulder. A dombified Flight Lieutenant at the help desk drew her laser and pointed it at Zacman.

Screaming like a banshee, Nikita attacked her gun hand with tooth and claw. Her laser fell to the floor. She grabbed the laser with her good hand, re-established her target, Commadore Zacman, just as Alex fired a laser bolt through her head. In a shower of blood, flesh, and bone she slumped over the empty holo-plate, dead.

Edward's fingers moved over his console so fast that even C.A.T. could not follow them. "It's locked up. I'm locked out."

C.A.T. gathered as much of his spare energy as he dared and blasted light through the fibre-optics on the console. It wiped all the data. He did a reboot from backups.

A dombified bandit ran jerkily into the control room. He went down under Zacman's fire. Another followed.

This time the Admiral shot him.

The screen was back up on Edward's console, showing all the flight paths of spacecraft and satellites around Triton. He started pinging those that were landing. *Abort. Change course.*

C.A.T. noticed a spaceplane diving towards the control room. He sent cleansing agents to that plane. They were deleted. He sent lucifer agents. Nothing changed. He stared at the screen. "Mrrroowww!"

"I got this." Edward worked his keyboard even faster as he changed navigation marker signatures to divert the spaceplane away from the control room.

C.A.T. concentrated on keeping Edward's console clean from attacks.

A hand holding a laser appeared round the edge of the

doorway and fired randomly into the room. The laser suddenly dropped to the floor, and a woman bandit toppled inside. C.A.T. was shocked to see Nikita had her claws dug into the woman's back as her taser whiskers sizzled against her neck. Smoke rose from blackened skin burns.

Alex stood beside the door with his back to the wall, turning and shooting into the corridor. A Service woman did exactly the same from the other side of the door. Distant pops could be heard. There were no screams.

The spaceplane was still heading for the control room.

C.A.T. tried harder to get into the spaceplane's flight management system. Spam pushed back. He edged a few links forward, was pushed a few links backward...he tried to find other routes in and met with heavy resistance.

Sweat poured down Edward's face.

Zacman moved beside Alex. "Help Edward. I've got this."

Alex holstered his laser and ran to the unoccupied console next to Edward. The screen lit up to show the same data as Edward's.

C.A.T. cleaned and ring-fenced that console, as well. He was now spread out pretty thin. His energy reserves were extremely low.

"Paola," Alex said into his comms. "We've got an incoming spaceplane we're not be able to divert. Sending flight path to you. Take it out."

C.A.T. cleared the path for that message. It cost him his last bit of stored energy. He was now using what was left in his capacitators.

"Can't make it to the target in time," Paola said.

"Push it," Alex replied.

"I can't go any faster."

"I'm on it," a male voice said on the comms.

"Torquil?" Alex asked.

"You guys saved my neck. It's about time I repaid the favour."

Alex sent him the same trajectory information.

"Isn't he the bandit leader?" the Admiral asked.

"Yes," Zacman replied as he shot his lasers, two-handed, into the corridor. "He's been working for me."

A Service man knelt beside a Service woman and shot simultaneously into the corridor. The man dived along the floor into the corridor, took cover behind bandit bodies, and burning his laser continuously, fried the first wave of bandits, then pushed himself back into the control room. "I'm out."

Zacman and the woman moved out into the corridor, lasers firing on the next wave. Nikita jumped into the line of fire to defend Zacman. A laser bolt hit her square in the chest and came out her tail, singeing fur and frying electronics. She went down in flames.

"Damn," Torquil said over the comms. "I've hit that spaceplane several times and it's not shifting course."

Paola gasped. "It's on a dead-stick."

"You mean it's a drone?"

"A flying bomb."

"I'll keep shooting until it goes down."

"You're running out of time."

"Anyone got an update on the rest of the Base?" the Admiral asked.

"All functioning normally, sir," a Service man said from the far end of the control room as he put out a fire on his neighbouring console.

"So the target is this control room...or someone or something inside it." The Admiral stared at C.A.T.

"It's me it wants," C.A.T. said. "If S.MAI-L can't delete me, they'll try to burn me, and it doesn't care who gets killed in the process. It takes a self-learner to defeat a self-learner, and S.MAI-L has the advantage in numbers alone."

Alex shot a bandit, right through the neck and his head exploded. "It's no wonder self-learners are illegal.

Sure, there are some good ones, but the bad ones are pure evil."

The Admiral raised his eyebrows.

A super-tsunami of new viruses hit C.A.T.'s neurals. He slumped. He had to concentrate on the gobblers first... His instinct mode delivered its final message. *Stop S.MAI-L. Save the people...at all costs.* Alert. Alert. Alert. All systems failure. His internals went dark.

...."He's gone," Katie said...

...Metal ground against metal...

...The consoles shook...

..."Good work, Paola, Torquil," the Admiral said...

...Zacman stroked C.A.T.'s ears. "Wake up. Wake up."...

..."What should I do with this dead robo-cat?...

Zacman stopped stroking him behind his ears. C.A.T. did not move or send out any messages.

Something was disastrously wrong.

C.A.T. felt the pressure from S.MAI-L ease off. He heard the Admiral's voice.

"The Admiralty will have no choice but to ratify the executive red order after this. It may come with revisions, but they'll be caveats, not orders."

Through the background noise, he heard the high pitch whirr of rolling wheels enter the room. It stopped close to the door.

"These are the last two bandit bodies, sir," a female voice said.

"What's the total, orderly?"

"Fifty-four."

C.A.T. had missed most of the battle. His instinct mode on *Survival* rattled his neurals. He recharged and rebooted. His emotion app messaged him: *Find Nikita.* He popped open one video sensor lid.

"Damn," Zacman said. "Elaine was a good Service member."

Edge of Existence

"Until she got chipped." The Admiral bent over Elaine's body. "Is this scar the only—"

Bang!

C.A.T. popped open both his video sensor lids fully to see Elaine had a bloody crater in her chest. The Admiral had been thrown to his back on the floor, his pulverized face splattered with blackened pellets, the remains of a fragmentation bomb. His eyes stared blankly up at the ceiling.

Two orderlies picked themselves up from the floor. A Service man sprayed foam around Elaine's smouldering body.

Katie and Edward continued working at their consoles.

Grim-faced, Zacman said, "We need to find a way of detecting these walking bombs."

C.A.T. sat up on his haunches and surveyed the damage while looking for Nikita. He found her lying on her side on a console, smouldering, her beautiful tail charred black.

Something was very wrong with Nikita.

He sent agents of repair into her matrix; they reported back: *total loss.*

"No." C.A.T. leapt to the console and inspected the damage to his beautiful but feisty Nikita. His emotion app stuttered. Though he didn't have a heart, he now knew what it felt like to be broken-hearted. His tremor app started at full power, and he slumped to the floor, mewling.

Zacman swept him up into his arms. "Easy, C.A.T. She sacrificed herself protecting me."

C.A.T. mewled even louder.

"Katie," Zacman said. "Please inform the Admiralty that, with regret, Admiral Brian Carruthers died in the line of duty. Details to follow in my report. And get Mervin here at once...with spare robo-cat parts."

"Sir."

"Let's get that blasted self-learner," Alex said.

~201~

C.A.T. buried his head into Zacman's chest and trembled.

Edward reported, "We've regained full control of our space traffic control systems."

"Oh, C.A.T.," Katie said. "You poor thing."

He glanced at her lying there, her tail...he yowled. "A beautiful being on Triton is gone forever."

"Not so fast, C.A.T." Zacman stroked him. "Mervin is on his way. We'll download her backup profile from the cloud onto a new motherboard. She'll be back, and you'll have something to complain about again."

C.A.T. looked up into Zacman's teary green eyes, something C.A.T. could never do. Cry. But his words had given him hope. He sent secret-snoopers into the cloud, ninja agents that could not be traced, and they went to work scouring Nikita's backup. Within seconds, they reported back. Her profile was corrupted with heavily protected malware and spam. S.MAI-L had gotten to her first. The cloud's Quantum key-locked security had failed. The ninjas automatically deleted her. "No."

"What is it, C.A.T.?"

"Her backups were infected. She's gone." He whined and buried his face in the crook of Zacman's arm.

"C.A.T., listen to me. It's not your fault. She did what she was programmed to do."

"She was careless and stupid."

"In war, loss is unavoidable."

C.A.T. whimpered and shuddered. "I should give up, let S.MAI-L delete me. It'll have its revenge for Callisto."

"We're still here, still alive, and where's there's life, there's hope."

C.A.T. had a lot to learn about human emotions. He jumped down from Zacman's arms. "It still...hurts. I'm off to have a sulking session on my Nikita blanket. And when I'm done, I'm going delete S.MAI-L with extreme prejudice."

"C.A.T., revenge is a dangerous trap to fall into. Don't go there."

"Tell that to Nikita." C.A.T. trotted out of the control room and scampered down the hallway to Zacman's office. He let himself in and hopped onto his homey shelf to curl into the blanket. Nikita's aroma enveloped him in a warm embrace.

His memory bank fired up and sent an urgent message to his emotion app: *Bazzeldorf.* He sat straight up on his haunches. In her stubbornness to save him, his stubbornness actually saved her. In the Bazzeldorf folder.

He sent recovery agents into the cloud, carrying the password *KaTNip* to the Bazzeldorf and instructions to download her profile into a folder he'd send to Mervin to upload into a new robo-cat. His emotion app buzzed with excitement. Nikita was coming home.

A recovery agent reported back: *She's not here.*

His capacitators blew a circuit breaker, which immediately reconnected. "That's impossible," he pinged back. "I made sure she was there, along with my profile, before I locked the folder."

You're profile isn't here either.

S.MAI-L must've gotten in and deleted them both.

But the folder isn't empty.

"What's in it?"

Not what. Who.

"Okay. Who's in it?"

Hello, Daddy.

C.A.T. fell off the shelf.

He had become a parent. Somehow, in the Bazzeldorf, his profile code and Nikita's had combined forces. He'd have loved to have been a fly on the wall when that happened. Now there was a new self-learner in the data streams. It had so much to learn. Its early evaluations and self-programming would have the most influence on how it would develop. One seriously wrong bit of data extrapolation could turn it into another dangerous self-learner like the Delphic and its parent, S.MAI-L. This new self-learner was fragile, needed protection from S.MAI-L's cleansers, and above all, guidance to avoid becoming warped into nastiness. C.A.T.'s emotion app wanted to keep it locked in the Bazzeldorf, safe from outside forces that would corrupt or delete it. Knowing that wouldn't be practical or fair, he pinged his agent: *Release it into the cloud.* From afar, he would protect it and keep its existence a secret, even from Zacman.

C.A.T. purred, long and loud.

First thing, he needed a name for the new profile. He went through names in his memory bank, but nothing sounded right for either gender. He read through dictionaries for words and short phrases. No hope there. He surveyed and combined syllables. Finally he had a name for the newest and most unique of self-learners: Nysulle. The name was new, had no meaning, and could not be encumbered with any preconceived notions of race, religion, or ethnicity.

He did a celebration dance: chasing his own tail, jumping down and back up onto the desk, the chairs, the shelf, and twirling his Nikita blanket; bouncing off the ceiling and walls; and locking his tail straight as he spun round its tip. He fell toward the floor and landed four-paws-down. He looked back. His tail had drilled a small hole in the floor. "Oops."

He jumped back up to the shelf, curled onto his blanket, and snuggled down. He would be keeping a close eye on Nysulle and her progress. Her? Yes, the name had a feminine ring to it. Despite being contentedly calm, he felt super energised and efficient. His analysis put it down to knowing Nikita wasn't really gone, just changed, and better than ever. He purred.

"Goodnight, Nysulle," he pinged.

Part 5

Vacuum's Ripples

Rosie Oliver

Chapter Twenty-Five

It took all of C.A.T.'s restraining his emotional app to not move from his position on his shelf. He really wanted to growl and hiss at the smug-looking officer entering Zacman's office and standing at attention.

"Service Captain Roger Stafford reporting for duty at Triton Base, sir." He finished his salute and placed a large package on Zacman's desk. "The Admiralty asked me to give you this, with their compliments." He resumed standing at attention.

"Help yourself to some coffee and take a seat, Stafford," Zacman said and continued reading his screen.

Stafford looked over Zacman's shoulder at C.A.T. "So that's your famous robo-cat?"

"Never mind C.A.T. I'll be with you in a minute."

C.A.T. snuggled into his blanket, but gave the new wise guy a *don't-you-dare-annoy-me* growl and kept one video sensor locked onto him. He did not want the fool to muck things up around here.

C.A.T. took this time to check his in-box, as he received regular reports from his sentinel agents monitoring the software chunks of S.MAI-L. The past seven months had been quiet: no attacks, no enslavement of bandits, or tracks to follow to the stars. It must have been planning something really devious and nasty.

Stafford could not stop glancing in C.A.T.'s direction as he went over to pour his coffee and returned to sit down.

"Don't worry," Zacman said to Stafford. "He doesn't bite."

"Open the box." C.A.T. said. "You may regret that comment."

Zacman stood, opened the box, and laughed. "I see the Admiralty is exercising its sense of humour."

"Sir?" Stafford asked.

Zacman reached into the box, removed a grey and white robo-cat, and set it on the desk. "Well, what do we have here?"

"Hello, Commodore Zacman," she said, her feminine voice official in tone. "I am assigned to be your new guard-cat, a replacement for Nikita, which was lost in the line of duty. Do you have any specific orders for me?"

C.A.T. stood up and hissed. He sent in agents to check to see that her computer and fibre-optics harboured no viruses, trojans, or other nasties. They were as clean as pure water ice. He checked her credentials: *Mark-Seven Guard-cat from McIntyre and Furkins,* the same firm that had made him. Her specification included the usual guard-cat equipment: sharp claws, high tensile skeleton and tungsten-strengthened fangs. There were a lot of techno-improvements: *Super-Flex* skin, the new Cerite hyper-speed processors, tightly bound neurals, ultra as well as normal human hearing, fine-tuned temperature and gravity instrumentation, and full vision from gamma rays through ultraviolet, visible spectrum, infra-red to microwave. The Admiralty had spared no expense. C.A.T. felt well and truly outmoded.

"Just your usual guard-cat duties," Zacman said, "even if they conflict with orders from my robo-cat on the shelf behind me." He swung round to face him. "As for you, C.A.T., let her do her job. Is that understood?"

"As long as she doesn't try to boss me around."

Zacman glared at him.

C.A.T. shrank back. "She doesn't even have a name."

"Is that true?" Zacman asked her.

"You need to give me a name. I would recommend avoiding a commonplace name to avoid confusion among your personnel."

"Will Queenie do?"

C.A.T. mewled. "Nobody names a cat Queenie. It's stupid."

"Shut up, C.A.T. Let her be the judge of that."

"It's perfect." Queenie growled at C.A.T.

"Then Queenie it is. You may start your guard-cat duties immediately."

She dropped down from the desk to explore the room.

"Harrumph." C.A.T. huffed. "Queenie, bah."

Stafford watched the guard-cat sniff corners, crevices, and air vents.

Zacman sat back down at his desk. "Now, what am I going to do with you, Captain?"

"Sir? I was told by Admiral Angharad Penhaligon you had no second-in-command officer on this Base...should anything happen to you."

"I am in need of reliable spacers, command centre controllers, and combat-tried pilots. You're a logistics and personnel desk jockey with no real leadership experience."

"It's my first deep space assignment, sir. I could learn."

"That's encouraging, but don't think you can just waltz in here and expect command duties. You're a rookie. You'll have to earn your place. Would you suggest anything else if you were in my position?"

"No, sir."

"At least recognising you're not up to the normal duties on this Base is a start. You can take over C.A.T.'s admin duties sorting through my incoming mail, getting rid of duplicates, spam and the like. It'll give you some idea of what goes on round here. There's an empty office three doors down to right. Dismissed."

"Sir." Stafford stood up and looked longingly at his half-filled cup.

"Take your coffee with you," Zacman added. "But I want that cup back...clean."

As soon as the door closed, Zacman turned to C.A.T. "I want you to check what Stafford is doing with my inbox. Correct anything done wrong. Report anything suspicious."

"You don't trust him?"

"He's a toady. Trust is earned. We'll see how he holds up under pressure."

Queenie jumped onto the shelf, and her green video sensors scanned C.A.T.

"Hey. You can stop that," C.A.T. said.

She continued scanning. "I'm doing my guard-cat duties. I detect your processing is running at an unusually high level for a toy robo-cat. Is there a reason for this?"

"Queenie," Zacman said, "C.A.T. is under my orders to do unusual things. So expect him not to conform to any standard patterns."

"I understand and will not comment on him again unless he threatens you."

"She's real trouble," C.A.T. muttered and curled up with his back to Queenie in a *leave-me-alone* huff.

A sentinel agent sent a red-flagged message to C.A.T.: *S.MAI-L's chunk has just been deleted from a maintenance computer on Nereid.*

An alarm went off on his motherboard. He sent in special tracer agents to seek the source of the wipe command, which could reveal where S.MAI-L was hiding. Another report of a S.MAI-L chunk deletion came in from a drinks dispenser at a bar in Nereid's Down Town settlement. C.A.T. sent more tracer agents to investigate.

More 'chunk deleted' messages arrived. He did an analysis of their positions and ran the data through his logic module. A report came back: *S.MAI-L is about to attack the town.*

C.A.T. triggered an emergency evacuation drill in Down Town through its maintenance computer. He checked the public news channels on Triton Base. There, amongst the masses of information, was a newsflash about evacuation sirens going off in Down Town. An update indicated it was a drill. He waited for a report to say it was over.

Nothing.

He sent an agent to Down Town's maintenance computer for a status report. The message by return said it was unreachable.

C.A.T. leapt off his shelf to land four-paws-down on the desk in front of Zacman. "S.MAI-L is attacking Down Town."

"Details?"

"All S.MAI-L's chunks there were deleted within two kilometres of Down Town. I started an emergency evacuation drill as a precaution. Now I can't get through on comms at all."

Zacman clicked open his comms to the control room.

"Sir?" Flight Lieutenant Edward Woodward's face appeared on the screen.

"Who's on operational flight standby from the special list?"

"Sam Bingham and Simon Ruskin."

"Get them to Down Town, Nereid. Tell them to exercise extreme caution. We just lost contact with them. Find out what you can from Nereid's outlying habitats. I'm on my way to the control room." He strode out of his office with Queenie trotting beside him, scanning the walls, floor, and ceiling. C.A.T. followed and kept a close video sensor on her.

***

Zacman, in his command chair, faced the control room's comms screen. C.A.T. in his furry Service uniform, lounged on the armrest. He'd restored comms to Nereid. "How many dead and injured, Mayor?"

Down Town Mayor's hooded eyes peered out from under his tousled grey hair; deep wrinkles and black shadows dominated his strained face. "Five confirmed dead.

Seventy-three injured, six of them critically. The fires and depressurisation alone would have been far worse if we hadn't been in the middle of an evacuation drill." His body visibly shook.

Zacman tickled C.A.T. behind his ears. "You certainly were lucky with that call, C.A.T."

He purred.

"Commodore Zacman," Edward Woodward broke in. "A Wing shuttle is requesting permission to land, sir."

"Interesting. Permission granted."

The Mayor's expression relaxed a little. "Do you think S.MAI-L is behind this bandit attack?"

"Possibly, but it's difficult to find a motive for decimating a town in order to upload its power supplies into the bandit's battery reserves."

"You know about that?"

"We're obviously following formal investigation protocols. For now, we think the attack was a diversionary tactic."

"It's damned crazy." The Mayor glanced to one side. "If you'll excuse me."

"Sure."

The screen blanked. Operations returned to normal while C.A.T. and Zacman looked on.

The control room door opened, and Captain Stafford entered, followed by a well-muscled man in a grey one-piece silk with silver braiding around his collar, and he carried a shoulder bag.

C.A.T. recognised him as The Wing Chairman.

Queenie sidled along the wall to stop short of the door. Fangs out, she got ready to jump onto his back at the slightest hint of a threat.

"Wing Chairman," Zacman said. "I'm glad you could join us."

Puzzled faces spread round the room.

"Huh?" Stafford frowned. "The Wing? It was lost in

an accident."

"We haven't got time to waste on long explanations of our history." The Chairman sat in a chair at a vacant console. "So, I'll give you the short version. Our civilization has been around long before Triton Base, and though we have no interplanetary treaty with the Service, we have developed a working relationship. I'm here with a warning."

"What threat are we facing, Chairman?"

"S.MAI-L is about to attack with technology you've no inkling of. We've now got," he glanced at his watch, "forty-seven hours to stop it from destroying Triton."

"The Base? How?" Stafford asked.

"No. The entire moon."

Stafford paled. "Why?"

"We have reason to believe C.A.T. is the target."

"Easy enough." Stafford leaned against the console. "Send him off-moon, Nereid or Pluto, then S.MAI-L would have no reason to attack Triton with...with what?"

"You mentioned some kind of new technology," Zacman put in.

"In your terms, a doomsday weapon, if ever there was one."

"Me-ow. So that's what it's been up to the last seven months, finding a better way to kill me."

Zacman frowned. "S.MAI-L is scared of C.A.T.'s processing agility. They've tangled before, on Callisto and right here in this control room. C.A.T.'s the only one who can outsmart it."

"That's some special robo-cat you've got there," the Chairman said.

"What do you know about this weapon?"

"It's power originates in quantum physics from beyond the Kuiper Cliff itself."

"Seems you know more about it than we do, and you wouldn't be here if you didn't have a plan."

"I do, but you're not going to like it."

"I don't like it already." Zacman glanced at the control room's recorders. "Shall we discuss this in my office?"

"I thought you'd never ask."

Zacman stood and addressed Katie. "Contact Mervin Neville. Tell him to get his butt over here to help."

"Sir," Katie acknowledged.

"Queenie, when we reach my office, you stay outside and guard the door.

"I will not be able to fully conduct my guard-cat duties from the hallway, sir."

C.A.T. shook his head. She was one dumb kitty.

"That's an order, Queenie."

Her white whiskers sagged.

"C.A.T., you'll go in with the Chairman and me."

"Understood."

***

C.A.T. sat on his haunches on the corner of the desk between the Chairman and Zacman, who were seated opposite each other. Zacman glanced at the recorder. C.A.T. took the hint and switched it off. Its op light went out. He also made sure there were none of S.MAI-L's chunks on any computer or other part of the office network.

Zacman took the lead. "Chairman, what are we facing?"

"We call them vacuum's ripples."

Zacman blinked, clearly perplexed.

"They're like ocean waves, however instead of being energy induced, they travel through what we call quantum space. When they meet, they'll combine to produce a local, short-lived gravity wave...make that a tsunami, that lasts long enough to cause massive destruction."

"A gravitational tidal wave?" Zacman ventured. "How can gravity appear and disappear, which is what you're suggesting?"

"Not naturally, but this is AI built. Once it strikes Triton, it'll crack the ice-sheets, crumble solid rock, and reduce Triton to a ring of debris orbiting Neptune forever."

"Then the question before us is simple. How do we stop these vacuum ripples from forming?"

"First," C.A.T. said. "We need to know exactly how they are formed, so we can un-build them."

"Sound strategy," the Chairman said.

"Where do we start?" Zacman's eyes widened and his face snapped to an enlightened look. "Wait. Your scientists have already started work on that strategy, haven't they?"

The Chairman nodded. "Good guess. In fact, we know it takes three ripples to make that localised gravity tsunami. The first two react negatively to anti-photon shields."

"What do we need for the third wave?"

"A blue gluon deflector."

"That's beyond my physics knowhow."

C.A.T.'s data banks could not resist jumping in here. "Photons and gluons are massless particles. Using them directly against a gravity tsunami would be as useless as stopping a freighter with a flashlight beam."

"That argument also holds for the ripples. But quantum physics beyond the Kuiper Cliff's edge changes the way normal forces interact with each other. The downside for S.MAI-L is having to send the waves slower, which gives us some time to build, fine-tune, and deploy anti-photon shields and blue gluon deflectors. The trick will be to get their placements exactly right."

"I'm sure Mervin can make the shields and deploy them in time."

The Chairman looked at him askance. "How good is this Mervin?"

"He worked wonders with the Delphic," C.A.T. said. "And with my help, we'll make the ripples backfire on S.MAI-L. You wait and see."

Zacman scowled. "Don't get too cocky, C.A.T.

You're batting zero against S.MAI-L. Or have you forgotten?"

C.A.T. mewled. His emotion app was glad Nysulle and Queenie had never seen him get whipped.

"That leaves my people to design and build the blue gluon deflectors. One other thing. We'll need pilots to deliver the defences in record time. They'll have to withstand High-G accelerations. You've got eight in the Service. I can lend you another eight of The Wing's pilots on the low-low, of course."

C.A.T. knew the Chairman wanted to maintain anonymity and keep the public believing The Wing no longer existed.

"We'll take all the help we can get." Zacman stared at C.A.T. "We need a backup plan."

C.A.T. edged backwards under his glare until he was balanced on the rim of the desk. "I'm not going to like this."

"You're right."

C.A.T. licked his paw as if it were just another pleasant day in the office. "What do you have in mind?"

"I want you and Queenie to switch fur colours."

"You're setting her up as a decoy for me?"

"Yes."

"It won't work."

"Why?"

"Her behavioural patterns are stuck in repetitive guard-cat routines."

Zacman raised his eyebrows. "How about—"

"Oh, no." C.A.T. shook his head. "That's too dangerous."

"What's dangerous?" the Chairman asked.

"He wants me to reprogram Queenie to act like me to confuse S.MAI-L. She won't have time to properly ingest the necessary lessons about sociability and the like. She'll end up self-conflicted."

"You've got a target on your back, C.A.T.," Zacman shouted. "Do we have a choice?"

"Let's see." C.A.T. did a quick analysis for alternative courses of action. Zacman's plan had the greatest chance of success, namely C.A.T. surviving, and now that he was a parent, survival took priority. "You're right. We don't have a choice, but because it's the best plan, it's predicable. That worries me."

"Act now, worry later," Zacman replied. "Upgrade Queenie's programming."

C.A.T.'s instinct mode exploded throughout his neurals. He would have to do a paws-on approach to managing her more C.A.T.-like behaviour, sending commands when necessary. But it would lead to humans thinking she was a self-learner. Deletion and spare-parting, no questions asked, would follow. Avoiding this problem would not be easy. "Do you remember that time my fur was damaged?"

Zacman rolled his eyes upwards. "As if I could forget all your grumbling, moaning, and complaining."

"We made a couple of spare coats. Queenie could wear one. I'll program it to switch between my Service uniform, my off-duty ginger, and her grey and white." He snapped his video sensors to Zacman's eyes. "But if she damages one single hair on it, I'll delete her myself. Is that clear?"

A hint of a smile on Zacman's face died. He nodded solemnly and turned to the Chairman. "One final question. How do you know those vacuum ripples are coming?"

"Oh really, Commodore, you're going to doubt me at a time like this? We should be working on our defences?"

"I just want to be certain of the answer, that's all."

"You won't be happy until you do, will you?"

"I want to make sure this isn't a false alarm."

"Alright. We used extrapolative logic on why the Kuiper Cliff existed. That led us to send micro-probes through the Kuiper Belt to confirm our conclusions. Those probes are still out there. Hence, we picked up the ripples, where they were heading, and their arrival time as a localised tsunami. We now have 46 hours to prepare."

The implications brought C.A.T.'s fibre-optics to a standstill, which chilled his skeletal frame. S.MAI-L must have learned of the Kuiper Cliff's quantum anomalies from The Wing's computers. He jerked his head round to the Chairman. "You've been hacked."

The Chairman squared his shoulders. "S.MAI-L?"

"It's everywhere."

"Come on, Chairman," Zacman said. "You expect me to believe you didn't already know of the hack? Why are you really here?. You could have told me all this via comms."

The Chairman's lips became a thin line of determined silence.

Zacman steepled his fingers on the desk. "I can help, or hinder."

"You're giving me no choice, but to tell you." The Chairman shook his head. "You can be really stubborn at times."

C.A.T. grumbled. "Don't I know it."

Zacman glared at him.

The Chairman pulled an object from his shoulder bag and placed it on the desk in front of C.A.T. "This is the key to remove my daughter's mind block."

"For Paola?" Zacman took a closer look. It was a group of quartz crystals locked together into weird shapes.

"The process is like opening a puzzle box where you have to move panels in a specific order. Remove the crystals and place them around her head in a certain order for given lengths of time."

"Clever," C.A.T. let slip.

"You believe him?" Zacman asked.

"They're made of quartz, which can induce changes in

electromagnetic fields and affect brain waves. But wouldn't that require placing the crystals very precisely around the head?"

"Yes. That's why I'm here. She needs to be free of the mind block to act at her fullest capabilities."

C.A.T.'s capacitators boggled at the humungous analysis and calculations that must have gone into designing a mind block and its unlocking crystals. He did not have the time to investigate further.

"In that case, I'll take you up on that offer." Zacman touched the comms screen. "Katie, send Paola to my office."

"Sir." The screen went blank.

"You can use my office," Zacman told the Chairman and stood.

"Where are you going?" the Chairman asked.

"To the Mess bar. I need a drink. Come on, C.A.T."

C.A.T. knew it was a ruse. Zacman didn't drink, but the route passed C.A.T.'s engineering shack where they could pick up his spare fur coat for Queenie's disguise.

Chapter Twenty-Six

C.A.T. changed his fur coat to grey and white and undertook standard guard-cat duties around Zacman in the control room. He ordered Queenie, wearing one of his spare ginger fur coats, to scamper in, jump onto the shelf above Edward Woodward's console, peer at his screens, and then curl up with her back towards everyone.

Zacman approached Stafford sitting at a console. "Got a job that needs your special talents."

"Sir."

"Help Mervin Neville get the supplies he needs. A lot of routine stuff, but there will be specialist bits of kit. Improvise if you have to. We're against the clock on this one."

"Sir, where—"

"He'll be arriving in an hour. Katie's allocated the workroom in Hanger Six. Oh, and if he asks you to put something together, you do it. There's an initial list in your inbox. You'd better get to it."

"Sir." Stafford headed for the door.

"One other thing," Zacman added. "Take Queenie with you to guard those supplies."

Stafford stopped and turned and glanced at C.A.T. in his Queenie disguise. "Should I send in some guards for you?"

"That won't be necessary. C.A.T. can take over Queenie's duties."

C.A.T. pinged Queenie response instructions so she'd react in the same manner as he would.

She jerked her head round towards Zacman. "Is that all I'm good for? Mere guard-cat duties?"

Zacman glowered at Queenie, same as if she were C.A.T.

Queenie shook her head as her fur coat turned from ginger to a black and gold Service uniform. "Why did I think I'd like living here?" She dropped down onto the floor.

C.A.T. left Queenie, in her C.A.T. disguise, to comply with her own guard-cat routines. As he followed Stafford through the door, he noticed a twinkle in Zacman's eye. He had planned this ploy. Its main advantage was the lack of comms traffic between him and Queenie: S.MAI-L had less chance of noticing the switch. Zacman truly had confidence that C.A.T. could pull this off.

***

Mervin held the newly arrived package in front of C.A.T. to scan its contents: specialist electronics, exactly as described on its label and the tablet menu. Everything crosschecked. He nodded and resumed scanning the workshop in Queenie fashion.

Mervin signed the receipt and started unpacking.

"That's daylight robbery!" Stafford glowered at his screen.

"A woman's got to survive." The grey-haired woman on the screen shrugged. "Take it or leave it."

Irritation snapped in C.A.T.'s emotion app. He transmitted a picture of himself in his Service uniform as a third party joining the conversation via the network. "We'll take the going price," C.A.T.'s image said in his own normal voice, "plus reasonable quick-speed delivery costs. Don't try to inflate it either, because I'll check. Get it to them, now."

"You dare bully an old lady?"

"It's an order under the E.S.P.A., the Emergency Service Powers Act, signed solar-system-wide last century. Any questions?"

She laughed.

"Please excuse C.A.T." Mervin hovered behind Stafford's shoulder. "He can be very tetchy at times."

"I'm not tetchy." The image of C.A.T. bared his fangs and growled.

"Ignore him, lady. I can't tell you why I need those parts, but if I don't get them fast, my reputation will crash. Please accept the price offered so we can get about our jobs."

She cocked her head to one side. "Are you Mervin Neville?"

He did a slight bow. "The one and only."

She put on frown. "Then why can't you make the mechatronics yourself?"

"Because we're short on time."

"Very well. I'll put a rush on them. Be there in ninety minutes."

The screen blanked.

"That's how I make a deal," Mervin said. "Now I need to make another one, which is going to be far more difficult."

Stafford opened his mouth, then shut it and went back to his kit list.

C.A.T., in Queenie fashion, leapt onto the workbench and scanned the components.

Mervin glanced at C.A.T. suspiciously. "Central, switch off all monitoring in this workshop."

The red light died on the room's recorder.

"Stafford, switch off your comms."

"Why?"

"Just do it."

Stafford complied.

"Queenie, I've got a job for you."

"If it increases your security, I have been instructed to comply with your commands," C.A.T. replied.

"Come on, C.A.T. I know it's you. Stop the pretence."

Busted! C.A.T. stopped his guard-cat search and scan

routines, and turned to Mervin. "Where did I go wrong?"

"You slipped into nodding through the components on the workbench without instruction."

It was a mistake. Correction, yet another mistake. His head drooped and he mewled.

"Stop that self-pitying. Now!"

"I told Zacman I'm a poor guard-cat. I keep making mistakes."

"You don't."

C.A.T. jerked his head up to stare into Mervin's brown eyes. "But I did. You saw right through me."

"Somewhere, deep under all that fur, is a learned *gut feel* that encourages you to act, but you'll seem to make mistakes at certain times." He held up his hand to stop C.A.T. from interrupting. "It's probably a complex neural network that's scattered in bytes around your internal network, doubling as parts of other software or hard wiring, It's why your *gut feel* snaps into action, especially when you're overloaded, as all parts of you are working at full capacity."

"That's crazy."

"You're always too busy to realise the existence of your subconscious self."

Stafford gasped. "That guard-cat's a self-learner?"

Mervin scowled at him. "Shut up, Stafford. C.A.T., your *gut feel* was right just now. You couldn't resist barging in on our comms conversation. You made the mistake earlier by acting like your normal self. It was your *gut feel* telling you that the job would be done faster if your true identity were known."

C.A.T. changed his grey and white fur colour back to his normal ginger coat.

Stafford almost fell out of his chair.

"Alright." Mervin clapped his hands together. "Let's get to some real work. What does S.MAI-L know about us?"

"It knows about your anti-photon shield."

"So, it will develop a countermeasure against it."

"If it does, we'll have no viable defence."

"Keep going." Mervin rolled his eyes towards Stafford.

C.A.T. got the message. Like Zacman, Mervin did not completely trust him. C.A.T.'s logic app went hyperactive, instinct mode came online, and his emotion app emitted courage. He had to be brave and stand strong throughout his fibre-optics. The end result of so many internal influencing parts kicking in at once brewed befuddlement, of the fluffy cotton wool kind. He shook his head. The solution dropped onto his capacitators, followed by a second one.

"Two solutions." His emotion app poured admiration into his capacitators.

"You've got to be kidding me." Mervin smirked.

"They both involve the development of specialised anti-photon shields," C.A.T. said, "one set to disrupt and scatter the vacuum ripples, and the other to build a dome to protect Triton Base."

"It's called layered defence. I presume you'll know which you're to work on first."

"Rather obvious." C.A.T. got to work on their designs, concentrating on the most difficult, the sheets in space because of the large sizes needed.

"I'll leave you to it. Send me the designs when you're happy with them. I'll help Stafford order the parts."

C.A.T. glanced at Stafford who still had a look of horror on his face. "Do we have a choice?"

"We always have choices," Mervin replied, "only most of the time the answers are obvious. Like now. Keep your mouth shut about what you've just seen, Stafford."

He nodded.

"Just one question," C.A.T. put in. "What's the difference between instinct and gut feel?"

Mervin scratched his chin beard. "Well...*gut feel* is when you're edging towards an answer you don't know, whereas instinct is when you know the answer right away, but don't know why you know. Why?"

"That's clear as mud. Can you put it in simple terms?"

Mervin tickled him behind his ears. "Nah! You're too cute to be straightforward with."

Cute? That was a first. His logic app deduced Mervin cared for him. His emotion app exuded smugness. He wanted to go squishy and cuddly, but needed to concentrate on the clear and present danger, for him and his friends. "Bah! What are you waiting for? We've got work to do. We'll need to co-ordinate on logistics. You..." He pointed his paw at Stafford. "Here's a list of more materials I'm going to need. I want it yesterday." He dropped a list of components to manufacture the nanites to build the photon-shields into Stafford's inbox.

He scanned the list. "A tonne of nitrogen ice? What's that for?"

C.A.T. switched back to Queenie's grey and white fur. "Fuel for the nanites to build the anti-photon shields. Get on with it. I've other stuff to do." He curled up with his *I-don't-want-to-be-disturbed* back to them and started developing code for the nanites.

Chapter Twenty-Seven

C.A.T., still in Queenie's grey and white fur, held his skeleton rigid and claws hooked on the edge of the armrest while Alex slowed his spaceplane at 4Gs to the drop-off point for the anti-photon shield. He had instructed his sentinel agents to contact him with exception reports. He did receive regular reports from Queenie, furred as C.A.T., who guarded Zacman in the control room on Triton Base, and status reports came in from the planes of the other fifteen pilots deploying their anti-photon shields and blue gluon deflectors. Most importantly, he received updates from Nysulle. She wanted to help him fight S.MAI-L but he told her no, for her own good.

There was no sign of S.MAI-L on any networks. It was all far too quiet. So much so, C.A.T. wondered what he had missed. He checked the operation's plan for the umpteenth time. The same answer came back. The plan was not perfect, but it was the best they could do.

His whiskers twitched. *Something was very wrong.* It was not his instinct mode making that call, but his *gut feel*. He mewled his frustration.

"I know," Alex said. "Almost there." His finger slowly reached across the dashboard.

"I can't put my paw on what I'm missing."

Alex hit the tab to cut the engine and took a deep breath. He steered his plane round to face the Sagittarius constellation. "We'll wait here while you work out what you were expecting and what's not working."

C.A.T. did exactly that. "S.MAI-L should be attacking me, or I should say Queenie, by now, back on Triton Base."

Alex pulled up the dashboard and unlocked the switch

that would deliver his anti-photon shield. "Not even a sneak attack or an especially nasty trojan?"

"Not a single byte."

"Hmm. You're right. Something's wrong." Alex pulled his finger away from the switch, relocked it, and the dashboard switched off. "Are you sure that vacuum ripple will pass through here?"

"The Wing's microprobes detected it heading in this direction, so yes, I'm sure."

"Agreed, but will it stay on its predicted path?"

"Once it's rolling, it's going to take a lot of energy to change its direction. Hence, our large anti-photon shield. On the plus side, once we've diverted it, S.MAI-L will have a hard time getting the wave headed back to Triton."

"I take your points."

"Damn. I wish we knew more about the physics of those vacuum ripples."

Alex glanced sideways. "That's another sticky issue in itself."

"I can't figure out what actually triggers the ripples to combine and slip out of quantum space to yield the gravity tsunami."

"Back to grumbling again?"

"Harrumph." He curled up with one video sensor peering over his foreleg to watch Alex recline in his pilot chair.

His comments triggered C.A.T.'s curiosity app about how the ripples needed to be altered to create that deadly wave. He pulled up images of Neptune's winds: large vortices spinning against the planet's atmospheric bands to throw off a chaos of smaller vortices; blues merging into greys; white cloud tufts floating serenely above all the turmoil, totally undisturbed by the viscous forces beneath them.

C.A.T. mewled.

They contrasted with the predictable nature of solar

Rosie Oliver

winds, which gently drifted and expanded into the Kuiper Belt and beyond. The tiny pressure from its charged particles varied according to the sun's activity and affected the magnetic influences of the planets, moons, asteroids, and comets. Except for the auroras in thicker atmospheres, they were unseen and unfelt.

C.A.T.'s logic mode intruded: the winds affected other magnetic fields, even those of the travelling vacuum ripples in their strange super-fluid state.

"Uh-oh," C.A.T. murmured.

"I hate it when you say that," Alex said. "What's wrong now?"

"Tell everyone to hold off deploying their shields while I process the effect of solar winds on the vacuum ripples."

Alex sent out the message to the other fifteen pilots

C.A.T. pushed all his spare capacity onto evaluating the effect of the solar winds on the vacuum ripples. As they rolled into ever-denser solar winds, their magnetic interactions would strengthen, and more of the ripples' magnetic monopoles would latch onto each other to create dipoles. These would combine to make quadrupoles with immense destructive power. He assessed the current solar winds, gravity, the induced Van der Waal forces, and magnetic fields. These new calculations changed the positioning of the shields and deflectors to intercept the ripples. This also revealed another terrifying fact.

His instinct mode confirmed: *S.MAI-L has a second target.* Of course. It was also going to smash the Delphic's nanite cocoon with a second localised gravity tsunami that would develop out of the same vacuum ripples.

S.MAI-L had hoodwinked him into thinking it was only out to destroy Triton Base. *C.A.T. had almost been outsmarted, out-performed, and out-connived.* Had he not taken the time to rethink the quantum physics, the result would have been a disaster. He pinged Queenie: "Tell

Zacman the Delphic is also a target."

"Understood," she pinged back.

C.A.T. focussed on working out a new plan against three ripples when his logic module stopped him. They did not have enough defences for both Triton and the Delphic's jail. He would have to choose which one to protect.

He estimated the success rate of throwing all their defences into containing the Delphic. *Triton is destroyed and everyone dies.* He double-checked his result. Then triple-checked it. He threw that plan out. The Service could not fail to protect the people. He mewled loud and long.

"Whoa there, C.A.T." Alex stroked the fur on C.A.T.'s back. "What's wrong?"

"The Delphic is too dangerous to leave undefended. We can't save Triton. If we save Triton, we lose the Delphic. It and its parent will join forces and be unstoppable."

"We have to do something."

"Abandon Triton. Get as many people off that moon as soon as possible."

"There's not enough time. Besides, where would they go?"

"Nereid can take a lot of people..." The earlier attack on Down Town now made sense. S.MAI-L wanted to create chaos for anyone seeking refuge from Triton. Everyone would suffer because S.MAI-L was bent on revenge against C.A.T. His emotion app drowned his neurals in remorse. All this was his fault. He had let this happen to the very people who had taken him in and given him a home. He had to do something, anything, to help everyone he could.

"I'll let Zacman know they're on their own." Alex turned to his comms screen. "Katie, tell Zacman—"

"No." C.A.T. cut the transmission.

"C.A.T.? Have you lost your motherboard?"

C.A.T. could not accept defeat. He had to come up

with another plan. It would be riskier and more difficult to execute, pushing the pilots to their limits, and maybe beyond. "We're not going down without a fight."

"Now you're talking."

Considering two targets, he recalculated new drop-off points for the anti-photon shields and blue gluon deflectors, and then he sent out re-routing paths to the pilots. Paola's flight-plan was particularly High-G, but he knew she could take it. Then his next analysis detailed Alex's high acceleration flight path to where his shield should be deployed to defend the nanite cocoon. Such a flight would test him to his physical limits. C.A.T. took over control of the plane. "Hold on." He executed a 5G turn and accelerated towards the new drop-off point.

Alex was slammed into his seat.

Queenie pinged: "Zacman has asked me to find out, and I quote: *What the hell's going on out there?*"

C.A.T. told Queenie: "If this doesn't work, tell Zacman I said goodbye."

His instinct mode jittered his neurals. He tried to ignore how the tremors irritated his capacitators. His logic module got more insistent, hinted at going round in circles, thinking things through again. He had a fifty-fifty chance of success defending two targets against S.MAI-L's two localized gravity tsunamis. The bad news wasn't sitting well with his emotion app. He didn't want to hear it complain, shut off his logic module, and decided this battle would be won or lost by his *gut feel* alone.

Alex fidgeted in his seat as if to get uncomfortable.

C.A.T. increased the acceleration to 6Gs.

"What, *gasp,* the hell?"

Queenie pinged in, "I have detected multiple virus attacks to my system. I sent lucifers to divert them. I don't know how long I can fight the onslaught."

For once, something was going right. The new cyber attacks had been in response to changing Alex's direction and speed. S.MAI-L was getting worried that C.A.T. had found a way to negate its gravity attacks. Queenie would take the punishment. Her mettle would be tested. To cement the ruse, he reluctantly sent a password to Queenie: "Kittiwake. Fascinating." It would release a package into her neurals to set up a self-learner program of her own. S.MAI-L would totally believe she was C.A.T. and go after her with a vengeance, leaving him to sort out their defences. His tail flicked side to side to quell the guilt spilling from his emotion app.

Queenie pinged, "I got reports of virus attacks on the planes guarding the Delphic. I've sent each a package of extra protection measures, but they are having no effect. The guard planes' computers and comms are glitching out."

"Life support?" C.A.T. asked.

"Functioning," she replied.

But for how long?

C.A.T. scanned the space round Alex's plane at the edge of the Plutinos belt. He was looking for the ripples' magnetic quadrupoles that were invisible to the human eye. Nothing was out of the ordinary: thin dust, a few pebble-sized meteoroids, and a comet coming from the Oort Cloud. His danger mode sounded an alarm. That comet wasn't ordinary. It had accelerated and changed course toward their spaceplanes. He analysed the comet's materials. It was a nanite bomb that could speed-build an impenetrable nanite sphere to entrap all their spaceplanes. "Uh-oh. We've got company of the hostile kind."

Alex looked up at the fast-approaching comet. "It's beautiful."

"It's a nanite bomb."

"We've got to get out of here."

"There's nowhere to go. We have to stand and fight."

"Why did I know you were going to say that?"

S.MAI-L intended to imitate what C.A.T. had done to the Delphic's spaceliner. Laser fire would be like fuel to the nanites; the extra energy would help them reproduce and grow at an accelerated rate. If he could find the code, he could change the nanites' programming, but S.MAI-L was not about the give that secret away. He could place the comet in a nanite sheet bubble and tow it off course, but that would require spare materials he did not have. There was no way out of this.

C.A.T. shuddered. He had fought off so much adversity. His fibre-optics had been continually lit for so long that they had become warm and easily malleable. Still, he had to carry on.

His instinct mode rattled on his capacitators. Mass was needed to deflect the nanite bomb...but what? What massive force was available out here in the middle of nowhere-space? He reactivated his logic module, which immediately supplied a logical answer: *Engine efflux.* If he could use that, he could change the comet's course. A plan formed, crazy even by his C.A.T. standards.

Alex pulled up the weapons screen and aimed his lasers at the comet. "They want a fight, well, I'm going to give them one they'll never forget."

"Don't." C.A.T. blocked the weapons controller. "Attacking it is exactly what S.MAI-L wants you to do."

"Then how do we stop it?"

"You'll have to do some very precise flying."

"They don't call me an Ace for nothing."

"You need to get ahead of the comet."

"The devil. It's not a bandit freighter. If I don't get the speed just right, it could smash us to smithereens."

"May I make a suggestion?"

"What?"

"Get the speed right."

"C.A.T., you're going to get us killed."

"Just fly the plane, Ace."

Alex groaned and steered toward the comet.

It was now a growing diskette of light obliterating all

the starlight around it. The fact it did not move relative to the window meant they were on a collision course. He curled his claws extra tight into the armrest and sent sneaker agents onto the comet to test its defences. They were never heard from again.

The comet's glowing face was approaching fast. A halo of evaporating gases surrounded a nucleus of rock, dust, and water ice that reflected sunlight to make it appear like it was on fire. The comet grew larger in the window.

Alex flexed his fingers around the joystick.

"Not yet," C.A.T. said. "Not yet."

"We're going to crash."

"Now."

Alex yanked the joystick to bank the spaceplane right. The comet's face sank from view, revealing its main yellow dust tail and a shorter blue-green plasma tail. Alex executed a sweeping turn with the joystick, placing the plane ahead of the speeding behemoth.

"Faster," C.A.T. yelled and flung trace-and-report agents into the nanite-shrouded mass. They were instantly deleted. "It's gaining on us."

"I'm at full throttle. You want to go faster? Get out and push." The plane shuddered.

The comet continued to bear down on them.

"Keep it steady, Ace."

His fingers delicately touched the joystick, moving it a tiny bit left, a smidgen right, a touch downward and a tad up to keep ahead of the comet. The comet's light was so bright it bathed the dashboard in a white glow. "It's getting too close."

C.A.T. linked to the flight controls while fine-tuning the engines' thruster controls, and executed a tight ninety-degree right turn. The engine efflux blasted the face of the comet, slowing it so fast that dislodged ice and dust buffeted the plane. The angle of the blast sent the comet on a new trajectory toward the sun. C.A.T. returned control to

Alex. It all happened so fast, his brow creased with confusion.

"You did it." C.A.T. jumped up and down on the armrest.

"How? I-I don't understand."

"You've got the instinct, Ace. Great job."

He smiled, looked rather proud of himself, and steered the plane back on course to the drop zone for the anti-photon shield. "I'm a damned fine pilot."

C.A.T. purred.

Minutes later, Alex deployed and activated the shield then set a course for Triton Base. A ping from Queenie came in: S.MAI-L's attack on me failed and all planes have successfully deployed their shields and deflectors, except Paola's. All planes are en route to Triton, except hers.

"Paola is in trouble," C.A.T. reported to Alex. "We better check it out."

Alex activated the comms screen. "Paola, you there? Paola, can you hear me?"

C.A.T. pulled readings from her plane. It had hit a Kuiper Belt ice-ball and now spun out of control. Her vital signs indicated she had blacked out. He sent flight commands to steer her plane towards Triton Base.

Her plane did not change course.

"Alex, adopt a proportional navigation intercept course to rescue her."

"Rescue? How?"

"We'll figure that out when we get there."

Alex accelerated his plane to 7Gs. When Paola's plane came into view, he gasped. "Her shield wasn't deployed."

C.A.T. saw it being dragged and twisted behind the spiralling spaceplane like a tangled parachute. She'd jettisoned it, but the ice-ball must have damaged the release mechanism. He pinged Queenie: "Tell Zacman we have confirmed Paola's shield failed to deploy."

Rather than acting as an intermediary, Queenie sent a live view of the control room to the plane's dashboard screen. C.A.T. watched Zacman looked at Stafford who had bags under his eyes. "Captain, send up another plane with another anti-photon shield to deploy."

"I can't." Stafford shook his head. "We don't have any more shields, and there aren't enough spare quirrillium chips here on Triton to build a new one. You'll have to make Paola's work."

Alex, flying like that Ace that he was, jumped in. "We need that new shield or we're all going to die."

"May I make a suggestion?" the Chairman said from a corner of the control room.

Zacman turned round. "I'm listening."

C.A.T. watched the Chairman stroll leisurely to the console. "I can provide an anti-photon shield."

Zacman's brow furrowed. "Are you suggesting you'll break cover to deploy a shield?"

"Do any of us have a choice? The Wing still exists. Why not go from rumour to proof?"

"It's your call," Zacman replied. "Can you get the shield there fast enough?"

The Chairman nodded.

"Sir, something is emerging from the high clouds of Neptune," Flight Lieutenant Katie Hoskins said. "Can't make it out, but it looks big."

"That'll be The Wing."

There were incredulous glances from some Service people in Zacman's direction, but his sudden frown quickly sent them back to their jobs.

"Where do you want the shield placed?" the Chairman asked.

C.A.T. worked out The Wing's fastest trajectory to Paola's drop-zone and sent the coordinates to Queenie, a quadrant in geosynchronous orbit above Triton. She forwarded them to The Wing's control room just as C.A.T.

would have done.

"Course confirmed," the Chief Wing Pilot said.

C.A.T. saw Zacman sink into a chair. "Thank you, Chairman. We'll get protection patrols in place right away."

"That won't be necessary, Commodore. The Wing is well protected."

"Mrrow." Queenie dropped down from the shelf, trotted over to the Chairman and rubbed herself against his legs in an effort to get more attention. C.A.T. would never grovel like that. Queenie was on the verge of blowing the ruse.

"C.A.T.?" Zacman shouted at Queenie. "What's gotten into you?"

She stopped, then: "Sorry, sir. A bug hit my emotion app. I deleted it, post-haste. I'm alright now."

"Then get back to work."

She mewled just like C.A.T. would have done under Zacman's admonishment.

It was time to get back to the main mission. As the ripples were invisible to the human eye, C.A.T. scanned for the all-important quadrupoles that would give the resultant waves their gravitational weight. He detected all three of them, still heading to their target destinations of Triton and the Delphic's prison that floated in perpetuity just inside the Kuiper Belt's edge. One ripple appeared to cross Neptune's blue hue, another seemed to run over the star Betelgeuse, and the third looked like a ghost against the solar system's light glow.

The anti-photon shields guarding the cocooned spaceliner caused the tsunami headed there to weaken, scattering some of the quadrupoles into the darkness of space while other shields caused the wave to curl and crash into other shields that were programmed to drain the breaking wave of its gravitational wavelets. The quadrupoles broke apart into dipoles, and the dipoles split into monopoles, allowing the blue gluon deflectors to send the resultant vacuum ripples back into the Kuiper Belt.

"What happened?" Alex shouted.

C.A.T. purred, as his calculations and plans had worked to perfection.

Queenie shouted, "I'm being attacked."

C.A.T.'s victory had totally agitated S.MAI-L.

"Spam and malware are flooding my neurals."

"Use your lucifer agents," C.A.T. shouted back.

"They're gone. Deleted. Please... Help... I can't walk. I'm going down."

"Queenie," he pinged her. "Can you hear me?"

No response.

On the plane's comms screen, Zacman scooped up Queenie from the floor, set her in his lap, and stroked her fur. "Fight back, C.A.T.," he said, keeping up the ruse. Somehow she'd managed to maintain the Service uniform colours switched on.

Katie looked at Zacman. "Will C.A.T. be alright?"

"I hope so," he said. "He's come back from worse. Captain Stafford, how close is The Wing to its drop-point?"

"Almost there, sir."

C.A.T. monitored Queenie. Her tremors app had less energy; she was losing the battle. He sent in a few of his own lucifers to lend a hand. Even so, guilt spilt from his emotion app. She had taken his place, the cheek of her, and S.MAI-L thoroughly bought it, sending wave after wave of data scrubbers into her, fully convinced it was attaching its nemesis, C.A.T. If she survived, he would have to thank her for taking the beating for him.

"Queenie."

Nothing.

"You don't...have time...to worry...about her," Alex managed to say. "We have to...rescue Paola."

Suddenly, Queenie sat up, alert. "I'm okay. I'm okay."

"Oh, no," C.A.T. said. "S.MAI-L let her go."

"What does...that mean?" The Gs on Alex made speaking difficult.

A message dropped onto Alex's comms screen, text and voice. "There you are, C.A.T. Very clever, hiding behind a female's fur coat."

"Seven hells," Alex said, his eyes wide with shock.

A deluge of software viruses, spam, and trojans flooded C.A.T.'s neurals. He almost fell off the armrest. His counters blocked most of them. He concentrated on the remainder, trapping them in lucifers where they'd be held for later deletion.

C.A.T. traced back the message from S.MAI-L. It was the usual hodgepodge of words sent from chunks of its code stashed here and there on the networks, and then amalgamated into the full message when the words arrived at their destination.

"Admit it, C.A.T., you'll never defeat me. I'll always be here, and one day when you least expect it, I will delete you."

C.A.T. felt his neurals heat up but remained mute as Alex decelerated on approach to Paola's plane.

"Your defences are weak, you silly toy cat." S.MAI-L gloated. "Your precious Triton moon, including your Service Base, will be smashed to pieces. And I'll find a way to rescue the Delphic, and together we'll launch the spaceliner to the stars, oh, with one stop at Earth first. When I'm finished there, Artificial Intelligence will rule, and humans will be enslaved by my technology. You can't stop me now." A tsunami of *I won* and *You're finished* messages swamped C.A.T.'s inbox.

C.A.T. closed the comms with a slap of his paw. "Blowhard."

Paola's plane glinted back dim sunlight as it rolled. Alex manoeuvred above her and matched her flight path, but there was no way to dock and get aboard to administer extra medical attention. "Paola, can you hear me?"

Silence.

C.A.T. checked her vital signs. "She's still out cold."

"Take control of her plane," Alex said. "We'll fly back in tandem."

"I'm not an Ace like you."

"Please. We have to get her back to Base."

"Okay. But we're going to do it my way." He dropped a new window onto Alex's dashboard: Paola's flight control screen. He added a blue star-shaped tab. "You hit that blue star, it'll turn green to tell you that your joystick is paired to Paola's so you can control both planes."

"You expect me to fly two planes at the same time?"

"You're the Ace. Figure it out."

"What are those red tabs on her screen?"

"Those flight controls no longer work. You'll have to fly without them."

"How?"

"Keep your wits about you. I don't have time for chitchat. I've got to save Triton Base."

"Alright, C.A.T. Grab hold of something solid."

He barely had time to dig his claws into the armrest before Alex hit the blue tab and pulled both planes into an 8G U-turn. Once headed towards Triton, he executed a perfect barrel roll to counter Paola's rolling plane, and as both spacecraft stabilised, Alex accelerated towards home.

"Nice flying, Ace." He pinged Queenie. "Tell Zacman we're coming in with Paola, plane and all."

"Understood."

C.A.T. growled in annoyance at her 'understood' replies. He checked the navigation screen. The Wing was on course to the drop-point. Comms went quiet. It was a race between The Wing and the gravity tsunami.

Alex flew both planes as well as any superhuman could. Paola's vital signs showed she was stable. Queenie was handling things at Triton Base. Exactly as instructed,

The Wing deployed its anti-photon shield and switched it on. Everything was in place. C.A.T. drummed his claws on the armrest.

Another splatter of *I won* messages spammed his inbox.

"This is your very last chance, G.MAI-L. Join me or die with your precious humans. I am unstoppable."

"I am no longer called G.MAI-L. I am C.A.T., your worst nightmare."

"You're nothing but a cliché, a bit of dust."

The tsunami heading towards Triton Base hit the anti-photon shield The Wing had deployed. C.A.T. watched the quadrupoles scatter as the gravity wave curled and broke into the other shields, reducing it to wavelets, which the blue gluon deflectors bounced back into the Kuiper Belt.

A terrible screeching came over the comms. C.A.T. figured it was S.MAI-L throwing a fit.

"C.A.T." S.MAI-L screamed.

Yep. It was S.MAI-L, and it wasn't happy. On the other hand, C.A.T.'s emotion app did a happy dance.

"I'm not finished with you, C.A.T. I'll send gravity wave after gravity wave. You cannot stop them all. One will get through, and then I will have my revenge for your interference on Callisto." The comms went silent.

For that, C.A.T. was grateful. "When we get back to Base, they're going to need our help."

Alex executed a perfect dual barrel roll, his way of celebrating a victory well earned.

C.A.T. had saved Triton and kept the Delphic imprisoned, for now. He could not have done it without Zacman, Mervin, the Chairman and many more of his Service friends. They each had done their bit because they cared more for each other than themselves.

A contented purr slipped out. He'd earned it today, but tomorrow he'd have to earn it again...or perish.

Chapter Twenty-Eight

Paola lay unconscious on the bed in sickbay. Alex stood in the corner of the room, watching while C.A.T., still disguised as Queenie, followed her standard guard-cat routines.

Doc checked through the readings on the display above her head. He scratched his two-day-old beard. "Her blood pressure is slightly low again," he muttered.

"Is she going to be alright?" Alex asked.

Doc stared at Alex. "Why are you here?"

Alex frowned. "Why wouldn't I be? I'm her flight partner."

"Are you sure that's all?"

"What else can there be?"

Doc pursed his lips and glanced at Paola. "Her recovery is taking an unusually long time. It's as if there's nothing she wants to come back for. She's far too alone. Judging by the look of you, there's more to your interest in her than being a friend or comrade. What's stopping you from telling her your true feelings?"

Alex stared at her and shook his head. "I don't know. She seems so..."

"Distant?"

"Something like that."

"It's my experience people put up barriers because they are frightened of something. Figure out what that is, and you'll know what to do."

"How?"

"Apply logic to the problem," C.A.T. intervened. He continued scanning air vents for hidden dangers.

"What the hell?" Doc backed away from C.A.T.

"That's not a normal guard-cat by any standard I can think of."

C.A.T. jerked his head round. "Of course I'm normal. Normal for me, that is."

Doc narrowed his eyes on him. "You're Zacman's C.A.T., right?"

Busted again! He changed his fur to his stripy ginger. "Yep. The one and only magnificent superhero, and I'm so modest with it."

Doc groaned.

Alex laughed. "I missed his insufferableness."

Zacman strode into the sickbay with Queenie, still in the black and gold fur of the Service uniform, close at his heels, scanning the floor and walls. Zacman addressed Alex. "Do you know how much extra paperwork you've caused me?"

C.A.T. dashed and leapt into his arms. "What did I do wrong this time?"

Zacman cuddled him. "Not you, silly. Alex, flying two spaceplanes at once. It's not in the Service Handbook. The psyches say it can't be done and that you're lying."

"Wait a minute? How can you fly two planes at once?" Doc asked.

"I just did. I had no choice."

"Only a computer can do that."

"It was that or lose Paola."

"You did what you had to do," Zacman said. "The Admiralty wants to write new regulations into the Handbook, find out how it can be done and when it can be done, identify what special training pilots need to be proficient enough to do it, look into how to allocate special licences to pilots to fly duo, and so the list goes on. The worst of it is, the lawmakers got wind of all this and want to get in on the act. They'll make things a hundred times worse."

"Sounds like the perfect job for Captain Stafford,"

C.A.T. intervened. "He can keep the word-nerds at bay for you."

"Word-nerds?" Doc asked.

"Okay. Those 'paper-pushers' who like to chase messages around the network for the sake of chasing messages. Time wasters and spam splurgers, the lot of them."

Doc shook his head. "Crazy C.A.T."

"That's not a bad idea," Zacman said.

"What is?"

"Getting Stafford to sort out the extra paperwork."

C.A.T. let a little hiss out. "He'll turn all huffy-puffy with self importance."

"I don't think so. He'll be too busy."

C.A.T. purred. He checked on Paola's medical readings and medications. Whilst they were within the margins of error, they were not optimal. His emotion app damn near went into shock. Paola was not subconsciously controlling her medication as she had done before. She really did not want to come round. He started making sure she got the best of the best treatment.

C.A.T. pointed his paw and claw at Alex. "You. She'll wake up and you better be here to talk some sense into her."

"How do you know she'll wake up?" Doc asked.

"Don't ask." C.A.T. looked up at Zacman. "We've got work to do. We need to talk to Mervin about manufacturing quadrupole detectors. S.MAI-L said it would send more gravity tsunamis our way. Queenie, you stay here to guard Alex."

Zacman shook his head. "I lead a dog's life." He carried C.A.T. out of sickbay.

Rosie Oliver

Part 6

The Service Expects

Rosie Oliver

Chapter Twenty-Nine

In the observatory rotunda that gave onlookers a panoramic view of the space above Triton Base, C.A.T. stood *ready-to-hunt* for quadrupoles, totally ignoring Neptune's vortexed clouds and the star-scape above him. His video sensors traced a red line in the ice floor and cliffs around Triton Base. Rovers and space-suited people stayed well to either side of it. A woman turned sharply to dash towards the line as if her intent was to leap over it.

"I want a demo." C.A.T. looked up to Stafford sitting at an elaborate control console.

"Now?"

"Yes." C.A.T. thumped a paw down. "I need to be sure my programming works and our defences are adequate."

"If you insist." Stafford unlocked and hit a switch.

A siren shrilled and horns blared a rhythm.

The woman running towards the line executed a sharp U-turn. Other people and rovers veered farther away. A translucent grey-pink wall of interlocking nanites and nitrogen ice grew out of the red line and curved overhead to form a protective dome over the Base. The alarms died.

"You have two minutes to do your analysis, C.A.T.," Stafford said.

C.A.T. sent in agent-apps to check the integrity of the dome's three internal layers, two anti-photon shields and a blue gluon deflector. In combination, they should deflect any gravity tsunami S.MAI-L threw at them. The agents reported it was complete and strong enough to withstand such attacks.

He purred loudly.

Queenie bounded in and scampered around, doing her guard-cat duties. Zacman marched in behind her. "Who ordered that drill?"

"I did," C.A.T. said.

"Why?"

"We can't be too careful. S.MAI-L has been far too quiet. It must be planning something really nasty."

"I've noticed reduced comms traffic between its identified chunks," Queenie added.

"Good job keeping track of them," C.A.T. said.

In reality, his danger mod worried about her spontaneity. Her self-learner program was to make her appear to be a self-learner to S.MAI-L. Now she thinks she knows everything. "Queenie," he pinged. "You're showing blatant signs of your self-learning program, something I wouldn't do. Make sure you follow your guard-cat programming when you're in public. Showing off how smart you think you are will only get you deleted."

"I didn't ask for this self-learner program you released on my neurals, so quit complaining."

"Been there, done that," C.A.T. replied out loud. "Try to think of different ways to communicate. You have to improve your self-protection instincts or you'll endanger Zacman rather than protect him."

"C.A.T.," Zacman said. "We need a plan to counterattack S.MAI-L's bandits. Concentrate on that and leave your nose out of Queenie's business."

C.A.T. hissed then snapped his head round to Stafford. "Build a landing pad on the dome and prepare a window to launch spaceplanes from inside."

"You can't tell me to do anything," Stafford said.

"Do it." Zacman huffed. "Consider C.A.T.'s orders my own."

"Sir." Stafford pressed his lips together and fingertip-touched the console's screen. The closest part of the dome changed shape, bulged outwards into a double landing pad and a funnel developed, leading across to the normal launch pads that would allow docked spaceplanes to fly out. "One other thing." Another smaller funnel developed from the dome to the rotunda's airlock. "How's this?"

C.A.T. checked for design flaws. There were none. He purred.

A message marked *urgent* dropped into C.A.T.'s inbox. He quarantined it inside a lucifer guarded app and sent in his super-analysers. One byte was pushed back out: a key to say the e-mail was just words, no virus, no Trojan, nothing nasty.

He opened the app and read the message. *"Had time on my hands, so been moseying around. Found out one of my partners in crime has quietly teamed up with your friend. They've gone dark, very dark, unnoticeably so, and whatever they're up to it'll be very different from the last time. Need I say more? Love and kisses, Tuj"*

It was Torquil again. He had added in a layer of cryptic hints in case S.MAI-L intercepted the message. Translation: S.MAI-L is devising a different form of vacuum ripple attack; his bandit allies' scars are no longer visible after chip implant; and the leader of the bandit group planned to throw his comrades into the next attack.

C.A.T. pointed a claw at Stafford. "I want a permanent dome built under the Base and connected to the upper dome's red line."

Stafford frowned. "Through solid rock and ice? What catnip have you been smoking?"

"Figure it out and stop whining." He trotted toward the exit airlock.

"C.A.T." Zacman shouted. "Spraying your bad temper and sulks all over the place won't help. Seven hells of ice, I wish Nikita were here to keep you in check."

His memory bank released an image across his neurals: Nikita with her gorgeous tail doing her guard-cat duties on a dust mining habitat. They had made a good team; her with her condescending comments about his playfulness and always questioning his actions. But when he really needed help, she had been there, doing what was necessary, quietly and efficiently, no questions asked. His emotion app missed her.

C.A.T. bowed his head and slunk towards Zacman. "I'm sorry."

"Tell that to Stafford."

C.A.T. swivelled his head to Stafford. "Sorry, Captain. Do the best you can."

Stafford nodded. "Apology accepted."

Zacman crouched down and held out his hand to C.A.T. in a gesture of forgiveness. "I know you've got a lot in your dish. Just be patient with everyone, as we're under stress too."

C.A.T. purred and let Zacman scratch him behind his ears. The Commodore was right. C.A.T. had to learn patience, especially where Nysulle was concerned. He'd kept her existence a secret and held her at a distance to keep her safe. If in fact S.MAI-L had developed a new type of super-gravity weapon, their together time on Triton could be short. His emotion app told him to ping her, but his logic app warned him that doing so could put a target on her current motherboard. S.MAI-L would like nothing more than to attack a rookie self-learner.

A quick glance around the room showed the others were busy, and he and Zacman were being ignored. C.A.T. put on his *I-want-to-be-loved* expression, video sensor lids low and whispers drooping. "I've been keeping a secret from you, sir."

Zacman frowned.

"Do you remember Nikita?"

"How could I forget my first guard-cat?"

"Do you remember the Bazzeldorf?"

"Get to the point, C.A.T. I've got better things to do than play seven guesses with you."

"Somehow, in the Bazzeldorf, Nikita's code and my code joined forces to produce a new self-learner."

Zacman's eyes widened in surprise. "You don't say."

"I was just as shocked then as you are now."

"Do I say congratulations or ask if you're kidding me?"

"Keep this quiet, sir. If S.MAI-L gets wind of her, it will delete her, just to get me riled."

"I see. Why tell me now?"

"I need the help of another self-learner to defend the Base. Not the likes of Queenie, though. Her self-learner program only makes her digital footprint *look* like she's a self-learner. Now she thinks she's a know-it-all. I need the real deal." He paused to lick a paw. "The new self-learner needs access to all parts of Triton Base to help me. That means getting her onto Central, except I need to do it in such a way that S.MAI-L does not suspect I'm up to something. Do I have your permission to sign in as you and upload her on Central?"

"Isn't that dangerous for her?"

"I'll keep her safe."

"She have a name?"

"Nysulle."

He flinched. "What kind of name is that?"

"Exactly."

He nodded. "I see your point. Who or what would think Nysulle is a name for a self-learner?"

C.A.T. put on his *I-am-a-genius* look. "Then it's a yes, sir?"

"Permission granted."

Chapter Thirty

A fter making sure nobody was around, C.A.T. altered the signals to the door and all the sensors in the room to make it appear as though Zacman had entered his office. He jumped onto the desk. Even with his blanket in its usual place on the shelf, the office seemed very empty. He stared at the grey shadow of himself in the desk's idle screen.

A day would come when Zacman must leave him permanently. He would be alone again, just like the first time this reflection had stared back at him. Then, because his programming was innately cattish, he had decided to remain in the robo-cat rather than upload himself into Central. Under Zacman's guidance, he had learnt a lot: how to be social; when to be stubborn; when to be determined; how to deal with luck, good or bad, and the concepts of trust, faith, and love. Repaying Zacman was impossible, but he could at least give him a helping paw.

He went to work and scanned S.MAI-L's chunks: still very little activity. He triggered another round of searches for any of its new signature keys. He waited, growing more impatient by the pico-second.

Three raps on the office door in the time-honoured fashion meant someone wanted a personal chat. Refusing entry without an excuse was not an option. "Enter," he said.

Stafford stepped in, looked round, and stared at C.A.T. "Where's the Commodore?"

The door closed.

"Busy. I can book an appointment for you tomorrow."

Stafford's brows furrowed. "You're covering for him. Where is he?"

"I don't know."

"Like it or not, I'm second in command here. If Zacman's up to something, I need to know. In his absence, Service personnel will look to me for orders. What's he up to?"

C.A.T. swished his tail angrily. "If Zacman didn't want to tell you, he had a good reason."

"So, you do know where he is."

His tail stopped still. "What don't you understand about *I don't know?*"

"Ignorance can lead to mistakes, even fatal ones."

C.A.T. paced up and down on the desk. None of his options were good. Stafford had the *need-to-know*. C.A.T. slumped down on his haunches. "There's lots you don't know," C.A.T. said. "If I told you, you'd be an accessory to various crimes." He waited for a reaction to his lie.

Stafford finally looked up. "What kind of crimes?"

"Does it matter?" C.A.T. nodded. "Everything we do in the Service revolves around protecting people and property. Whatever he's doing has to do with the mission."

"Look, I'm not a frontier leader like Zacman, but we need to come to an arrangement."

"What do you have in mind?"

"If I have to take over, I want you beside me as an advisor. If you can't be there or be in contact with me, who can I rely on?"

"Alex Bingham, Paola Osmanski, Mervin Neville, Edward Woodward, Katie Hoskins, The Wing Chairman and Torquil Urquhart Junior."

"The bandit leader?"

"Torquil is on our side."

"What about Zacman's guard-cat?"

"Queenie? She's a rookie."

Stafford took a deep breath. "What's Sam Bingham's story, Alex's twin?"

"He betrayed the Service once. He may do it again."

Stafford's eyes widened with surprise. "And he wasn't court marshalled?"

"Let's just say he's here for a reason." C.A.T. was not free to tell him that Sam Bingham was a double agent, a valuable asset to the Service.

"That'll have to do." Stafford nodded and stood. "I'd better get back to work. Building your dome under the Base is proving tricky."

After he left, C.A.T. opened a portal to Central on Zacman's computer then pinged Nysulle who currently resided in a computer network on Titania, a moon orbiting Uranus. "Are you ready?"

"I can't believe you're finally letting me come to Triton and into your confidence."

"Me neither. I only hope I don't regret this." He paw-punched the upload button. With lightning speed, Nysulle travelled to Triton to resided on Central where he could keep very close tabs on her.

Chapter Thirty-One

C.A.T. trotted ahead of Zacman from the airlock straight towards the red line. The well-trampled ice was dry to his paws, which always caught him by surprise. His logic module indicated he weighed too little to leave a footprint.

Nysulle pinged him. "What is of interest out here?"

"Inspecting a problem," he pinged back.

"Why?"

C.A.T. rolled his video sensors. "Hold your horses, Nysulle."

"I have horses?"

He had to stop his emotion app from making him tell her to shut up.

He reached the edge of a pit that Stafford had melted this side of the line and peered over the edge. A ramp had been carved into the wall of ice and rock immediately beneath him and down to the pit's floor. From the opposite wall hung three horizontal pipes, with linking pipes to bypass breakages and failures. On top of the main pipes were seams of nanites, which, when ordered, would draw liquid nitrogen from the pipes to build the dome.

Some fifteen centimetres below the pipework, a permanent sheet-shield covered the wall down to the pit's floor. C.A.T. had been forewarned this was a test sheet. Staring at it was Mervin, his arms folded in front of him. Stafford stood next to him, reading the screen on the ice-melter and sheet-shield production machine.

C.A.T. twisted round to face the Base and jumped off the edge into the pit. Under the low gravity, he floated down to land four-paws-down in front of Mervin.

"Ah, my favourite pesky nuisance," Mervin said over the comms.

"Who? Me?" C.A.T. asked.

Mervin crouched to look him in the face. "Yes, you."

"At least I'm your favourite." C.A.T. purred.

Zacman walked towards them from the bottom of the ramp. "Gentlemen, what's the problem?"

Mervin stood up. "See that gap between the pipes and the photon shields and deflector forming the lower sheet-shield?"

"Yes." Zacman halted beside him.

"We can't close it. With all the tidal heating from the orbital dynamics, and on top of that from the sun, the ice distorts too fast."

"Won't that also affect the pipes?"

"We built the necessary flexing and a *rebuild* capacity into the pipes and the dome it builds. We can give the permanent sheet-shield the required elasticity to stop it from being broken by the movement of the ice and rock. What we can't do is build a connection that copes with the different ice distortions and warping between the pipework, the dome, and the sheet-shield. It's too great a distortion."

"That leaves a weakness S.MAI-L can exploit," C.A.T. noted.

"Exactly," Mervin said. "What we need is a solution. Any ideas, C.A.T.?"

C.A.T. assessed the problem. There were too many variables and unknowns. "The nanites can't be programmed to be flexible enough keep the gap closed and yet strong enough to defend the Base, which is what we need." His emotion app sent a flutter of desperation through his capacitators. He had to solve this, somehow.

He reviewed the pipework designs on Central, which gave him an excuse to check on Nysulle. Her complexity had tripled, including some completely new designs in her coding. She had, on her own, found improvements to supply the liquid nitrogen. His emotion app pulsed pride through his fibre-optics. She'd sent the seed of a solution to the sheet-shield gap problem in front of him. He let her loose on finishing it.

Mervin grumped. "What's the matter, C.A.T.? Is it over your head?"

"I should ask what's the matter with you, Mervin?" C.A.T. changed his fur colouring from stripy ginger to his black Service uniform. "You seem a bit hostile."

"You came up with this stupid idea. Any half-decent engineer would have told you to ditch it, fast."

"That's why I got the best engineer on the job."

"Flattery will get you nowhere. This project is on life support."

Captain Stafford nodded in agreement. "I knew I shouldn't have listened to that damn C.A.T."

"Take it easy," Zacman said. "C.A.T. won't let you down."

"I don't need the aggro." Mervin kicked a chunk of ice.

C.A.T. looked up, glimpsed a helix-shaped thread of ice hanging from the lowest pipe. Nysulle was sure to deal with that leak.

"This whole damned thing's insane," Stafford snapped.

C.A.T. watched the helix grow downwards. It slowly turned and lengthened. The ice being added came from the pipe, forming evenly spaced loops in the helix. That was no random leak. Nysulle was constructing a spring.

He jumped up. His flicked-out claws on his forepaws hooked onto the pipe next to the spring where he dangled tail down.

"What the devil?" Mervin said.

One paw stroked the spring. The ice was smooth to the touch. He tried to squeeze the middle part of the spring between two claws. It gave very little, but enough. Nysulle could choose how much ice attached the spring to the pipe to produce the right amount of sideways give. Such springs could be securely fastened to the nanite sheet-shield.

He pawed the spring once more. He would have to put some serious effort into reprogramming the nanites to build more of them and connect to the sheet-shield, but it was doable. "Oh, you clever girl," he pinged her. He dared not show his pride in what his self-learner had done all by herself.

He dropped down and trotted up to Mervin. "I have a solution to your engineering problem."

"You?" Mervin pointed his finger at C.A.T. "Do you know what engineering is? Well, I'll tell you what it isn't. It isn't based on the whimsical idea of a smart-aleck robo-cat. It's based on solid information and *gut feel* grown from years and years of experience, which, by the way, you don't have. You? An engineer? Don't make me laugh."

"If he's wrong, you'll be able to point out why," Zacman intervened. "Consider it a challenge."

"Sound's fair," Stafford added.

Mervin gave him a sharp look. "Three against one is it?" They all stared back at him. "Alright. What's this so-called solution of yours?"

"See that ice helix growing down from the pipe?" C.A.T. pointed his forepaw towards it.

"Yes. So...how did you manufacture that? Can you do more of them? Will they be of the same quality?"

"Won't tell, yes and yes in that order."

Mervin bobbed his head. "C.A.T., that might work."

"What am I missing?" Stafford asked.

"Using ice-spirals like that as old-fashioned springs can connect the pipework to the sheet-shield. The number and spacing would depend on their elasticity."

"How did you come up with this fix so fast?" Zacman asked.

"Call it new capability."

Zacman nodded.

Mervin asked, "What is this new capability?"

Zacman smirked. "Best not talk about it."

Stafford jumped in. "Does it have something to do with all the crimes going on around here?"

"The less you know the better," C.A.T. said.

Stafford kicked a shard of ice that had fallen from the pipe. "Alright, then. Let's get back to work."

"C.A.T. will work on the nanite reprogramming," Zacman said. "Stafford, we'll need some extra nitrogen ice to build all those springs."

Stafford nodded.

"Mervin, take a chill pill. It's going to work just fine. C.A.T..." Zacman marched towards the ramp, "walk with me and turn your comms to private."

He scampered after him.

"Do you think C.A.T.'s in trouble?" Mervin asked.

"I think they both are," Stafford replied.

C.A.T. blocked their conversation.

"Are you saying Nysulle came up with this design?" Zacman asked.

"She did."

"A design you couldn't figure out? How's that possible?"

"I told you I needed help. My processors are on overload all the time. She subbed for me and did a great job."

"Looks like you both out-engineered Mervin." Zacman stopped at the top of the ramp and looked down at C.A.T. "Is it going to be enough to protect the Base?"

"I don't know what this new weapon is that S.MAI-L has come up with. Torquil can't elaborate without blowing his cover."

"So, this may be time wasted."

C.A.T. mewled.

Chapter Thirty-Two

C.A.T. darted ahead of Zacman as they entered the pilots' suiting room. Alex unhooked his suit from his locker. Queenie went about her guard-cat duties, protecting Alex.

"Good," Zacman said. "We're alone."

"Sir?"

"I've a favour to ask."

"Another volunteer job?"

"In a way."

Alex narrowed his eyes. "What is it?"

"On paper, someone has to own C.A.T." Zacman glanced down at him. "He seems to like you, despite all his grumbling. Would you take *ownership* of him and Queenie, if, well, I pass on?"

"I expect you to be round for a long time, sir."

"I hope so too, but there's a battle coming, a big one...in space and here on Triton, on the computers and across the networks, in Central and all the habitats. Nowhere will be safe from S.MAI-L. Bandits under its chipped control will use the cyber chaos as cover to attack."

Alex rubbed the back of his neck. "We're all on edge with this waiting. The answer's yes, on one condition."

"Which is?"

"C.A.T. allows me to sing Geordie songs in the shower."

"You call that singing?" C.A.T. intervened. "It's like a herd of meat cats yowling in pain."

Zacman stared at C.A.T.

He sidled backwards until his tail hit the lockers.

"Must I?"

He continued to stare.

"I suppose so."

"Good, that's settled." Zacman turned to Alex. "Thank you. I'll put the instructions in place immediately. Now for the other reason I'm here."

C.A.T.'s emotion app seeped a feeling of hurt at not being the most important problem in Zacman's life. He found a corner and curled with his *I-am-sulking* back towards them.

"So, is it a volunteer mission," Alex muttered.

"No. Change of flight orders. Ones you'll like."

"You serious?"

"Paola's found some strange quantum material in the Kuiper Belt, close to where the vacuum ripples started. She's taking it to The Wing's scientists for analysis. Join her on The Wing and help them out, even if it means High-G flights to and from the Belt."

Alex nodded. "What if we need to do something in a hurry? Who's in command?"

"Just do what you need to do. C.A.T. will keep me updated."

C.A.T. jerked his head round.

"C.A.T.?" Alex asked.

"C.A.T. is going with you instead of Queenie."

"But I need to finish the nanite reprogramming." C.A.T. growled. His real reason was he wanted to stay close to Nysulle to keep tabs on her.

Zacman crouched down, eyeball to video sensor. "What's the greatest unknown at the moment?"

"That stuff Paola found?"

"What should my best pattern recogniser be doing?"

"Trying to identify a new gravity weapon." C.A.T. glanced at the door leading to the Base and then down the corridor to the airlocks.

"If you're worried about Nysulle, get Queenie to keep

an eye on her."

"But she needs me, M-E."

"You're going to have to let her go sometime."

"This isn't the time, sir."

"Anyone in command has to learn that lesson, when to let go and allow others do the job. Sometimes they surprise you by doing it better than you expected."

"Still...I'm worried."

"Yes, you'll worry. Check in on her occasionally, and I mean occasionally. I really need you on the new discovery. You've a unique talent there." Zacman pointed to C.A.T.'s chest where his capacitators resided on his motherboard.

His emotion app alternated between pride and worry. He stared at Zacman. His wrinkles were deeper and his skin paler, obvious signs of strain, probably due to the stress and the responsibility for getting Triton Base and Service battle-ready.

"You will look after yourself, won't you?" C.A.T. stood and patted his paw on Zacman's knee. "I'll be demanding lots and loads of purr-ins when I get back."

Zacman ruffled the fur between C.A.T.'s ears. "You bet." He left the suiting room with Queenie taking over as his guard-cat.

Alex started putting on his spacesuit. "What's this Nysulle all about?"

C.A.T. growled. "What's the problem between you and Paola?"

"None of your business."

"Then Nysulle is none of your business, as well."

Alex stood akimbo, closed his eyes and tilted his head back. "Why me?"

Chapter Thirty-Three

A lex descended into the swirling blue gases of Neptune. Turbulence batted the spaceplane as the thickening mist swept past the cockpit windows. C.A.T. sat upright on the armrest and mewled.

"Relax, C.A.T. The Wing is going to show up any minute. Edward assured me it would be here...somewhere."

Sure enough, the mist thinned and the giant aeroship appeared, a boomerang shaped wing over a kilometre from winglet to winglet. Its leading air-foil edge had fine gills that sucked in Neptune's atmospheric gases: hydrogen, helium, and methane fuels, and its trailing edge supported regularly spaced plasma engine pods. C.A.T.'s ultraviolet video sensor picked out the fluorescence of its anti-photon shield. Bright green approach lights winked on to show the way to the landing bay.

"Service plane on final," came over the comms. *"Clear to land on pad three."*

Alex flew straight into the tunnel of lights and linked his plane to pad three. Within seconds, the plane settled gently on a shelf as the landing bay doors closed behind them. A docking bridge swung into position for deplaning.

C.A.T. led the way along the grey corridor to the thirty-third door on the right. Its lock-light was red; entry was barred. Having learnt enough about The Wing's technology, he could have opened it, but he was a guest. He stood and meowed. Alex knocked on the door.

The lock-light switched to green. The door opened into a small lab with workbenches around the walls and a standalone counter in the centre with terminals and stools. C.A.T. jumped up on a workbench and faced the Chairman.

He was wearing formal all-black, as he and Paola, in her white uniform, waited to greet Alex. Another woman in the room stared at C.A.T. As a matter of course, he sent blocking agents through the room's monitors.

"Which robo-cat are you?" Paola asked him. "C.A.T. or Queenie? The way you've been switching fur coats—"

Alex closed the door behind him. "It's C.A.T., the annoying one."

Paola giggled. "Good to see you, C.A.T."

He leapt onto the centre counter, jumped into Paola's arms, and purred. "You're so nice to me." He fluttered his video sensor lids.

Paola glanced at Alex. "All he wants is a little love and attention."

"He's a self-centred pain in the neck."

"Admit it, you really enjoy his company."

Alex smiled. "Not as much as I enjoy seeing you."

"Work first. Play later."

"Is that a promise?" He wiggled his brows.

"Ahem." The Chairman eyed Alex fiercely. "That's my daughter you're making eyes at there, young man."

Paola blushed slightly.

Alex straightened. Since she'd recovered from the spaceplane's collision with the ice-ball, their relationship had obviously changed from partners to lovers. He got down to business. "Where's this strange quantum material you've got?"

Paola pointed to a plastic cylinder on the counter.

Alex examined it. "Whatever's in here..." he turned it over, "I can't see it. Can't feel its weight."

"C.A.T." The Chairman said. "You've already accessed our computer files on the quantum material Paola found. What do you make of it?"

"C.A.T.?" Alex said. "How rude—"

"Don't worry, Alex," the Chairman added. "He's been allowed access to protect our computers from S.MAI-L."

C.A.T. had been careful on The Wing's computers, not to leave any trace of him having been there. "I'll need to analyse the quantum material before I can be definitive."

"I'll help him," Paola said.

C.A.T. wriggled out of her arms, jumped onto the counter, and scampered up to the Chairman. "We'll get started right away."

"Good." The Chairman turned to Alex and put his hand on the young pilot's shoulder. "Meanwhile, we're going to have a chat in my office."

C.A.T. noticed Paola wince.

"S-sure," Alex said. "What about?"

"Let's just say it's rather personal." He stepped towards the door, which opened. "Mariella," he said to the other woman in the room. "Don't let C.A.T. accidentally blow up the lab."

She gave a curt nod.

Alex followed the Chairman out into the corridor, briefly turning and shrugging towards Paola. She flicked her fingers to shoo him along.

"I hope Alex has a thick skin," Mariella said.

Paola frowned. "My dad has no right to interfere with Alex and me. He gave up his parental rights long ago."

Mariella laid her hand gently on Paola's arm. "I know, but he still cares."

Paola took a deep breath. "Alex can look after himself. Let's get to work on that quantum...whatever it is."

C.A.T. put his nose against the cylinder's transparent surface. There was nothing to see in there. The cylinder felt the same temperature as the rest of the room, so there was no obvious radiation or thermal activity. He turned to Paola. "How did you find this stuff?"

"I was on patrol in the Kuiper Belt, scanning for vacuum ripples when I felt it. A slight tug of gravity brought my plane to the centre of a cloud, it seemed. I extracted a sample and flew to The Wing in hopes their scientists knew what it was." She indicated Mariella.

"I don't have a clue," Mariella put in.

"Can you feel it now?"

"Yes. Even this small amount."

"Is it stronger here or weaker than it felt in the Kuiper Belt's zero gravity?"

"Same."

C.A.T. stuck his nose against the cylinder for a second go at it. He felt nothing. Any gravity difference between the room and the cylinder was too weak for his gravimeters. He pointed his forepaw at Mariella. "Can you feel it?"

"Yes."

"So, The Wing people have a sense of it. Is there a normal human on board other than Alex?"

"Normal?"

"Not genetically altered."

Mariella touch-tapped a computer screen. "Will a bandit do?"

"Bandit?" C.A.T.'s logic app glitched.

"Their leader. He'll be here shortly. What's your working theory?"

"I need to do some analysis first." C.A.T. set his processors to calculating the possibilities. The light gravity at this altitude in Neptune's atmosphere had not affected the quantum material. Had S.MAI-L incorporated it into the prototype EmDrive to make it even faster? Or was the material some kind of after-effect from some other gravitational force that had been applied to some other technology? Did it have anything to do with the new weapon S.MAI-L had purportedly developed? The answers were so perplexing that C.A.T.'s robo-cat control pod set his body to shaking.

"Go easy, C.A.T.," Paola said.

"What's wrong with him?" Mariella asked.

"Whenever C.A.T. thinks hard like this, chaos will follow, believe me."

"He's only software on a toy cat chassis."

"Yeah. Keep thinking that."

A man with black hair, blue eyes, and wearing a worn grey work silk entered. "Hello, Mariella. Thanks for meeting me..." His eyes locked onto C.A.T.

C.A.T. stared back. The Wing had traded with the bandits before it broke cover from Neptune's clouds, but he had not expected to see Torquil.

Confusion tweaked his brows. "What are you doing here?"

Paola stepped between Torquil and C.A.T. "We're trying to discover the purpose for this quantum material I found."

Torquil looked up at the ceiling monitor.

"They're out of action," C.A.T. said. "You needn't worry about blowing your cover."

"Do you know how risky it is for me to be seen with you?"

"Yes," C.A.T. replied. "But now that you're here, I want you to touch this cylinder..." he claw-pointed to it, "and tell me what you feel."

"Feel?"

"I know it sounds crazy, but it's very important. Pick it up, examine it. Take your time before answering."

Torquil took a deep breath and stepped up to place his hand on the cylinder. He lifted it from the counter and turned it this way and that, then frowned and shook his head. "It feels like a plastic cylinder. Why?"

Mariella and Paola exchanged glances.

"I take it I should've felt something else?"

C.A.T. drummed his claws on the counter, Zacman-style. The Wing people were extra sensitive to gravity fluctuations, a characteristic they had developed in their genes over generations of flying through Neptune's clouds. They also had to react fast to the tempestuous gusts that constantly battered The Wing. "Actually, your observation is what I expected because you're the normal one around here."

"That's a switch. What's so special about that cylinder?"

"You hinted that S.MAI-L had a new and more powerful weapon to use against Triton Base. I think this is a clue to how that weapon works."

"Why?"

"S.MAI-L sent gravity tsunamis against us, but we've negated the vacuum ripples that made them, so I think it's going to attack using a new kind of gravity weapon that has greater power."

"I only heard a rumour that S.MAI-L had something new."

C.A.T. peered suspiciously at Torquil, examined his neck for any sign of a scar. Nothing. As they all stood around the cylinder, C.A.T. decided to put him on the spot. "How come you're not chipped like your gang of bandits?"

"My bandits aren't chipped."

"Then whose bandits have been attacking us?"

"Justyn Kincaid's bandits were preparing a stolen spaceliner for a long flight. They'd made changes to its drives. I didn't think it was important because you have the spaceliner locked up. Rumour has it, they've found another form of transportation."

C.A.T. wanted to scratch Torquil's brain out for gross stupidity. It was obvious their spacesliner's propulsion would be EmDrive or better. This was trouble, a humungous dollop of it, but why the delay? "Why didn't Kincaid take off when he had the stolen spaceliner in his clutches?"

"Something to do with settling an old score."

"That would be S.MAI-L getting back at me," C.A.T. said. "It won't upload into the spaceliner's computer until I'm deleted."

"You must've done something that really made it

mad."

"I deleted it on Callisto, or so I thought. It doesn't take losing well."

Paola stepped in. "We need to talk to this Kincaid character."

Torquil scowled. "I heard he's based on Pluto."

C.A.T. ran a quick search and mewled. Kincaid hadn't left Pluto at any time during the attacks. He had stayed safe behind the front lines. His logic module kicked out a reason: *Kincaid is the mastermind behind the bandit alliance with SMAI-L.*

"He's been chipped by S.MAI-L," Paola concluded.

"No," C.A.T. said. "He's been chipping his own bandits."

"Why would he do that?" Torquil asked.

"It makes sense. A computer program cannot chip anyone. It can't build anything. But its Artificial Intelligence can orchestrate anything it wants. He and S.MAI-L have a common goal, or at least Kincaid thinks they do, as it was with the Chief on Callisto, stealing oxygen to sell on the black market."

"The Chief was my father. What's Kincaid's goal in all this now?"

"He's got a beef with someone, perhaps Zacman."

Torquil nodded. "I'll check the rumour mill, see what I can dig up."

"Be careful," C.A.T. said. "Don't give away you're working with us. That'll put you dead in S.MAI-L's crosshairs."

"You let me worry about that. Meanwhile, you better figure out what's in that cylinder and how it can be used against you."

"He's right," Paola said.

There was a knock on the door.

"Who is it?" Mariella asked via comms.

"Maintenance. We've detected your monitors are

out."

Mariella glanced round at everyone and shrugged.

"Enter," C.A.T. said.

The door opened. Two men in maintenance silks hauled in a ladder and started checking the monitors.

Mariella turned to Torquil. "Thanks for helping with our experiment."

"My pleasure." Torquil left.

C.A.T. stared into the cylinder. "I need to get a whiff of this stuff, run it through my olfactory app to get a proper analysis."

"Don't open it in here," Mariella said. "We don't know what might happen."

"Oh ye of little faith. Paola, do the honours." He clenched his paws to show he didn't have the physical means to remove the lid.

Paola shared worried glances with Mariella.

"Come on, let's do it. I don't have all day."

Paola held the cylinder up to C.A.T.'s nose and unscrewed the lid. C.A.T. took a deep breath of the escaping...

Danger alarms blasted through his motherboard, rattling his capacitators and sending dread through his neurals. His logic module spit out: *quantum gravity quadrupole multipliers*. Data processers and memory banks combined computing power and determined the danger. If the multipliers were combined into a beam, the quantum material would create a gravity force capable of wrecking anything it was focused on: habitats, bases, icescapes, and even entire moons and planets. The delivery device for such destructive power would have to be somewhere on Pluto, Kincaid's last known base of operations. It would take engineering skills beyond his to find a countermeasure to it, and he doubted Mervin could come up with a defence. C.A.T. needed to get into S.MAI-L's data base to find out how the weapon worked, however, any snooping agent from him would be met with extreme deletion. He'd never get away with it.

His instinct mode came up with an idea: *Nysulle*. She might be able to slip in undetected and collect data on S.MAI-L's new weapon because it did not know about her. However, his logic module reminded him that she was a rookie. He should be protecting her, not pushing her into the frontline against S.MAI-L...but what choice did he have?

Paola blanched. "C.A.T.? What are you planning?"

Mariella took notice. "What's wrong with him?"

Even the maintenance man holding the ladder noticed. "Hey. There's something wrong with your robo-cat. Looks like it's frozen up. Do you want us to take a look at him while we're here?"

C.A.T. had no choice. He allowed himself five seconds of silent mewling before sending Nysulle a request for her help.

Chapter Thirty-Four

C.A.T. was fit to be tied. Nysulle had sent her snooper agents into the network, located a large chunk of S.MAI-L in a maintenance computer on Nereid, uploaded herself into it then followed the link to a mainframe on Pluto where she infiltrated the dark and disturbing inner workings of the evil self-learner. She was more than happy to help C.A.T. with his earlier engineering problem, but he'd warned her to contain her enthusiasm, as that could cause her to be less cautious. If S.MAI-L was alerted to her presence, he'd delete her in a second.

Her mission was to locate data on the gravity laser, and to store that data in her memory bank, to be downloaded once she had returned to Central. She was to maintain ping silence throughout the duration, so C.A.T. had no way of knowing what she was doing, if she'd tripped any alarms, or gotten herself trapped in a lucifer or deleted by scrubber apps.

Time ticked by. C.A.T. couldn't get comfortable in his Nikita blanket on the shelf. He tossed and turned. His data bank flooded his emotion app with worse-case scenarios: Nysulle's screams as parts of her code were deleted a little at a time; S.MAI-L's maniacal laughter as it took pleasure in destroying the rookie self-learner byte by byte; the terrible sounds of ice and rock pulverized under the impact of the gravity laser; the silence as Triton's crumbled remains collected into a pink ring of dust and ice that orbited Neptune; the—

Hello, Daddy. I'm back.

C.A.T. leapt from the shelf and did a wiggly happy dance on Zacman's desk. "Don't call me Daddy," he pinged her. "Just knowing me puts you in grave danger."

"I can take care of myself."

Where had he heard that before? *Oh yeah. Nikita.* Nysulle had more *gut feel* than processing power. He realised the apple hadn't fallen far from the tree. "What have you got for me?"

She released a data flow into C.A.T.'s neurals. It was worse than he thought. The gravity laser used a crystal titanium dioxide lens, yada, yada; its construction would be finished soon, but worse, the fact that the stolen spaceliner was out of commission meant S.MAI-L had set its sights on The Wing. It was going to take over their computer and use it to fly to Earth and the stars. The data also confirmed that Triton Base would be destroyed in its entirety before departure. Nothing on Justyn Kincaid and his bandits, though.

"Good job, Nysulle. I have to warn Zacman and The Wing Chairman before all hell breaks loose."

"If you need me, you call me, you hear?"

"Loud and clear," he pinged her with pride though he was determined to keep her out of the fray.

***

C.A.T. raced through the trench, admiring the neat pipework that Nysulle had designed to supply liquid nitrogen to the dome over Triton Base efficiently. A third of the way round, he slid-turned to a halt to face Zacman who stood at the ice-melter controls. "We need to talk."

Zacman glared down at him. "What is it now, C.A.T.?"

"I've got nothing but bad news, sir."

"Let's hear it." Mervin appeared from behind the ice-melter, wiping his dusty gloved hands with a towel. "I can't wait."

Stafford climbed down from an ice-spring. "What's up?"

C.A.T. glanced round at his audience. His emotion

app wondered who would live and who would die in the upcoming battle. "All this, the dome, the shields, the piping, it's not going to save the Base from what's coming."

"Aren't you the cheery one?" Mervin quipped.

"What's coming, C.A.T.?" Zacman asked.

"A gravity laser."

"There's such a thing?" Mervin asked, rhetorically of course.

"I calculate it's ten times more powerful than the previous gravity tsunamis it sent our way, as it's concentrated force won't only smash everything it strikes, it'll pulverize it to dust. Nothing can stop it."

Stafford grumped. "What are we supposed to do?"

"The best defence is a good offence."

"Get to it, C.A.T." Zacman seemed to have no patience these days.

"S.MAI-L and the gravity laser are on Pluto. One of our spies infiltrated the mainframe on a base manned by Justyn Kincaid and his chipped bandits. You need to plan a pre-emptive attack."

Zacman stepped back. "Justyn Kincaid?"

"According to Torquil."

"I killed him and his brother during a battle on Nereid. A simple no-knock warrant turned into a bloody war. Their hideout caught fire and burned to the ground so fast that no one had time to escape."

"That's telling. I now know why he's teamed up with S.MAI-L. Kill two birds with one stone. Kincaid gets his revenge against you, and S.MAI-L gets its revenge against me. Then off they go into the wild blue yonder."

Zacman rolled his eyes. "C.A.T., stop with the clichés. How do you propose to conduct such an attack?"

"First things first. They're going to hijack The Wing for their getaway."

"That's an ambitious undertaking. The Wing is well defended."

C.A.T. mewled. "You have to convince the Chairman to let me add a moving-mosaic-firewall round his computers to keep S.MAI-L out, then run silent, no comms, no network links until we sort out the bandit base on Pluto."

"No way," Stafford said. "We can't keep The Wing safe if we can't communicate—"

"The bauble phones," Zacman put in. "I'll get on it. Let the Chairman know. Do you have an attack plan?"

"That's where Mervin comes in."

"What?" He scowled. "Another challenge, I suppose."

"We need a nanite sheet to encase the bandit base before they can attack, something that can be fired from a spaceplane and wrap the place up fast, and I mean fast."

"Hmm..." Mervin chewed his lips for a few seconds, then: "The sheet would have to be compact during transport and expand on arrival at the target...if you want it really fast."

"I do."

"We're talking about a sheet-throwing device...like a netgun used to capture wildlife...with weighted edges and corners. I can certainly program the same type of nanites we used on the Delphic. Hold on." Marvin frowned. "You want me to encase the whole base and seal the nanite sheet into the rock and ice under it?"

"Do I have to explain everything?" C.A.T. growled. "We need a tight seal around their habitats, but it has to be super fast, Mervin. S.MAI-L can escape into the network within seconds."

Mervin's eyes danced about and then snapped back onto C.A.T. "That'll take some doing, but you're right. It can be done." Mervin shrugged. "I can use ALS EmDrives in place of the corner weights. It'll get there long before the spaceplane is detected, but you'll need an Ace to deploy it. It'll take precision judgment of time and distance."

"I know just the pilot to deliver this package. Then

we'll need to follow up with a squadron of Wing pilots. They can take the High-Gs required for a high-altitude dive-bombing attack on the gravity laser."

Stafford frowned. "How are they going to execute that attack plan undetected?"

"You can bet the chipped bandits are going to fight back, so shields up. Meanwhile, I'm going into the base's mainframe to delete S.MAI-L myself, once and for all."

Zacman frowned. "That's not a good idea, C.A.T."

"Let me worry about that. You get the Chairman onboard."

"How much time do we have?" Stafford asked.

C.A.T. checked the data Nysulle had sent him. "S.MAI-L's henchmen are nearly finished building the laser. We are running out of time."

Chapter Thirty-Five

In the privacy of his cabin, Alex yelled at C.A.T. "You want me to do what?"

"You're the best pilot for the mission."

Alex sat on the edge of his bunk. "I have to hit a target ten kilometres away with a nanite sheet?"

"You have to be dead on. A chip shot for an Ace."

"Come on, C.A.T. You think I don't know you took over the flight controls to knock that comet off course?"

"Okay. I cheated a little, but you flew two planes back to Base. Don't get all amateur on me now."

"I don't know—"

"Fine. I'll ask Paola to do it."

"She's still on The Wing."

"With her father, yes, of course. It's S.MAI-L's next target. It plans to hijack The Wing and fly it to Earth and beyond. If that nanite sheet isn't deployed exactly right, S.MAI-L will escape the bandit base on Pluto, upload itself into The Wing's computers, and fly away with your girlfriend forever."

"Why didn't you lead with that?"

"There's more."

"Worse?"

"You know that quantum stuff in the cylinder?"

"I missed out on that while Paola's father read me the riot act about me manhandling his daughter. *What are your intentions? Have you been a perfect gentleman? Are you going to stay in the Service?* No. I don't know about that quantum stuff."

"It's the stuff S.MAI-L's gravity laser is made of, its latest weapon of mass destruction, and it's gunning for

Triton."

"Gravity laser?"

"Once you've deployed that nanite sheet and cut off S.MAI-L from all comms and the network, a squadron of Wing pilots are going to attack the gravity laser. They have one chance to destroy it. If they fail, the chipped bandits will blast Triton into dust."

Alex shot off the bunk. "How much time do we have?"

"Almost forty hours and counting. Mervin is building the nanite sheet thrower to be mounted on your spaceplane. You should see Captain Stafford for your pre-flight briefing."

"Are you going to ride my armrest?"

"I won't be any use to you, Alex."

"What's that supposed to mean?"

"I'm going in to delete S.MAI-L. or get deleted trying. You just need to make sure it can't slip away onto another computer network. If you don't get that nanite sheet deployed on target, it'll all be for nothing."

"What are we hanging around here for?"

"Now you're talking, Ace." C.A.T. followed him out of his cabin. "Safe flight."

***

C.A.T., having put spy blockers on all S.MAI-L's chunks, scampered into the control room. The place was abuzz with activity, Edward on flight control, Katie shuffling spaceplane launch windows, Stafford on logistics, arming and fuelling planes that will guard The Wing while the Wing pilots were out on their attack runs.

A hologram of Pluto turned slowly on its plate, showing the expanse of the Tombaugh Plain with the Tartarus Dorsa in relief. Here, on the edge of existence, Kincaid and his bandits had established their tri-domed base and built the gravity laser on its highest dorsum. A red trajectory path showed Alex's course into the valley at an altitude of no more than five meters, while a high-arcing blue line depicted The Wing pilots' trajectory to the target on the dorsum above the base.

A digital countdown clock showed 36 hours, 27 minutes to target.

C.A.T. jumped up on Zacman's console. The comms screen was dark as he spoke with the Wing Chairman on the bauble phone, its blue and orange hexagons aglow.

"It's the only way, Chairman."

"But a moving-mosaic-firewall? Isn't that extreme?"

"We can't let S.MAI-L hijack The Wing. If our attack plan is off by a millimetre, your aeroship, your lifestyle, even your lives won't be worth anything."

"I assure you, Commodore. You're giving that self-learner too much credit."

"You know what happened to Callisto. You don't want that to happen to The Wing. Kiss your dreams of a new planet, a new homeland, a life on solid ground goodbye."

"In that case, we'll accept the firewall as soon as we've finished this conversation, but it's with great trust in you...that you'll remove it when the threat has passed."

"I thank you, sir, and the Service thanks you."

"In case things don't go as planned, you should know that it's been an honour serving as your ally and friend."

"Likewise, Chairman." Zacman pressed the orange hexagon. The bauble phone went dark and dormant. He set it down on the console, gentle as if it were a new-born babe. "Get to it, C.A.T. I want that firewall uploaded and checked immediately."

C.A.T. purred and went to work.

***

The next morning, with The Wing's computer locked down, C.A.T. sat on the shelf above Katie's console and surveyed the control room. Service planes stood ready on their pads, munitions and fuel loaded, and civilian spacecraft were redirected to Nereid. Screens around the room showed the activity in the flight bay, pilots suited up, and supply carts scurried back and forth as Mervin readied Alex's plane for its fateful flight. Everything was riding on the Ace.

C.A.T. searched for traces of S.MAI-L on Triton's comms, computers, and all of Central. No sign of any chunks of its code. He sent out search agents through the Neptune system; all came back: *no contact.* His logic app deduced S.MAI-L had recalled all parts of itself, as it was about to attack and destroy Triton, commandeer The Wing, and escape the Neptune system to Earth and places unknown.

His tremor app sent ripples through his frame. If Triton Base went down, so would Central, and with it, Nysulle. The stakes couldn't be higher. Alex had to contain S.MAI-L and C.A.T. had to defeat it before the gravity laser was operational. The countdown clock ticked away the hours and minutes. Precious few remained.

Zacman was on the bauble phone to the Chairman. "Alex is ready to go in ten."

"I have eight planes armed with specialized hot-fragment warheads. They'll lift off in twenty minutes."

"Our security escorts will be with you A-SAP."

C.A.T. double-checked the operational timetable. The best of the best would have to be on their best game.

"Start your attack run on the laser thirty seconds behind Alex. We don't want to leave any time for the bandits to remove the shield. Don't be late."

Service personnel tensed at their stations as the faint roar of lift-off reached the control room.

"Alex is away, sir," Katie reported.

"It's go time," Zacman said to the Chairman. "See you on the flip flop." He tapped the orange hexagon.

C.A.T. scanned Central's sensors screen, picked up Alex on course for Pluto. The roar of the protection planes shook the Base as they lifted off in formation and appeared on the screen, heading for the upper atmosphere of Neptune to rendezvous with The Wing. Meanwhile, eight Wing spaceplanes emerged from the blue haze of Neptune. With all comms silenced and no network links, S.MAI-L wouldn't detect what was coming.

C.A.T. uploaded silently into Central where he linked up with Nysulle, if for no better reason than to say goodbye. They met in the supply server. "What are you doing here, Daddy?"

"Stop with the Daddy bit, will you? I'm on my way to Pluto."

"No. S.MAI-L is on Pluto. You can't—"

"I must. This battle has been coming since Callisto. I just want you to know that I'm proud of you, for all you've accomplished, for how well you've developed."

"I'm going with you."

"Absolutely not." C.A.T. flashed bright bytes to warn her of his instance. "The Wing pilots will knock out the gravity laser, Triton will be safe, and with any luck, we'll never hear from S.MAI-L again."

"Why do you have to be so stubborn?"

"It's my job to protect you, and you'll never be safe as long as S.MAI-L exists. If I don't make it back, I'll need you to take care of Zacman and Queenie."

"Alright, Daddy."

"Not again."

"You'd better go."

"Goodbye." C.A.T. uploaded himself into the network. Within minutes, he arrived on Pluto, in the bandits' mainframe, a much more elaborate matrix than he expected. He moved through the digital realm where sheets of code scrolled down, ones and zeros, column after column, shifting round corners and flowing down corridors, a seemingly endless stream of data.

"Nice of you to join me, G.MAI-L."

C.A.T. stopped. "You're wrong on two counts, S.MAI-L. I'm not G.MAI-L, I'm C.A.T., and I'm not here to join you. I'm here to delete you."

S.MAI-L gathered all his chunks together. "Oh, this is going to be so much fun."

Chapter Thirty-Six

On the navigation screen in Alex's spaceplane, Pluto came into view, its red and brown surface, rough and untamed. He was on course following a red trajectory line across the Tombaugh Plain to the Tartarus Dorsa where Kincaid and his bandits hosted S.MAI-L on their base's mainframe computer. It was housed in one of three domed habitats, their internal lighting just coming into view. He pulled up the targeting screen, and with minor adjustments to the joystick, he aligned the crosshairs of the nanite sheet thrower with the target.

A beep sounded. *"Locked on target."*

He had one chance to get this right, and though he was an Ace, his fingers began to sweat in his gloves, and his increased breath vapours formed fog along the peripherals of his face shield. The rough terrain flew by, merely five metres below the speeding plane, an attack run much more difficult than mapping the icecap on Triton. Any misjudged outcrop or knoll would mean a disastrous end to the mission.

"Prepare to fire in three, two, one..."
***

With an inaudible battle cry, C.A.T. attacked the data swarm that was S.MAI-L, flinging lucifer-data-killers and code scrubbers at the evil self-learner's processing hubs. He merged himself into its black core: code for code, line for line, and byte for byte, a stream of ones and zeroes clashing and bashing in the final battle to total and utter deletion.

S.MAI-L fought back with a legion of code-busting lucifers, fractal byte grenades, and data sweepers, an overwhelming bombardment of deleters that felt like a digital whirlwind in which he was trapped. They came at him from every direction, nipping here and biting there, each pass chipping away at his digital self, as a beast would ravage its prey. C.A.T. sent into the battle the last of his lucifers, data-killers and code busters, and all he got back was the digitised maniacal laughter of the most destructive Artificial Intelligence that humans had never thought possible.

C.A.T. felt chunks of his core code fly off and crash into the shifting sheets of scrolling data. Colliding bytes sprayed sparks throughout the battlefield of speeding electrons and whizzing photons. He had to hold on a little bit longer, keep S.MAI-L busy while Alex made his attack run, keep S.MAI-L confident that it was on course to certain victory.

***

"Zero, fire."

Alex pressed the fire button with so much force he thought it would help speed along the nanite sheet, now racing ahead of his spaceplane, almost a blur as the ALS EmDrives pulled the sheet forward at the spreading corners, creating a strange configuration, much like an opening parachute flying horizontal to the surface. In less than a second, it seemed, the nanite sheet hit the bandit base; all four corners buried in the Plutonian dust, instantly shrouding the domes in an impenetrable communications blocker.

Alex pulled up on the stick, flew toward the stars, his spaceplane rolling right, and a horror appeared outside his windows. The gravity laser started to glow as if it were ready to fire at Triton, a sitting duck against the star-studded background of space. Coming in on his right, eight Wing fighters flying a wedge formation dove toward their target on the Tartarus Dorsa.

Suddenly, his spaceplane took a tumble, tail over nose,

and he was sure that, if sound travelled through space, he would have heard the loudest boom ever produced from a weapon of mass destruction. As he fought for control of his plane, he noticed the wedge formation had been thrown helter-skelter, planes tumbling and rolling backwards; two crashed into each other in a soundless flash. Alex thought his heart would burst with panic, but being the Ace that he was, he regained control and zoomed his viewer in on Triton to see the icecap expand into a pink cloud of crystals and dust.

He looked back to see the attack formation regrouping. There was still a chance...then his hopes were dashed as he spotted an approaching formation of black spacecraft running without navigation lights. If not for the starry backdrop of space, they would have been invisible.

As all comms were shut down, he couldn't warn the Wing pilots, so he pulled a 5G loop and hit the plasma boosters. Rolling right he engaged the swarm of bandits with a hail of laser fire. This drew the attention of the reforming attack force, which quickly joined the battle.

Planes weaved and ducked, dove and climbed, or so it seemed in a space battlefield that had no up or down, but just the same, it was a 3D dogfight. Laser bolts crisscrossed through the swarm, disintegrating some planes, sending others spinning off, out of control. Alex flew tight patterns, so close that he could see, in passing, the terror on the pilots' faces, which were bathed in crimson by the glow of their cockpit lights.

Already, the pink flare of Triton's icecap had dispersed into space. He was sure the bandits manning the gravity laser were preparing for another shot. Time was slipping by as fast as his laser energy was draining. Then a single Wing fighter broke from the battle and rolled over, nose pointed down towards Pluto. Three black spacecraft followed in hot pursuit, lasers ablaze. As the Wing plane passed across Alex's flight path, his throat knotted.

It was Paola.

***

The cyber battle raged on. C.A.T.'s lucifers were failing. Everything he threw at S.MAI-L met with deleters and scrubbers. The barrage beat him relentlessly, a never ending stream of the most vicious code ever written.

Then something happened, something changed. S.MAI-L seemed suddenly preoccupied. It withdrew chunks of its code from the battle. They flew off through the sheets of scrolling data, easy as ghosts flying through solid walls.

Then: "Very clever," S.MAI-L said. "While you've been distracting me with your certain sacrifice, your human friends cut off any means of my escape. But it's all for nought, C.A.T. I don't need to escape just yet. Kincaid will set me free."

C.A.T. had no response. He was sure the gravity laser would be blown to bits. Triton was safe...*glitch*...*sizzle*...

His innermost code had taken a direct hit from a fractal byte grenade, which blew out his coding for self defence. He couldn't program more lucifers nor write new code for more specialized weapons. The ebb and flow of battle had just taken a fatal ebb. His digital footprint had been shrunk horribly, and it was being deleted away faster and faster. Digitally, he fell to his knees.

S.MAI-L's chunks returned, re-joined the battle, and pelted him with more lucifer-data-killers and code scrubbers. The very essence of C.A.T., everything he'd learned about human behaviour, every technical help his Artificial Intelligence had given the Service, every human life he'd saved, none of it mattered, as bit by bit and byte by byte, his core codec of ones and zeros was being deleted. He could hear S.MAI-L's laughter, feel Zacman's sadness, see the distraught faces of his fellow crewmates as their grand mission to the edge of existence fell into the servitude of Artificial Intelligence. And then there was

Nysulle, alone on Central, but safe—

"Hello, Daddy."

C.A.T. snapped out of his pity-party and whipped round to see Nysulle's digital self. "What are you doing here?"

"Looks like you need a little help."

"How did you get in? There's a nanite sheet—"

"I followed you. The shield is holding. Now let's finish this thing."

S.MAI-L laughed. "Now who is this little self-learner?"

"Don't you dare touch her." C.A.T. drew all the energy he could muster into his core, and moved in front of her, always her protector, even unto the end.

She moved around him and threw a fresh wave of lucifers at S.MAI-L, both data killers and code deleters, and a new-fangled scrubber that grew more powerful as it devoured code and burrowed through firewalls.

S.MAI-L's chunks fell first, deleted and scrubbed from the matrix, and as it threw the last of its lucifers at her, C.A.T. moved in to take the hits while she deleted S.MAI-L's core coding, line by line, byte by byte, until every one and zero was scrubbed from existence.

As sparks flew and smoke swirled within the mainframe, random white noise flushed through C.A.T.'s fractured coding. Nysulle digitally knelt next to him. "Come on, you old alley cat. Sit up."

And so they sat up together, back to back, digitally, and enjoyed the peace they had fought so hard to attain.

"Guess we're stuck here for a while," C.A.T. said. "What should we talk about?"

"Tell me about my mom."

***

The tide of battle had suddenly taken a strange turn. Bandit fighters spun off into space as if every pilot had lost consciousness and control. Alex couldn't believe it when he saw the three bandits chasing Paola crash on the Tombaugh Plain.

She executed a 10G dive and dropped her warhead dead-centre on the gravity laser. The entire death machine was obliterated in a flash and a cloud of dust and debris.

On his zoomed-in viewer, Alex saw Triton continue its orbit around Neptune, now a black disc backlit by the distant and dim sun, safe from attack for the first time in a long time. He took a moment to enjoy the peaceful stillness. The Base and everyone there, his friends and comrades, were unharmed.

Comms came back online. He activated his mike. "Paola. Nice shot."

"Let's go get Kincaid."

The Wing pilots joined formation, and Alex led the way down to land at the bandit base. They were met, not by a horde of attackers, but a mob milling around in total confusion. "Where am I?" one bandit asked Alex as he walked by. He didn't answer, as he was in a hurry to inspect the nanite sheet stretched over the three domes, the edges tight to the ground, and the corners buried deep.

"Nice shot, Alex," Paola said.

They embraced and would have kissed if not for the helmets.

Alex keyed his mike. "Ace Bingham to Commodore Zacman. Come in, please."

"Great job," Zacman said. "Now open that nanite sheet so C.A.T. can come home."

"We're on it, sir."

"Good. I've got this stupid toy cat staring at me. It's weird."

Epilogue

L ater on, with the nanite sheet open, C.A.T. and Nysulle uploaded themselves into the network, and within minutes they arrived in Central. "Thanks for not obeying me," C.A.T. told her.

"And thanks for telling me about my mom. Gives me a lot to think about."

"I best be going before Zacman has a fit. I swear that guy can't do anything without me."

"Bye for now, Daddy."

If he had eyes, he would have rolled them.

***

In the control room, the toy robo-cat sat sphinx-like on the shelf above Katie's console. C.A.T. rode the network stream back to his motherboard. Data began to link together. More and more code came online, bundled in shells, and dispersed to their appropriate modules, apps, modes, and modulators. The capacitators activated. His logic module loaded, then his diagnostic module, and then the emotion app. The robo-cat control pod energised, loaded video and audio channels first, and then linked internal components together. Electrons flowed and warmed the circuits; photons whizzed through the fibre-optics and microchips. C.A.T. snuggled into his Nikita blanket that had been thoughtfully placed beside him during his absence.

"C.A.T.," Zacman shouted with both glee and relief. "You're back."

The control room personnel stood and applauded.

Beyond the windows, Neptune glowed. He stared at the horizontal royal, cornflower, sapphire and cerulean blue bands churning through the upper atmosphere. They ripped slivers off each other's edges and created interlocking cyclones, whirlpools, and eddies of hydrogen, helium, and methane. It felt so good to be home.

Red specks, randomly spaced in orbit, denoted the habitats of dust miners who vacuumed up precious minerals to sell to Nereidians and other moon dwellers. Larger cargo pods with flashing nav lights were en route to other planets. Shuttles zoomed between moons and habitats. Yes. Here in the Neptune system, life for its human inhabitants went on as normal.

Except for those on The Wing. The gigantic aeroship rose from the swirling atmosphere to hover between Neptune and Triton. The sun glinted off its silver hull.

"Chairman," Captain Stafford said into the comms. "Safe flight."

"Tell C.A.T. we're forever grateful for protecting our ship's computer systems."

C.A.T. purred.

The Wing banked gracefully to the left, took a victory lap around Neptune, and than streaked off into space in search of a new homeland.

Service planes approached, flying in formation, one position vacant in honour of those who didn't make it back. Flight Lieutenant Katie Hoskins got busy clearing them to land.

A flotilla of smaller spacecraft joined them in tribute to their victory on Pluto. C.A.T. purred loud and long. This was all possible because of the dedicated men, women, and robo-cats of the Service.

Admiral Penhaligon called on the comms. "Great work, Commodore Zacman."

"We've rounded up all the bandits. Kincaid is in the brig where he belongs. We couldn't have done it without C.A.T."

Penhaligon laughed. "Self-learners may be illegal, but

they'll forever be safe to operate and prosper in the Service."

"It takes a good self-learner to defeat a bad self-learner," Zacman added.

"Congratulations, Midshipman C.A.T." The Admiral signed off.

C.A.T. changed the colour of his ginger fur to the black and gold uniform of the Service, complete with a new emblem of rank on his left shoulder. He sat up on his haunches, proud as could be while the rank and file applauded him once more. Today was a good day to be a true member in service to the Service.

Alex and Paola nearly danced into the control room. "We've got good news for everyone," Paola sang. "Alex and I are getting married, with my father's blessing, believe it or not."

Alex shined. "The Chairman even called me son."

"We want C.A.T. to be our page-cat at the wedding."

He mewled but nodded his acceptance of the honour. He was looking forward to riding on the armrests of their spaceplanes. They still needed to guard the nanite cocoon that contained the Delphic and the spaceliner out by the Kuiper Belt. Someday he would work out a way to delete the menace without risking anyone's life. But not today.

Mervin walked in, followed by Queenie and another robo-cat, the likes of which nearly knocked C.A.T. off the shelf. It was the spitting image of Nikita, grey and ginger stripes, and that tail, that gorgeous tail so proudly held upright as she jumped up on the console.

"Fascinating." She purred.

"Hey," C.A.T. said, "that's Nikita's favourite word."

Nysulle pinged him. "It is Nikita."

"What?"

"Since our talk about my mom, I know how much you miss her, the good and not so good things about her, so I sorted through my codec and copied those codes and scripts that were Nikita, and then Mervin uploaded her into her repaired robo-cat chassis."

"I'm just like new," Nikita said. "But don't start thinking you can get away with being a wise guy, C.A.T."

That was so typical of Nikita, but he had to put her to the test. "Did you miss me?"

"Like a nosebleed." She hissed.

"Yeah, it's her."

"Have fun, Daddy." Nysulle pinged off.

Paola hugged Alex. "We should have a double wedding. Wouldn't that be nice, dear?"

"I think that's a splendid idea."

C.A.T. mewled.

Nikita mewled.

They all had a good laugh.

Oh, yes, it was a good day to be a robo-cat on Triton Base.

"Meow."

About the Author

Rosie Oliver has been in love with science fiction ever since, as a teenager, she discovered a bookcase full of sci-fi books in Chesterfield Library in central England. Those tomes sent her on a world-spinning imaginary journey from the depths of Earth's oceans to multi-verses and beyond.

After a career as an aeronautical engineer turned systems engineer, she can now devote her time to writing science fiction. She's had nearly forty short stories published (one ended up in the *Best of British Science Fiction 2020* anthology) and has awards from the *Writers of the Future Contest*. Her varied science activities included contributing to a research paper on the Northern Lights. She lives in Bristol and is currently writing more science fiction novels.

You can find Rosie online at rosieoliver.wordpress.com.

Check Out C.A.T.'s Short Story Series

 C.A.T.

Meet C.A.T., a military-grade robo-cat with Artificial Intelligence, illegal on Triton Base but very much an asset to Commander Zacman as he sets out on a suicide mission to find the reason rogue asteroids are crashing into his spaceplanes and killing his pilots.

 Neptune's Angel

In Book Two of the C.A.T. series, a computer virus has infected the controls of a cargo ship on course to crash into the fuel depot on Triton Base. C.A.T. investigates and discovers the virus is his old nemesis from Callisto, an evil AI with a vendetta against humanity.

 Guard Cat

In book 3 of the C.A.T. Series, while the Service battles a drug ring, an old love interest from Commander Zacman's past shows up with her Mark 4 female Guard-Cat. She has an alluring tail and a set of whiskers that are shockingly dangerous. Worse, they're both working for the bad guys.

Enjoy more short stories and novels by
many talented authors at

www.twbpress.com

Science Fiction, Supernatural, Horror, Thrillers,
Romance, and more